Looking Glass Theory

Vivian Catfield

CATFIELD
PRESS

Looking Glass Theory

By Vivian Catfield

Published by Vivian Catfield on her imprint, Catfield Press

2692 Madison Rd.

Ste. N1-354

Cincinnati, OH 45208

www.viviancatfield.com

www.catfieldpress.com

First Edition, Published 2025.

eBook ISBN: 9798992771534

Paperback ISBN: 9798992771527

Printed in the United States of America

For Roberta,
Who showed me that being a woman alone was just fine

Contents

Chapter One

The green mountain sat there on the desk between them. Nora didn't dare touch it. Four million dollars. It was the greatest amount of cash she'd ever seen in one place.

"I assumed that large bills would be more convenient," the attorney said. "Was I correct?"

Nora's throat was dry. "Yes," she whispered.

"Good. It should be more easily portable that way. Are you certain that you wouldn't prefer a wire transfer? I assure you that it's very secure. Much more so than physically carrying it."

"No, I... I have plans for it already. Thank you." Nora replied.

"I'm sure that you do," Julia smirked from the opposite side of the green mountain.

Why do you hate me? Nora thought. If she'd had any hope that Jasper's death might have brought her closer to her husband's mother, Julia, Nora was mistaken. If anything, Julia had become even nastier to her over the settling of Jasper's estate. Having spent the past decade begrudging every second that she had to spend in her daughter-in-law's company, it seemed that Julia's behavior would be consistent to the very end.

At least it's almost over. Taking a deep breath, Nora slid back into her chair. It was a lot of money, she knew, but it seemed insufficient to represent everything that Jasper was. The fight for it had been epic, though, in Nora's eyes.

When Jasper died the previous year, Nora was just as surprised as everyone else that he left the balance of his trust fund to her. Throughout their relationship, they'd always kept their finances separate. Although Nora had a job (not a *good* job, she always told people, but *a* job) with an interior design firm in downtown Nashville, it paid at the lower end for her level of experience. Jasper, in contrast, never had a job working for anyone else. He'd always been able to devote his time to music and whatever whims interested him at the moment. Their relationship existed in a quiet state of mutual acknowledgment of that fact. Jasper never pushed money on her, and Nora had never asked for any. And yet there it sat. The green mountain between her and Julia.

The attorney, Clifford Tuttle, continued. He pushed his little round glasses a bit higher on his nose.

"Of course, we've already taken out our fees, so it's less than the original amount. However, I have supplied an accounting sheet itemizing all costs, should you want to double-check."

Tuttle attempted to hand the sheet to Nora, but Julia lunged forward. The lawyer snatched it away. Nora noticed Tuttle was much quicker than he looked for his age. *Perhaps you get faster after a lifetime of keeping things away from people like Julia.*

"No, no, Mrs. Chandler, this is not for you," Tuttle said, rolling up the sheets loosely in his hand and wagging them at her as if she were a naughty child. "Your counselor will be providing you with a full accounting of everything, I'm sure. These are for Nora. *Confidential.*"

The lawyer slipped around the desk efficiently, yet a step or two further away from Julia than was truly necessary. He handed the papers to Nora. "Would you like my assistant, Daphne, to wrap this up for you? We can put it in brown paper, unmarked and separated into parcels as we discussed."

"I would appreciate that," said Nora, nodding at the pair of enormous, wheeled, hard-shell suitcases parked next to Tuttle's desk. "I brought those to put it in. I hope it all fits. I didn't think that there would be so much."

"So much? Well, I did. It's a hell of a lot of money," Julia broke in. "Years worth of the hard earnings from a good Christian man who worked himself into an early grave slaving every day for the only son he'd ever have. Only to have it frittered away to some..." She searched for a word that would express contempt without appearing elitist or prudish. Failing, she settled for "some... *stranger.*"

"Julia, I'm hardly a stranger," Nora began, but Julia dismissed her with a wave of her bony, heavily bejeweled hand. The rings spun between her knuckles.

"Are we done here?" Julia asked the attorney.

"Almost," Tuttle replied, letting out a heavy sigh. Nora sensed that Tuttle was just as eager to be free of Julia as she was. "There are a few more papers left to be signed and notarized. I'll call my girl in and we'll see to it."

"Fantastic, *see to it* then," Julia mocked, drawing her lips into a thin line that curled into a contemptuous smile on the ends. She gave another wave of her sparkling hand, like a witch casting a spell over the room.

Tuttle pushed the intercom button and summoned his assistant, who entered with the notary seal. Daphne managed to complete the entire process of reviewing their identification and observing their signatures without uttering a single word. Nora was slightly impressed. Few people could complete a task involving Jasper's mother without provoking her unnecessary, derisive commentary.

When she deemed the process to be over, Julia raised a thinly penciled eyebrow at the attorney, who nodded silently. Plucking her oxblood designer bag from the seat between them, Julia unwound her reed-like stems from their cross in the chair as she straightened up to the full six feet of her height. The soft popping of her Nicorette gum echoed the much louder clack of her expensive pumps as Julia strode across the marble floor and down the long hallway, slamming the door behind her.

Tuttle and Nora watched each other, feeling every second pass as they heard the elevator ding at the top, and sighed in unison when they heard it start down again.

"Well, we did it!" Tuttle said, grinning. "Care for a drink?"

Nora checked her phone. "It's only 10 am!"

"Ah, but you forget, Miss Hewitt, this is Nashville. Here, it's five o'clock *all* the time."

Nora almost laughed, then caught herself. "I'm going to miss you, Cliff."

"Likewise, kid."

Clifford Tuttle was the kind of man who called anyone under fifty a kid. He crossed over to the mahogany minibar and poured them each a shot of whiskey into crystal tumblers, adding one large spherical ice cube from the mini-fridge beneath his desk. Handing one to Nora, they clinked glasses and drank together.

"It's encouraging to see someone stand up to Julia Chandler and *win* for once. Jasper would be proud of you. You did something that boy could never do in his entire life, poor kid. His father either."

"What's that?"

"Tell Julia *no.*"

Nora nodded. "I think that was the start of his problems. Always did."

"Me too," Tuttle replied, swirling the ice cube around in the empty glass as he smacked his lips. "Jasper was a good boy. Quiet, but smart. A real still water type. How could he be anything else, with Julia sucking up all the air and his father being... Well, Jubal?"

Again, Nora nodded. Jubal Chandler had been a legend in gospel music. Both for his ministry work onstage and for his less-than-Christian exploits offstage.

"God, I hate how it ended for him, though. For you, too." Cliff motioned at Nora with the glass. "How long had Jasper been sober?"

"Almost seven years. He worked hard at it," Nora said.

"I know," Tuttle replied, pouring himself another whiskey. "We talked about it several times. How hard it was to be part of the music culture without drinking. He wasn't drinking at all in the end, I'll tell you that. When Jasper came to see me a few days before he died to go over those copyrights on that last bunch of songs he'd written for Tommy Ponder, he wouldn't touch a drop. And you know me; I *try.*"

"I know," replied Nora, trying her best to hurry through the conversation she'd already had at least a hundred times with others. "Jasper didn't drink at home anymore either. Didn't do anything. Didn't go out. No drugs. All he did was go to the studio and work. Kept saying he was making up for lost time. Having his mind clear at last was opening him up to all sorts of new ideas."

"Well, Jasper was certainly talented. More so than his old man. Jubal was just an old showbiz ham who got hooked up with the God Squad when it became cool, and he made millions off it. But Jasper? If he hadn't gotten mixed up with drugs and all that shit, he'd have been *somebody.* That kid was the real deal. I bet I've still got an old tape somewhere from when he was just a little boy... maybe you'd like to have it." Cliff turned to begin rummaging through the cabinets behind his desk.

Nora couldn't take it. She swallowed the last of her whiskey and stood up. "Cliff, I hate to have to run, but I need to pick up my sister at the airport. Over in Asheville. Then I have to head over to the coast tonight. Could you get your assistant to wrap the money for me? Put one million each into two separate bundles, then the rest together. Please?"

Tuttle's glasses had slid completely off the end of his nose in his search for the missing tape. Straightening, he pushed them up and then sensed Nora's urgency.

"Oh, Lord, kid, I'm sorry. I know it's still hard. I didn't mean to start going into all that. It's just... I miss Jasper too. A lot of people do. And I know you..." Cliff trailed off.

"Yeah, I do. All the time."

They stared at each other for a moment. Tuttle once again summoned his assistant, who wrapped the money into three large packages and then secured them inside the pair of wheeled suitcases that Nora brought for the occasion. Nora tried to shake hands with him, but Tuttle wouldn't have it, insisting on a hug instead.

"If you ever need anything, kid, just call me. Promise."

"I will, Cliff."

Nora steered the heavy suitcases into the hallway. When the elevator door opened, she turned her head just in time to avoid the man who exited. *Tommy Ponder. Ugh.*

Tommy was Jasper's producer. When Jasper tried to get sober, Tommy constantly pushed Jasper to drink and party with the kinds of people whom Tommy claimed would take him places. Most of the time, Tommy Ponder chose to ignore that Nora existed. That day, Nora reciprocated the snub. Tommy Ponder represented everything Nora reminded herself that she would *not* miss about Nashville, from his garish sleeve tattoos to his long hipster beard and the mirrored sunglasses that he wore everywhere, even indoors. To Nora, Tommy's every gesture screamed poser.

Nevertheless, the brush with Tommy caused a temporary break in the armor of her thoughts, which Nora managed to keep up through the meeting with Cliff and Julia. Nora didn't cry until she got onto the elevator, alone at last. Putting on her sunglasses as the elevator stopped on the ground floor, Nora stepped out onto Sixteenth Avenue in the glaring August sun.

Chapter Two

The drive through the mountains of East Tennessee and into Western North Carolina on the Blue Ridge Parkway was as beautiful as Nora remembered. The long, gentle green roll of the Appalachians always reminded her of a sleeping dragon from a fairy tale. She'd promised herself years before that she might start writing illustrated children's books if she ever had the time.

No excuses now, Nora thought to herself. *You have all the time in the world.*

Still, the drive was long, and it was only the first leg that she'd have to travel that day. As Nora pulled off the exit for the Asheville Airport, a text message dinged from her phone. Calista and Sheridan were on time, for once. They were standing in the loading area as she arrived, with what appeared to be two carts full of vintage luggage, Sheridan's Sphinx cat, Isis, and a pale pink piglet on a leash. Calista and the piglet, Nora noticed, were wearing matching snap-front Western shirts with pearlized buttons, tied up Daisy Duke style around their waists. Or, in the piglet's case, what one might suppose was its waist.

"Where in the world did you get a pig?" Nora asked.

"Oh, Zelda? She's my emotional support animal. I got her at a rescue upstate," replied Calista, as if it were the most normal thing in the world to arrive on an airplane with an unannounced pig.

"They give away homeless emotional support pigs in New York? How have I slept through this new trend?" Nora covered her mouth with her left hand in mock horror as she reached to pet Isis with her right. Isis purred and slow-blinked contentedly at Nora from her perch in the crook of Sheridan's arm.

"Oh, hush your mouth, Vanna Van Winkle!" Sheridan chided, in a playful, mock Southern accent. "Calista didn't get her in the city. We went to pick up a few things from my folks in New Hampshire and saw an ad for a petting zoo rescue. And then... well, you know how it is with Calista."

"We fell in *love*," gushed Calista, swooping the piglet into her arms and booping noses with her. "After I saw those sad little eyes pleading at me, I couldn't say no. Since I knew we were coming down South, I thought that we were meant to be. Because she'll have room to run around. She's very smart, too. Already house-trained, and she can do tricks. Watch!"

Calista set the animal down on the ground and snapped her fingers around her head several times. The piglet stood up on its hind legs, waddled around in a circle, and then plopped back down, bouncing and chortling happily. Calista beamed. "Isn't she wonderful!"

"Simply delightful," Nora said, rolling her eyes. "A love story worthy of a novel."

Calista continued unfazed, "Her name is Zelda. Like Scott Fitzgerald's wife. She died in a fire in Asheville. I thought it sort of went with what we were doing, you know?"

Barbecue? The darkly humorous thought passed through Nora's mind, but she dismissed it as awful, knowing that her little sister could be overly sensitive to jokes. "I'm positive that the late Mrs. Fitzgerald would be honored to know that her untimely demise had been memorialized in the 21st century by having a pig named after her," Nora said instead.

Calista stopped petting the piglet and looked up at her sister. "I'm sorry, Nora. I thought that it might cheer you up, you know. If you arrived, and the first thing you saw was me and Zelda. I mean, it's so goofy, you just can't help but be a little bit happy, right?"

"*God*, I'm tired of everyone telling me they're so *sorry* all the time. As if they're the first person to think of consoling me. It's been over a year now. I've had time to get used to it," Nora sighed.

At this, Calista looked a little deflated. She stared down at Zelda, who was examining a sprig of clover growing from a crack in the sidewalk. Sheridan turned to Nora with crinkled eyes and winced, shaking his head. *No, no.*

"Okay, hey... I'm the one who should be sorry," Nora backpedaled. "She's an adorable pig. Really. And I know you've had a hard year too. I guess I'm just not in a smiling sort of mood right now. I had to deal with

Jasper's mother this morning, and then five hours in the car. Just to bring you *this*."

Nora pulled out the smallest brown paper-wrapped package from the lawyer's office. "Because I wanted to see the look on your face when I handed it to you. What did you wish for when we were girls? Remember? In that game where there were three wishes between us, and we could each make only one?"

"I wished that I had a million dollars," Calista answered.

"And why did you want the million dollars?" Nora asked again.

"So that I could open a dance studio of my own."

"Well..." Nora handed Calista the package and took a bow. "Here is the million dollars. Let's go look at your new studio."

Calista's eyes glistened, grasping the package tightly in disbelief. "Oh, Nora! Are you sure? Are you really, *really* sure? You've already done so much! I could have found another job in New York."

"Yes, honey, I'm sure. And you shouldn't have to. You've already danced up there for twenty years. Think of this as your retirement. Come here." Nora moved in for a hug, and Sheridan joined them. "Knowing I've made you happy is worth more than anything to me. Jasper would have wanted to know that you were secure too, for the future. Both of you." When Nora stepped away, big rivulets of mascara were running down Calista's face.

Sheridan pulled the red pocket square from his navy blazer and began blotting her, as the traffic behind them started honking. "Girls, this is all lovely, but can't it wait until we get to the studio? Before someone makes this a drive-thru and presses poor little Zelda into a panini?"

Calista sniffed loudly and chuckled, picking up Zelda and putting her into the back seat with the package, as Nora and Sheridan began unloading carts into Nora's Tahoe.

***

Although Nora normally hated to admit when her brother-in-law Pierce had done anything right, she had to say that Calista and Sheridan's studio looked amazing when they walked in. The remodeling crew that Pierce recommended had followed Nora's instructions precisely about how to place the mirrors and barres along the back walls and to put down new wooden flooring for the dance practice rooms. It helped that the building was architecturally ideal for the purpose. In its former life, the building housed a Cadillac dealership, and the enormous showroom floor on the first level covered half a city block. With the large, beveled glass windows at their backs when they practiced, Calista and Sheridan's dance students would have the option to turn around and see all of downtown.

Sheridan was impressed with the lighting and sound system that she had installed. They'd agreed it would make their students more excited to rehearse because it was like being on a real stage. Calista loved the dressing rooms. Done up in old Hollywood glamor, they featured big makeup lights and lushly upholstered chaise lounges. Nora was particularly proud of the rows of reclaimed vintage cabinetry that she'd refinished herself in whitewash, tinged with a little sparkle and gold leaf. It was the sort of practice space they'd wished for as girls when she and Calista first began taking ballet lessons together many years ago.

Nora had converted the former second-floor office spaces into two large loft apartments. Coming from decades of tiny spaces in New York, cramped with roommates, Calista and Sheridan marveled that they had places with all the midcentury urban details they loved but with the square footage of a house. Nora had taken care to represent both of their personalities in their respective units.

Sheridan's was very minimalist East Coast chic, with black and white honeycomb tile details in the kitchen and bath, warm textured gray walls, a slate floor, and a splash of his signature red in the modern artwork and furnishings. Even Sheridan's cat, Isis, had a special place. Nora had turned one corner opposite the fireplace into a three-dimensional piece of abstract modern art that resembled the petals of a rose, which cleverly concealed multiple lounging places for a cat, covered in snag-resistant red velveteen. Pleased with Nora's choice to turn her afternoon naps into sculpture, Isis leaped from Sheridan's arms and into the central petals of the rose immediately. Nora had a feeling that Sheridan's social media would soon be filled with new pictures of his little queen in her rose garden.

For Calista, Nora had made an ethereal green space, blending bamboo floors and natural woods with many plants and textiles in shades of deep violet and soft, warm pinks. Knowing her sister's preference for handmade things, Nora had selected all the furniture from local artisans and kept a scrapbook of sources for every piece, so that Calista could know the stories of the craftspeople who'd made them. Although Nora hadn't accounted for Zelda's arrival, she was already going over ways to accommodate a pig in the loft.

Solving problems like that was one of her favorite parts of being an interior designer. For the second time that day, Nora had to drag herself away from well-wishing to finish her journey.

Chapter Three

B y the time Nora made it to Wilmington, it was almost midnight. She called ahead while on the road to Pierce, who claimed he was staying there for a few days to see some clients about beach houses. Nora asked Pierce about keys and where to drop off the money. Pierce seemed preoccupied. From the noise in the background, he was clearly at a bar. Nora wondered in passing whether he was there for business or pleasure.

Early last year, after getting fed up with calling Pierce's office repeatedly as she tried to set up appointments to see properties but got no response, Nora decided to go to his office in Durham. There, Nora accidentally walked in on Pierce and his assistant Harper getting it on in the file room. Catching them in the act only confirmed what Nora had suspected for years. Pierce, the dumb college football jock, married her oldest sister, Victoria, thinking that he was hitching his wagon to a rising star. However, Pierce had no genuine interest in Vicki. An ambitious, blonde, former cheerleader like Vicki, who came from a family of somewhat successful social scientists, was the best that Pierce, an orphan from the sticks whose only discernible talent was being able to hold onto a football, thought he could ever hope for. Thus, Pierce proposed, and they married.

After Nora discovered the affair, Pierce's level of responsiveness changed. Normally a lackadaisical broker at best, Pierce instantly became super-attentive to Nora's every real estate need. He helped Nora find her new house in Wilmington and the place that she'd bought for Calista and Sheridan in Asheville. Both in short order and for great prices, taking no commission.

Nora hadn't yet decided whether to tell her sister Vicki about Pierce's ongoing fling. She hoped that Pierce would be careless enough to tip her off himself, but that wasn't likely. Ever since she won her first fellowship in graduate school at Duke, most of life ceased to exist for Victoria outside of her lab.

The fact that they had twin sons mystified Nora somewhat. However, considering the amount of time and money Vicki spent finding the best nannies in the world to corral them over the years, Nora thought they were as well off as any other two young men of their wealthy set. Between Vicki's obsession with work and Pierce's obsession with himself, they didn't even have time for a pet, let alone children.

Standing at the front door while waiting for Pierce to text back the location of the key, Nora had time to marvel at the house that was now hers. In Nashville, Jasper was insistent on living in East Nashville, in one of those god-awful, prefabricated, tall-and-skinny condo monstrosities that, despite being desperately ugly and generic, still cost over half a million dollars. Inside was the most horrific mix of faux cowhide, reclaimed barn wood, and random farm implements morphed into lamps that she'd ever beheld. Jasper thought they were authentic. To Nora, they were wretched impersonations of rural poverty, from which she was only one generation removed.

Nora's father, Dr. Henry Hewitt, had grown up poor on a small tobacco farm near the Virginia border of North Carolina. Once, before Calista was born, he took Nora and Vicki to see what remained of the old family farmhouse. Henry's expressed intention was so that the girls would remember where they came from, but his underlying message was clear. Get an education and move forward in life so that there was no chance they'd ever end up back there. Thus, the house in which Nora grew up during the 1980s in the Durham suburbs was filled with Pottery Barn sofas, but nothing that in any way resembled an actual barn. Bland, yes, but rustic? Never.

The house that Nora purchased in Wilmington would have looked perfect along a cable car route in San Francisco, although it cost a third of the price and was in much better shape than many of those old painted ladies. There were many trips and conversations back and forth with painters, carpenters, and roofers in Wilmington as Nora finished out the house from a distance in Nashville while she waited for the settlement of Jasper's estate. The result was lovely. As Nora paced the wraparound porch, admiring the care that had been taken to repaint the sunshine yellow exterior walls and white gingerbread trim on the cupola exactly to her specifications, she was pleased that the floorboards did not utter a single squeak.

Finally, the text came back from Pierce. *Look under the turtle rock next to the front door.*

Marveling how she now lived in a neighborhood that was not only far more aesthetically pleasing than East Nashville but also where it was safe to leave a key hidden under a not-inconspicuous, moderately turtle-shaped rock, Nora texted Pierce back. *Thanks.* As she went inside, Nora wheeled the suitcases of money with her from the Tahoe. *This might be the historic district,* she thought to herself, *but I still like to keep my eyes on the cash.*

The living room of the house was almost exactly as Nora had left it two months ago, only now most of the light fixtures she'd last seen in boxes were installed. Nora flipped the switch and was greeted by the warm glow of Edison bulbs in the foyer's bronze Sputnik chandelier. She noticed that the dimmer dial worked perfectly, and all the switches faced the correct way. It was the little things, Nora nodded to herself, foggy with tiredness, that made all the difference.

A quick circuit through the kitchen, dining room, downstairs powder room, and former parlor produced another series of satisfied nods, as did the squeak-free heart-of-pine staircase that led her up to the second-floor bedrooms. She'd purposefully left them unfurnished to add things one at a time as she refinished antiques and acquired new pieces to achieve the whimsical look that she was going for. Parking the suitcases of money in the pantry, even as she shook her head at the cliché of her hiding place, Nora headed upstairs.

Everything appeared to be in apple-pie order until she arrived in the master bedroom across from her soon-to-be study. On the center of the wall facing the street, to the right of the cupola with its little round window seat, hung a large, old-fashioned looking glass in a wrought iron frame. It was directly over the fireplace, and there was a note on the mantel next to it.

Found this in the basement. Fit the pattern on the paint, so I left it for you. Thought you might want it.

Who thought I might want it? Questioned Nora as she peered behind the corner of the frame.

The glass was very thick and heavy, and the ironwork on the frame appeared to be handmade. *Silver-backed, probably,* she thought. *Very old.*

Curious to investigate further but too tired for it, Nora resigned herself to going back downstairs to the Tahoe and pulling out what she would need for the night. Carrying her suitcase of clothes and air mattress upstairs, she turned it on to inflate while she went back down to the kitchen for a glass of wine.

Taking one of her old work mugs from the small box of kitchen things that she'd brought until she bought new dishes, Nora smiled at the quote on the side of it. *Well-behaved women seldom make history.* She'd bought it knowing that the line would drive her former boss at the design firm crazy. *Bet the old bat's out getting more Botox injections*, Nora chuckled to herself.

Without her Brentwood Barbie boss to annoy, the mug made a perfect wine cup. Nora poured it full of Sauvignon blanc and went back upstairs to check on the progress of the air mattress and unpack her linens. Although she could have stayed in a hotel, Nora preferred the quiet emptiness of a house waiting to be decorated. Sometimes, if it were a historic place that she was fond of, Nora occasionally stayed overnight like this in clients' spaces. Whenever possible, Nora liked to take her time and breathe in the personality of a house before she sought to release its character.

Finding the air mattress fully inflated and mentally congratulating herself on purchasing the deluxe model that raised it to the height of a normal bed, Nora began to pull the fitted sheet flat around the corners when she saw a flash out of the corner of her eye. Thinking it must be the headlights of a passing car, Nora was in the process of typing a note into her phone to *begin looking for window treatments tomorrow* when she saw it again. Not really a flash this time, but more of a shimmer across the bottom. The lights were off in the bedroom, so Nora looked down the hall. She'd purposefully left that light on so that she could see to get to the bathroom. However, the bulbs were brand new, and the wiring had been checked thoroughly. She'd seen to it herself. There was no reason for those lights to flicker. Wishing that she was more decisive and had already chosen the overhead light fixture for the bedroom, Nora pulled out one of the aromatherapy candles that she brought for the bathroom and lit it. A reassuring scent of calming eucalyptus mint filled the air.

In the glow of the candle, Nora could discern the other source of light. It was coming from *inside* the looking glass. Nora walked slowly toward the glass, holding the candle in front of her. *It must be some odd trick of the light*, she thought. The glass appeared water-damaged around the bottom edge, perhaps in some kind of long-ago flooding incident in the basement, giving whatever was reflected in it the appearance of sitting on a cloud. As Nora moved her candle back and forth in front of the glass, she noticed that the light source did not budge within it. No matter how Nora moved her candle, she could see its reflection and hers move in unison, but the other light remained steady.

Nora inched closer and closer until her candle was almost touching the surface. As she did so, it seemed that the water stain around the edge was coalescing into another form. Nora set the candle down on the stone mantelpiece so that she could get even closer. With her nose a centimeter away, Nora could see that what she thought was merely a water stain beginning to take the shape of a person. He seemed to be asleep. At the foot of his bed was a fireplace, just like the one that Nora was standing on. The other light—the only bright thing in this shadow world—had grown bigger. Nora could see that it was a fire in the fireplace.

This must be one of those Victorian illusion paintings, not a mirror at all, Nora thought. *The kind where you could walk across a room and the seasons changed or a young man turned old.* If it were, though, it was a very unusual one. Rather than following her from left to right, as one might walk across a room, the covers lying over the man in the bed seemed to be rising and falling up and down as if he were breathing. Nora stood watching the shadowy sleeper inhale and exhale slowly for some time, with nothing else moving except the curiously bright light in the fireplace and the flame from her candle.

Then, all of a sudden, Nora heard footsteps ascending the staircase behind her from the first floor. Not just one, but two sets, heavy and labored, as if they were carrying something. Nora jumped back from the glass with a small cry, knocking the candle off the mantel. The glass cylinder holding it hit the rock hearth below and shattered. Nora scurried to the closet and slammed the door shut before thinking, *You idiot, have you ever seen a horror movie? If someone's here, the first place they'll look is the closet!*

She strained to hear more, but the footsteps stopped. Unable to remember whether or not she locked the front door, Nora took a deep breath. *Maybe it was a stray animal that walked in. Four feet would make four steps, right?* Nora tried to reassure herself but wasn't convinced. The footsteps had sounded human. Her brain raced for an acceptable answer.

Maybe it was a couple of homeless people, she wavered. Although this didn't seem like the right kind of neighborhood for random homeless people to be wandering into houses. She circled back to the more comforting first guess. *It has to be a big dog or maybe a deer. Regardless, you are not going to stand cowering in the closet of your own home. Especially with three million dollars hidden in your pantry. Go!*

Summoning her courage, Nora swung open the door to the closet and jumped toward the corner of the bedroom. She faced the open door with her back to the wall. *Nothing.*

Not wanting to step on any pieces of broken candle jar in her sock feet, Nora put her shoes back on. Hurriedly, she dug through her suitcase for anything that might be used as a weapon and pulled out a pair of spiked high heels. She'd seen a movie once in which someone impaled a villain's eye with one of those. It would have to do.

Peeping around every corner with a heel in each hand, Nora re-explored her house, room by room. Trying the front door, she found that it was unlocked and breathed a sigh of relief. Whatever was on the stairs must have run out the door that, like some kind of idiot, she'd left standing open. Nora locked the door, drew the chain, and pulled on it three times for good luck. Then she made one more round of the house, checking all the doors and windows again. Pouring herself another mug of wine and gulping it down, Nora considered a third but decided against it, remembering the broken glass still on the dark floor.

That can wait until morning, she thought, heading upstairs. Flopping down on the air mattress, Nora fell into an exhausted sleep and did not dream.

Chapter Four

The next morning, Nora awoke at seven, with the late August sun already streaming in hot through the windows. She padded downstairs for a broom and dustpan to sweep up the remains of the candle jar and afterward spent several minutes staring into the looking glass. Seeing nothing but a water stain, she chalked up the previous evening's strange events to excessive tiredness and went about her morning routine. After a yoga session from her favorite YouTube channel and a granola bar and diet soda from the stash she'd brought in the car, she took a quick shower with stress-relieving eucalyptus and mint essential oils. Then, she put on an easy outfit of a chambray shirt, crisp white linen shorts, espadrilles, and diamond earrings, along with swift swipes of tinted moisturizer, lip gloss, mascara, and artfully tousled, sea-salt sprayed hair. Nora was out the door in under an hour.

While getting ready, Nora texted Pierce twice but received no answer. She was not surprised. A man usually slept in when away on an impromptu vacation with his girlfriend. Rallying, Nora Googled *things to do on Saturday mornings in Wilmington*, and the weekend street market popped up. *Perfect*, she thought, deciding to walk from her place on Dock Street down to the riverfront. After an excellent brunch of an omelet and two Bloody Marys, Nora felt sufficiently fortified to face the day.

Once outside in the marketplace, Nora took her time browsing around. There were the expected stalls for handmade jewelry, inspirational wall hangings, and somewhat artistic artifacts incorporating driftwood or shells, but one merchant, in particular, caught her attention. The booth displayed all kinds of vintage mirrors. After perusing the collection for a few minutes, Nora stopped.

She had seen *that* mirror before. Nora was positive she had *bought* that mirror before, or at least one identical to it, in a Nashville antique shop near the 100 Oaks Mall. The massive gilded frame was over six feet long—not a piece that anyone would forget after she'd attempted to hang it, that was for sure. The other one that Nora had bought lived for years in her husband Jasper's studio. *Until...well*, she thought, *the end*. Spying the merchant, Nora asked for the price.

The old lady sidled forward on her cane. She wore a navy polo shirt with a pack of Newport cigarettes in the pocket and a pair of black, polyester dress slacks, even in the heat. The outfit contrasted oddly with her 50s-style horn-rimmed glasses and shiny marcel-waved hair, stiff with gel. She introduced herself simply as Dean Goodnight, without a handshake.

Eyeing Nora with suspicion, the old lady croaked. "How much ya willin' to give?"

Having spent innumerable hours at antique shows before with her clients, Nora refused to take the bait. Deciding to play dumb, she replied, "How much do you *have* to have? To not take it home this evening, I mean?"

The old lady cackled, a raspy sound that ended in a cough, and then took a deep draw from her cigarette. She clenched the long black holder between her teeth like Winston Churchill as she sized up Nora's ability to pay. Propping one fleshy elbow on her opposite hand, Dean exhaled a perfect ring of smoke. Then she said saucily, "That depends on whether ya gonna take one or the lot of 'em."

"The lot of them?" Nora asked.

"I mean, there's two more in the warehouse," Dean finished.

"Well, I'm not sure how much room I have," Nora replied, not wanting to tip her hand that she most likely intended to use as many of the mirrors as possible for resale.

The frame style was truly unique—almost a foot wide of hand-carved wood into which was set an antique silver-backed glass. Not only was the mirror beautiful, but it *leaned into* her. Having no other way to describe when a piece that begged to be reused or restored seemed to call her name, over the years, Nora had taken to calling it *leaning in*. This particular mirror *leaned in* so heavily that Nora felt the full weight of it as if she were the wall on which it was hanging. If she let go of it, or even if she breathed hard, Nora had the strange feeling that it would merge with her hand.

Dean nodded. She was shrewd, Nora noted. She knew the value of what she had, and that Nora was interested.

"Why don't I set this one aside for ya, and then this afternoon, we go an' take a gander at the other two? I can meet ya 'round three." Dean asked, with a sparkle in her blue eyes that disclosed the satisfaction she knew that she was near a sale.

"Sounds good to me," said Nora, attempting to appear noncommittal. "I'm waiting on someone anyway."

"I have all the time in the world," replied the old woman, settling back into a camp chair in her stall.

Nora perused the remainder of the street market but found nothing else exceptional. She was somewhat relieved when Pierce finally texted her back, even though his reply was abrupt.

You ready? I am. Do you have the money?
Yes. Where should I meet you?
Your place is fine. Around one?
Great. I'll be there.

Already heading back, Nora stopped to take a picture with her phone outside of the Black Cat Shoppe. It offered ghost tours every few hours. *Should be an interesting way to spend a Saturday evening,* she thought as she hurried to meet Pierce.

Back home, Nora waited only a few minutes before Pierce pulled up in his Mercedes S-class. *Always trying to prove something to someone,* Nora thought, rolling her eyes. She could see Harper was with him. *Just great. Now I have to be nice to her too.*

"Hellooo, beautiful!" Pierce called, stepping out of the car. Nora was nonplussed. Her brother-in-law called every female beautiful. Nora endured the side hug of his muscular, yet orange, spray-tanned arm for the absolute minimum amount of time that was socially acceptable before breaking away.

"Got everything ready for you. Already wrapped. You're free to count it, of course." Nora said as she handed Pierce the package of money for the amount they'd agreed upon, hoping to expedite the transaction.

"Aw, Nora, I trust you," Pierce waved her off. "Hope Harper and I didn't scare you shitless last night. I was going to show her around the house, but I forgot you were comin'."

"You mean... you were too drunk to remember I'd be here, even though I texted you," quipped Nora, quietly breathing a sigh of relief that the pair of footsteps she'd heard the previous evening must have belonged to Pierce and Harper.

"Naaaw," said Pierce, drawing out the word with a growl that Nora felt sure he thought was cute. It wasn't.

Harper piped up. "We only got to the front door to unlock it before I told Sweet Pea that I thought that was your car in the driveway. Then, he was like, *shit*, we better get outta here pronto." Harper's upturned blue eyes sparkled adoringly at Pierce.

Jesus, Nora thought to herself. *Vicki's eyes never sparkled like that at anyone. Maybe that's why Pierce had... anyway.*

"Everything looks great, *Sweet Pea*," Nora replied, leaning heavily on Pierce's nickname. He winced, but she kept on. "Except, what's up with that old-looking glass in the master bedroom?"

"Oh, that," Pierce said, blowing out air and making his lips vibrate like a camel. "I just saw it in the basement and thought you might like to restore it or somethin'. Isn't that sort of what you do? Make old shit new? Anyway... it kind of had a spook-ass vibe to me. Whad'ya think of it?"

"I thought it was..." Nora searched for the right word. "Interesting. Very interesting. Regardless, can I get either of you anything? I only have diet soda, water, and wine at present."

"Naw, I figured we'd just pick up the payments and head on back to Durham. You've already done all the paperwork online, right?" Pierce winked at her. Nora looked away. She hated men who winked.

"Right, everything's done except this." Nora nodded in acknowledgment once again at the money. She wondered whether they were still drunk from last night or if they had started early that morning. Ever since she caught the pair together but hadn't gone immediately to tell Vicki, it seemed as though Pierce thought the two of them had some kind of secret. Nora found this assumption mildly disgusting.

"Alrighty then. You have a good life, Eleanor," Pierce said, winking at Nora again feebly. She grimaced. Harper, slightly better off, whispered loudly in Nora's general direction, "I'll take care of him."

"Great," Nora breathed as the Mercedes trundled haltingly backward out of the driveway.

Nora was relieved to see them go. She looked down into the empty suitcase, remembering her reasons for carrying so much cash. *A quarter to Calista, another to Pierce, and the last half for store stock, because it's easier to bargain for deals with cash in hand.* Glancing around the exterior of her house, Nora whispered to herself. *Yep. Worth every penny.* She checked her phone. 2 pm. Dean, the old lady at the market, had said she planned to meet Nora at the warehouse by three. According to the directions app, she'd have to book it to get there on time.

***

An hour later, Nora stood outside one of the sketchier warehouses that she'd seen in her life, which was saying something. Over her sixteen years in upcycling antiques, Nora had found herself outside innumerable shady warehouses. This one was made worse, Nora thought, by its weathered appearance. The last bottom foot of the exterior, although metal, was eaten away by rust, leaving the insulation exposed.

Probably from past flooding in the area, Nora thought. Given the condition of the warehouse exterior, Nora's hopes were not high that the other mirrors would be in usable shape. She didn't have long to wait. Dean Goodnight came rattling up in an ancient Volkswagen van a few minutes after Nora arrived.

"I hope ya brought cash," the old woman crackled in her smoker's rasp as she swung open the creaky metal door. Nora was surprised to see it was unlocked. "We got hundreds of mirrors like them you was interested in here."

Walking into the warehouse, Nora immediately began sneezing. *I should have taken a Claritin*, she thought. Still, through her watery-eyed haze, Nora could discern stack upon tiered stack of mirrors. They were sitting on a raised metal platform, about a foot off the ground, each swaddled in protective foam and plastic wrap. All of them were large and appeared to be antique.

"Where did you find all of these?" Nora asked Dean.

"A lot of 'em I got at estate sales. Some of 'em was set on the curb. Yanno. Death mirrors."

Nora took a deep sniff. Wishing she'd brought tissues, she settled for the back of her hand. "Death mirrors?"

"Yanno... the ol' wives' tale." Dean continued, her congested voice dimming with phlegm that erupted into a coughing fit, then revived to its full strident vigor. "If a person dies in front of a mirror, his soul is supposed to be trapped in it."

"I didn't know that was a thing," Nora said. Although uneasy, she couldn't help but wander among the stacks. She'd never seen so many antique silver-backed mirrors in one place.

"Well, it's a pretty near universal fact 'round these parts," Dean replied, stopping to cough up something that Nora cared not to think about at the end of her phrase before beginning again. "If ya die in front of a mirror then your soul gets trapped inside. I guess, forever."

Nora studied the old woman for a moment, trying to judge whether or not she was putting her on. Her business sense said to table such speculation for a later time. "Where are the other two like the one you showed me in the market?"

Dean's eyes twinkled mischievously. "Ah, ya wantin' to see those other two from the ol' Blue Post. Hold on, just a minute... I have 'em right back over yonder."

Sensing another sale was imminent, the Dean scurried over to a stack near the back wall of the warehouse. She struggled to pull out two other large mirrors, one in each gnarled hand, so that Nora could see the outside edges of their frames. They exactly matched the one that Nora had found in the market. Before Nora could make an offer, the old lady decreed a price. "I'll take $200 each, or $500 for the lot of three."

Nora could see no point in arguing. Each mirror was at least as long as she was tall. They'd easily fetch ten times that on the decorating market once they'd been spruced up and restored. "I'll take all three."

"Faaan-tastic!" Dean cackled, drawing out the word as she clapped her hands together. "Lemme help ya get 'em tied down quick in the car. They say a storm's a-brewin'. Comin' up from the ocean tonight, yanno."

"No, I didn't," replied Nora, looking at the weather app on her phone. "Weather doesn't say anything about it."

"Well, it's a comin'," said Dean as she unfolded an old sheet and handed it to Nora along with a length of cord from a shelf nearby. "I always get that not-quite-right feelin' yanno, with a storm. Like the air itself is tight. A' holdin' its breath for when it's 'bout to blow." The old woman mimicked a sneeze with a sound that might have come from an angry kitten. Nora laughed and took one more glance around the warehouse. *What other treasures might be lying in those dusty stacks?*

"Do you have a card? So that I can find you again if I'm looking for something else? Here's mine. I didn't want to give it to you straight away." Nora produced a business card from her purse. *The very first*, she thought, handing it over, *for my new studio.*

"Eh, ya thought I'd go up on the price, huh?" Dean smiled as she read the card. "Eleanor Hewitt Designs. Phone number, website, email, and everythin'. I don't have no email. My granddaughter does all that computer stuff for me. She's real smart. But I'll hang onto this." Dean tipped the card at Nora before slipping it into the back pocket of her polyester slacks. "But no ma'am, I don't have no cards neither. Just come back to the market any Saturday or Sunday that ya need anythin' further. Ask for Dean. Nadine Goodnight." This time, the old lady extended her hand and Nora shook it.

An hour later, Nora shoaled slowly home with all three mirrors tied precariously in the back of her Tahoe. She decided to put the first mirror, the one that she'd spotted on the street, behind the desk in the office of her new design studio at the Cotton Exchange.

Parking behind her house, under what once had been the carriage shed, Nora called her sisters and mother to see if any of them wanted the two other mirrors. Calista agreed instantly, saying that hers would make a perfect addition to the dance studio. Nora's mother, Marjorie, flatly declined, which didn't surprise Nora at all. Her mother's house was extremely minimalist and had been ever since Calista, the youngest, moved out. To Nora, her mother's house was like some sort of singular version of Noah's Ark. There was only one of everything: one armchair to read in, one stool to sit at the kitchen counter, one desk at which to work, positioned by one narrow bed. All of which were completely covered in stark white. Whenever the family got together for the holidays, they always went to Vicki's in Durham. To go to their mother's would have been like entering some sort of surrealist nightmare.

Although Vicki was loath to waste too much time on anything that she considered frivolous, such as decorating, she was very particular when it came to anything new being brought into her home. To Nora's surprise,

Vicki asked that she send the last mirror to her office at Duke. "It will look perfect over my desk. I never spend time at home anymore, now that the twins are gone off to college."

Vicki's response gave Nora pause. Here was the opportunity that she had been waiting for. The real estate deals were done. *Should I tell Vicki about Pierce and Harper?*

"Are you sure?" Nora probed, asking without asking, for a natural transition in their conversation. "It's more of a homey piece. Very intimate. I'm not sure why, but I get the feeling that it's the sort of mirror a person would want to keep for her whole life. Maybe longer. To pass down, or something."

Vicki hesitated. Nora could hear her thinking... breathing really... on the other end of the line. "No, no. If I want to be able to enjoy it, you'll have to send it here to the office. Pierce won't care about it, and you know the boys." Nora did know Vicki's twin boys all too well. Blonde, tanned, perfectly muscular, and equally brainless replicas of their father. The only difference between them was that they each played soccer at two opposing Ivy League schools, to which they had gained admission on otherwise nebulous credentials.

Avoiding further comment, Nora agreed to send the mirror to Vicki's office at Duke. Having just under half an hour to get to FedEx and send the two mirrors on their way, Nora rushed out the door. Although she hadn't admitted so to herself, Nora liked the fact that each of them would have one mirror from the set and be able to look into it at work every day. Somehow, it made the three paths of their lives braid together again, like when they were girls.

After the rush of making the FedEx shipping cutoff and dropping off her mirror at the design studio, Nora was at a loss for what to do next. She wasn't used to having Saturday evenings idle. Ever since Jasper passed, she'd volunteered for overtime on Saturday nights to see clients who had no time available during the rest of the week. Restless, Nora searched through her phone for some sort of activity that didn't involve Netflix and polishing off the bottle of wine at home.

At last, Nora remembered the ghost tour starting at seven o'clock outside the Black Cat Shoppe. It promised a recollection of the spirits of Old Wilmington, starting with Paradise Alley. Although Nora considered herself firmly in the *I'll believe it when I see it category* of paranormal speculation, she loved a good tour of local folklore. Plus, she reasoned, it would be a great way to pick up the little tidbits of history that helped move a client's opinion on a piece from *maybe* to *yes* if they waffled. Having been in the design business for many years, Nora knew that narrative prompting helped. Antiques for sale didn't tell stories on their own.

Chapter Five

After a liberal dousing of mosquito spray bought at a nearby bodega while she waited for the tour to begin, Nora joined the group on Front Street by the Black Cat Shoppe. The tour guide appeared to be a college girl whose name Nora didn't catch. She had burgundy hair and was clad in an elaborate garb halfway between postmodern steampunk and pirate wench.

If I dress up for Halloween this year, Nora thought, surveying her outfit, *finding something around this town should be a piece of cake.*

Nora was intrigued to find that their first stop was down the same Paradise Alley where she'd sighted the mirror at Dean's stall in the street market. She pulled up a note-taking app on her phone to record any details that might add color to her sales stories later.

"Right here behind us," the tour guide gestured toward the window she was standing in front of, "is the site of what used to be called the Blue Post. A prime spot for traveling sailors and local men about town to meet up for a pint whilst enjoying the entertainment of dancing girls." She scanned the crowd for children before going on. "Among other amusements, they could also purchase favors from ladies of the evening in the rooms up-stairs."

The entire group glanced skyward as if by doing so quickly, they might glimpse some long-ago lovely in her lingerie, smoking out of the window. Nora noted this was the same Blue Post that Dean Goodnight mentioned in connection with the mirrors. *Probably won't be selling those to any preachers*, Nora chuckled to herself as the tour guide continued.

"Imagine if you can, the scene through this window. Dozens of beautiful girls in stockings and corsets, with long-feathery plumes in their hair, entertaining guests, all under the watchful eyes of Gallus Meg." Here, the guide paused for effect, awaiting the question she was poised to answer, yet no one said anything. Nora peered through the window, seeing the broken remains of cut-glass chandeliers dangling from the ceiling and several dusty silhouettes she perceived to be the same shape as the mirrors she'd purchased that afternoon.

Waiting for someone else to talk while she typed, Nora finally noticed the lecture had stopped. Taking the bait and feeling a bit as she had in high school when she'd always been the first to speak in class, Nora asked the obvious question. "Who was Gallus Meg?"

"Glad you asked, my dear," replied the guide, smiling slightly with relief that she'd been prompted and could continue with her story. "Gallus, or Gallows, Meg was the original owner of this establishment. No one knows where she came from, but she stood over six feet tall, and she was stronger than most men. Any time someone tried to start something, Meg threw them out. And if they roughed up one of her girls, she'd bite off one of their ears and spit it into a large pickle jar that sat right there on the corner of the bar."

Every head in the group turned to the spot where the guide was pointing, visibly trying to imagine the jar full of pickled ears. She had them all in the palm of her storytelling hand at last. Nora could see she was pleased with herself as she finished.

"Meg made quite a fortune in her line of work and was nearing the age that she thought she might retire. However, one night, as she was locking up, a group of at least half a dozen men lay in wait for her. They stole the bag of money she had from that evening and beat her to death right on this very spot." Here, the tour guide paused to shake her head sadly. "But if they thought that would be the end of Gallus Meg, her murderers were all wrong. It is said that she can be seen in this alley every night around 3 am, the same time she was attacked. Also, many men who frequented the various bars that were housed in this building over the years have reported being accosted by her in the bathroom. Gallus Meg seems to enjoy catching rowdy patrons off guard when they least expect it."

A whispering round of bathroom jokes circulated through the crowd as the tour continued through several other stops. One was at the allegedly haunted house of a doctor on whose basement table dead bodies were laid out for autopsies. Another stop was near a street crossing where a wealthy Welshman was murdered. Curiously, his killers hadn't bothered to steal his horse, which ran home and alerted everyone of his disappearance. Nor had they stolen his distinctive serpent ring, which also mysteriously disappeared. The motive was most likely pure malice or old-fashioned jealousy, the tour guide said. The man was known for his exquisite manner of dress and was generally well-liked about town. Having trouble with the spelling of his unusual name, *Llewellyn Markwick*, Nora added an emoji with glasses in her notes to remind her to look up more about his story later.

The last tour stop was the St. James Parish graveyard. Noticing that her phone had just blinked the *under 10%* warning at her, Nora put it away in her purse. She decided to focus on the final tale without taking notes. The tour guide continued to solicit engagement from the crowd and was getting a quicker response time. The wind started to pick up. A sure sign of the summer thunderstorm rolling in, just as Dean Goodnight predicted.

"Have you ever heard the phrase *dead ringer*?" The tour guide asked. Several in the group murmured *yes*. A few replied *no*. She explained the concept for the benefit of those unaware before proceeding. "Well, that certainly would have helped poor Mr. Jocelyn here. Perhaps Wilmington's most famous ghost, Samuel Jocelyn was buried alive, right here in this very churchyard." Those in the group who'd begun checking their phones for last call times at nearby bars pricked up their ears to listen.

"Samuel Jocelyn was a successful young lawyer in Wilmington, with a thriving practice among the shipping merchants of town. One night, he and his best friend Alexander Hostler were out drinking. They began discussing what happened to a person when they died. Did they simply pass on, or was there some sort of afterlife waiting for them? And, even more importantly, was there any way to communicate with those who had died?

The two men swore to one another that whichever of them died first would come back and tell the survivor what was on the other side. Unfortunately, for Mr. Jocelyn, the opportunity to honor that promise came less than a year later. According to the accounts of several witnesses, Samuel Jocelyn argued with his young wife. He took off, riding his horse recklessly through Holly Shelter Swamp near their plantation house late on a bitterly cold evening in 1810. Startled by something in the road, the horse fell, pinning Jocelyn underneath and knocking him unconscious. Jocelyn was found by a search party two days later, on March 18th, lying in a frozen pool of water. He suffered from severe hypothermia, a skull fracture, traumatic brain injury, and a broken back. Although he lingered for several agonizing hours after being found, Samuel eventually slipped into a coma, causing the doctors attending to him to believe that he had died.

Only, Samuel Jocelyn *was not dead*. Embalming was unknown in those days. He was simply buried in a wooden coffin. On the evening after his funeral, Jocelyn appeared to his best friend, Hostler, in the form of an apparition. Pointing an accusing finger at his friend, Jocelyn cried out to him, *How could you let them bury me alive when I was not dead? Open my coffin and you will find I am not in the position in which you placed me.* At first thinking it was a delusion based on the sudden loss of his friend, Hostler later became convinced that Jocelyn was trying to reach him from beyond the grave after the spirit appeared to him for a second night.

Hostler went to Jocelyn's family to attempt to gain permission to exhume his body, but they refused. Now desperately certain that he must do something to help his friend, Hostler enlisted the help of another mutual acquaintance, James Toomer. The pair proceeded to dig up Jocelyn's grave after midnight. What they found haunted Hostler for the rest of his life and continues to haunt Wilmington to this day. Samuel Jocelyn was found in his coffin, his fingers ground down to bloody nubs. In his delirium, Samuel Jocelyn had tried to claw his way out, first up through the lid of the coffin and then later through the dirt."

The crowd was shocked into silence. "Any questions?" The tour guide prompted. There were many. Regarding the second medical examination and reburial and the historical lecture that revived interest in the story, which continued to the present day, the guide provided a plethora of information. However, she admitted that little was known regarding Jocelyn's widow or the fate of his best friend, Hostler. "Some things," she shrugged, "are simply lost to history."

As the crowd peeled off into couples and small groups, Nora glanced at the clock on her phone again. Not quite 10 pm. The tour had made a big loop of the historic district downtown, and she was within a few blocks of her office at the Cotton Exchange. With her curiosity piqued about the possible origins of the mirror now sitting in the storage area at the back of her studio, Nora wanted to stop by quickly before getting a nightcap and heading home.

Rolling up the big loading door at the back of the studio, Nora noticed the wind continued to gain strength. She remembered what Dean said about the air feeling tight before a storm and decided the old lady must be right. It certainly felt like rain.

Inside her office, Nora found a couple of furniture moving pads to put under the corners of the mirror so that it slid gently into the front room. The old lady at the warehouse was stouter than she looked and had helped Nora get the three mirrors tied down easily in the Tahoe. However, the piece was simply too unwieldy in shape and length to handle any further on her own. Nora plugged in her phone to charge and flipped on her desk lamp.

After removing the sheet tied around it, Nora could see that, although dusty, the mirror was in surprisingly good shape for its age. No water stains as with the looking glass that had lain in the basement of her house for who knows how long, although it was silver-backed too. She could tell by the level of tarnish under the glass that gave it the color of hematite rather than bright silver. The glass itself had tiny air bubbles here and there, tipping Nora off once more to the fact that it was genuinely old and probably handmade.

While still examining the wide, ornately gilded frame for cracks as she wiped it off with a soft cloth, Nora stopped to make another note in her phone to look up period paints for the restoration of tiny chips here and there. *Could this really be one of the mirrors that left its imprint along the walls of the Blue Post?* Nora considered.

There were no markings to indicate such. A quick flip through the pictures on her phone from the evening's tour told her that it seemed to be the right height and width, which was exceedingly rare, considering that the mirror was at least six feet long. Glad that she'd bought extra insurance at FedEx for the other two, Nora knew that they were worth a fortune.

Still, rather than making her usual mental calculations on how much the other two might have sold for since she'd already given them away, Nora focused on the remaining mirror. Looking around the room for a place that she might hang it, she noticed an empty wall. Pulling the mirror over on its little felt runners, Nora leaned it back against her desk so that it reflected the door. Crossing her arms and stepping back to appraise the effect, Nora smiled at her reflection in the dark glass.

"Meg, Meg, *Meg*," she said, walking closer to the surface. "You certainly had an interesting life. Do you think you'll like living here with me? We can be working women together."

Just then, a magnificent thunderclap shook the entire building, followed by the sudden *whoosh* of oncoming rain that blew a chilly breeze through the door. Nora rushed to slam it shut as a few dead leaves, leftovers from the previous fall, blew in.

When Nora turned back, a broad, flat face surrounded by a mane of curly red hair leered back at her from the surface of the mirror. Nora screamed and bolted out the door, slamming it shut. Standing under her awning, shivering in the summer rain, Nora peered back through the front window of her studio. *Nothing.*

I've heard enough ghost stories to scare myself tonight, she thought.

Deciding against a drink, Nora caught her breath and went back inside to retrieve her purse and phone to summon an Uber. She turned on every light in the studio and left them on overnight.

Chapter Six

Sunday passed uneventfully. Nora rose early as usual. She stopped into Java Dog for coffee before rounding the block to her office, admiring the assortment of happy canines milling about within. She especially liked the smiling blonde corgi whose pudgy butt greatly resembled the fluffy muffins in the bakery display case.

As a child, Nora was never allowed to own a dog because her mother, Marjorie, was allegedly allergic to pet dander. Later, as an adult, she'd spent so many hours away at work that it didn't seem fair to whatever prospective pet she might have hoped to adopt, not to mention that none of her landlords in Nashville allowed dogs. Plus, Jasper hated the thought of animals in the house. Nora made a note in the ever-growing to-do list on her phone to start searching the shelters as she picked up her coffee and headed to the studio.

Peering into the front window in an overabundance of caution from the previous night as she unlocked the door, but seeing nothing, Nora shook her head in wonder at this new direction her life had taken. A direction that not only allowed her to walk to work (an absolute impossibility in Nashville, without fear of being mowed down by lost tourists) but also the opportunity to own a dog and to walk it to work as well. *What's next?* Nora thought, smirking. *Time for a yoga class in person?*

Also, for the moment Nora was intent on enjoying the effect of partial digital detox. Even though she was addicted to her phone, Nora wanted to see how long she could go without internet connectivity at home. At Nora's former job, her Brentwood Barbie boss and similarly entitled clients had expected Nora to be on call twenty-four hours a day, by phone and email, as if designing the remodel of their home office or overly elaborate playroom were equal on the urgency scale to brain surgery. Here, however, as her own boss, Nora was free to set her hours, and she intended to stick to the ones that she'd painted on the door. Ten to six, Tuesday through Saturday. Anyone who came by at another time could leave a message.

After firing up the laptop, Nora browsed several mattress websites online before selecting one to be delivered. She could tolerate the air mattress for a few days, she reasoned, if it meant sparing herself a trip to the mattress store. Even as someone in the business of decorating spaces and restoring furniture, Nora still could not bring herself to shop for mattresses face-to-face. She'd never liked mattress salespeople. They always seemed too pushy and slightly shady, like used car salesmen only worse, because they spent their entire careers pondering how to get their products into people's bedrooms.

Once she'd ordered the mattress, Nora shoaled through a few furniture auction sites and then stopped herself. *Nope.* She thought, clicking away to another page. *I'm going to take my time and find every piece organically.*

Throughout her college career, and in the years afterward until she'd met Jasper, Nora had spent countless hours at thrift stores and auctions, buying broken-down relics of furniture for what she rationalized as experiments in refurbishing and restoration. Then, she'd worked for weeks at a time on each one, until it became something completely different—bright, modern, and alive. Although she'd completely enjoyed this time and counted it as supremely useful to developing her signature style, it hadn't always resulted in the most aesthetically pleasing living spaces. At the time, Nora rationalized, she was still finding herself, so the search was worth it.

All of that came to a screeching halt, of course, when Nora and Jasper moved in together. At first, she'd chalked up what she'd seen as his abysmal lack of creativity in decor to a combined lack of time and interest. Jasper was, she reasoned, a straight man unconcerned with interior design. However, after her initial encounter with his mother, Nora knew otherwise. The wretched amount of repurposed barn wood, whitewash, and upscaled, yet outdated, recycling of what appeared to be Rachel Ashwell's shabby chic movement from the 90s originated with Jasper's mother, Julia. As an adult, Jasper was content to live in it that way, so long as the endless cycle of recording equipment moving in and out of his studio was not disturbed.

Any attempt that Nora made to change the status quo in their little bungalow had disappeared. Several times, before she gave up entirely, Nora arrived home to find that whatever unique piece she'd chosen or fabricated mysteriously vanished. In its place appeared yet another overpriced, bland yet expensive "something" from Restoration Hardware or some other such faux bohemian monstrosity, often with the price tag still attached. Thus, Nora had been forced to content herself with decorating only for her clients, while her own home remained bereft of any resemblance to her signature, brightly colored style. In short, Nora thought, closing the laptop and resolving to be patient in her quest for pieces with which she planned to adorn her new home, Julia always made sure that everything in the space that she'd shared with Jasper appeared as if Nora had never lived there at all.

As she pondered the possibility of being able to reclaim her home space at last, Nora's cell phone rang. It was her mother, Marjorie. As usual, Marjorie didn't say hello but merely launched into random motherly niceties and questions about the house and studio before at last coming to what was really on her mind.

"Have you spoken to Vicki lately?"

"Not since before I drove out to Wilmington," Nora replied automatically. Even though she'd called her sister about the mirror, her blanket response to her mother was to deny everything. It just made life easier. "Why? What's wrong with her?"

"Everything."

"Could you be more specific?"

"Where do you want me to start? With that sham marriage of hers, or how she's sabotaging her career?"

"Let's start with the marriage," Nora sighed, readying herself for the onslaught of her mother's commentary, and only slightly surprised when it involved Harper. She should have known that Pierce's dalliance with his intern would not have escaped Marjorie's omniscient gaze.

"How long have you known about Harper?"

There it was... out in the open. *Here we go*, Nora thought.

"Since I began searching for properties. Around Valentine's Day, I guess."

"Valentine's Day... a fine time for such a thing. Well, I've known since Christmas."

"How did you know at Christmas?"

"Because I caught that little rat talking to her on the phone in the bathroom."

"You were listening to Pierce in the bathroom?" Nora asked, with the appropriate amount of shock in her tone, but she was not surprised. Her mother had no concept of privacy.

"Well, it was a house that your sister paid for, after all. Why would I not, as her mother, want to be on the lookout for her best interests?"

"I have no idea," Nora replied absently as she reconsidered the rug in the reception area. Although her initial thought had been for something low pile, so that it would absorb the flow of tourist traffic for several seasons, now she wondered if something with a bit more texture might be a better choice.

"Nora, are you listening to me?"

"Yes," replied Nora, mentally returning to the conversation. "I had no idea it had gone on so long."

"Well, it has. It's all over the Faculty Club. Pierce dared to bring *her* to the faculty barbecue this weekend. Without your sister, who is the *reason* that he was invited in the first place!"

"The unmitigated gall," Nora replied, half-mockingly. It was her favorite Eudora Welty phrase.

Marjorie caught her sarcasm but not the reference that Nora intended. "This is no laughing matter, young lady." Nora would always be a "young lady" as far as her mother was concerned. "Pierce is making your sister the laughingstock of the town. You have to *do* something. You have to *reason* with her before it spoils everything she's worked so long for."

"Why me?" Nora asked, knowing full well *why her*.

"Because you're the only one in the family that she *will* listen to!" Marjorie countered, growing more emphatic with every word. "Vicki *has* to get a divorce from him. Pierce is nothing but dead weight. He'll ruin her career. Academia is a hard enough field for women to begin with. We're always discounted for not being forceful enough in our work, but when we are, we're called bitches. And if a lousy husband runs around always drunk and banging interns, then what does *that* look like, I ask you? What message does *that* send? If a woman can't control her household, what *can* she control?"

"You know, Mom..." Nora sighed, eyeing the walls. *Textured wallpaper*, she thought. *It's on trend, and it would add some dimension.* She'd look for it online this afternoon. "Vicki seems pretty distant from Pierce anyway. She's so involved in her work."

"And that's *another thing*!" Marjorie continued, oblivious to the *yeses* and *mmm humming* that Nora's end of the conversation had otherwise devolved into. "You've got to speak with her about the utter insanity of taking up your father's experiments."

"What experiments?" Nora was only ten when her father passed, and her mother had only spoken of his final work dismissively at intervals, if at all.

"All of that nonsense with the mirrors," Marjorie said, audibly exasperated.

"I just sent her a mirror this week," Nora said, absentmindedly stepping off the square footage again for the rug and wallpaper and rummaging through her desk for sticky notes.

"Oh no! That will only give her further incentive to keep going!" Marjorie exclaimed.

"What are you so worried about, Mom? It's only a mirror."

"Only a mirror, pah!" Marjorie spat. "It was a mirror that started all of it."

"All of what?"

"Your father's expulsion from Duke, from all his important work, that's what. And what launched us into that nightmare of him getting fired and my having to find a way out for us to *survive?* For *you* to have all the *privileges* you've had."

Oh Lord, not the privileges discussion again, Nora thought. She had to push the conversation in another direction quickly. "What in the world are you talking about, Mom? You're going to have to start at the beginning."

"Well," Marjorie paused, taking a deep breath. "In the *beginning*, your father was a brilliant social psychologist. He was making great strides in behaviorism. Studying inmates and what motivated them to commit crimes based on the environments in which they were raised. It's an established theory. Social Behaviorism. A person can be expected to act in accordance not only with how he or she was raised but also in concert with the expectations that surround their life. If a person is expected to act in a certain way by his or her environment, then he *will* most likely end up acting in conformity with those expectations. Surely you remember that much?"

"Mom, I follow what you're saying, but I don't remember. I was ten."

"Well, yes, *anyway*..." Marjorie continued, drawing out the word and eager to get onto her next point. "It was great work. Your father had an excellent book almost finished and could have done a lot for society as well, but *no*... *Henry* got pulled into all of that hocus pocus mirror nonsense."

"What mirror nonsense? Get to the point, Mom!"

"It all began as a joke. Your father and I were in the *real* psychology department, and those quacks were over in parapsychology. Henry made a joke to one of those pseudoscientists in the dining hall that if *he* was working on the looking glass theory and *they* were working with the concept of whether it was possible for mirrors and other objects to be haunted, then *perhaps* they should combine forces. That's when it started. Once Henry began observing their experiments on cognition and paranormal activity, all his other work went out the window. He became obsessed with their crackpot theories. Started saying that he'd seen ghosts come out of mirrors when they did their ridiculous experiments. Anyway, Henry tried doing this asinine co-presentation at the faculty research day with all that bunch, and the next thing you know, he got the boot. Then, there I was, left alone to provide for all of us until he finally..." Here, Marjorie's rant trailed off.

"Until he killed himself. I know, Mom. And I'm sorry," Nora replied gently. "But what does all of that have to do with Vicki?"

"She's replicating some of your father's experiments! One of my colleagues told me. She's completely abandoned all her other research, her students, everything. Just like your father, she's become obsessed with the idea that she can summon things out of mirrors! That it's not some kind of weird folktale." Marjorie sounded desperate, on the verge of tears. "You've got to speak with her, Nora. She's always listened to you because everyone knows you're the most level-headed one in the family. Vicki has my *real* intellect, but you've got *common* sense!"

Trying to ignore her mother's usual brand of backhanded compliments, Nora complied. "Okay, I'll give Vicki a call this afternoon. See what her side of the story is and try to reason with her."

"There is no *side* to the story," Marjorie mocked. "You've *got* to stop her, or she'll lose her chance for tenure. With Pierce acting the way he is, and the boys already off to college, she has nothing else."

But she has herself and her work, Nora thought. *Maybe she's found something else that truly interests her.* However, to her mother, she expressed none of these sentiments. Instead, she only replied, "I'll do my best."

"Your best isn't good enough unless you *make it happen*." And with that, Marjorie's end of the line cut off with a definitive chirp.

"So much for enjoying a leisurely day," Nora thought, eyeing the clock. It was almost noon. If she could get Vicki on the phone and secure some sort of response to placate her mother, she might be able to salvage a peaceful afternoon. Nora pressed the icon for Vicki's number and was relieved when her sister responded on the second ring. After exchanging pleasantries, Nora got right to the point.

"So, Mom called, and…"

"Spare me," replied Vicki, sounding exasperated. "Let me guess. I'm ruining my career, and my marriage is a sham, and Mom called you because she wants you to do something about it."

Nora sighed, relieved at least of the burden that she'd have to break any news to her sister delicately. "You're right on the money, honey. Do you want to talk about any of it? Just between us? I can always check the box on Mom's duties by saying that I tried, but your decisions were already made."

"I guess, although I'd rather discuss your escape from the Nashville Rash. It gives me hope." Vicki paused. "That's one part you might not have heard yet. Pierce and I are separating in anticipation of divorce. Or are you among the legions who know about him and Harper moving in together? They're getting a place in Wilmington near the beach. She's becoming a Reiki healer or something like that."

Nora was a little surprised by this part. *So that's why Pierce was so willing to help me find a property down here*, she thought. *Might have known there was another ulterior motive. He was looking for a place to be with Harper too.* Pierce could rarely be incited to industry.

However, to Vicki, Nora merely answered, "Yes, I did. I'm sorry that I didn't say anything. But it's hard to be the bearer of bad news."

"I'm not, really," replied Vicki. "It needed to happen for a long time. Everyone knew about it. We grew apart years ago but tried to hold it together for the boys. Now that they're in college and too cool to speak to us, it sort of doesn't matter anymore."

"Well, at least that's something that I can pacify Mother with. Your impending divorce. She'll be thrilled. Why haven't you told her? Wouldn't it be nice to have her off your back about at least one part of your life?"

Here, Vicki paused for a long time, which was unusual, and Nora noticed it. Vicki had always been the sister most ready with a snappy retort of some kind. Something more was bothering her. Finally, Vicki continued.

"I'm trying to avoid speaking to Mom altogether right now. It's not just her usual nagging. Something else this time. I can't say what it is because I'm afraid that it will sound crazy, even to you. I'd rather wait until I'm sure."

Here, Vicki stopped again. Nora could hear her sister tapping her ballpoint pen to some unheard rhythm in her head. She could envision her flipping the pen back and forth around her fingers, unconsciously mimicking her baton-twirling days in which Nora had rarely seen her idle. Changing direction, Vicki continued. "Tell me about Wilmington first. Is it everything you'd hoped? Distract and dazzle me with all the pleasures of life as a single woman. I need something to look forward to."

"Mmm, yes and no. The city is lovely, and the house and office are amazing for the price. Still can't believe Pierce did such a good job helping me pick them out." Nora paused, but Vicki didn't respond, so she went on. "I've stumbled upon a couple of little pieces of local folklore too, if you're interested. Oh, and I sent you a present!"

"What kind of present?" Vicki asked. The tapping and clicking from her end of the line stopped.

"Well, it's that mirror. Huge one. Over six feet long. Really old. It once hung in a place called..."

Vicki interrupted her. "Oh yeah, yeah, yeah. You called the other day about it. The one for my office. God, I've been so totally absorbed in everything else, I forgot." She cackled strangely.

"Yes..." Nora started, shaking her head. *Her sister, the absentminded professor.* "If you don't like it, I can always pick it up again when I come over to see you."

"No, no, it's not that. Actually, it's sort of ironic and perfect at the same time. Oh, Hell's Bells. I might as well tell you. But *don't* talk to Mom about this part. I mean, she knows about the experiments, but she doesn't know the latest developments. Give me a minute, and I'll go outside and sit in the car so that I can explain in private."

Nora heard her sister swiping out of the secured door to her lab and then hurrying down the metal staircase before going through a second secured exit to the faculty parking area. *Whatever this is, it must be pretty hush-hush,* Nora thought, wondering why Vicki not only didn't want her mother to know but also didn't want any of the other researchers in her lab to overhear. After the soft beeps of her Mercedes unlocking and relocking, Vicki returned to the phone.

"Okay. First of all, do you remember that mirror that used to hang in Dad's office?"

Nora replied that yes, she did, also recalling that the same mirror now hung in Vicki's study at her house.

"Well, a few months ago, after Pierce started spending so much time away with Harper, I needed something to occupy my mind. So, I started going through some boxes of Dad's old papers. His colleagues in the lab gave them to me years ago, remember? Because I was the one into science."

"Yes, I remember," said Nora, cautiously. Her oldest sister had been almost sixteen when their father died and was the closest to him of any of his three daughters. Vicki had taken it the hardest. She'd begged their mom to allow her to attend a special boarding high school for math and science, claiming it was because she wanted more of a challenge in her studies. Nora knew it was really because Vicki just wanted to spend her last two years of school before college away from home and anything that reminded her of their dad.

"Good. Anyway, amongst all the behavioral analysis stuff you'd suspect, I found several unmarked folders about these mirroring experiments. Dad was working on a project jointly with some other researchers in the parapsychology department. They were trying to debunk some of the myths behind the ghost stories. You know... the ones where you say something in front of a mirror, and it's supposed to make a spirit or something appear in the mirror? Bloody Mary and all that other nonsense? Well, guess what he found out?"

"What?" asked Nora, sensing where this was going.

"That it's not just folklore. The things that people claimed to see in the mirrors were often real. Some sort of spiritual imprint. They'd recorded several of them, both in person and on video and audiotape. I found them in separate boxes. Had to dig out the old VCR and boombox from the attic to play them, but they still worked! Naturally, I needed to see the phenomenon for myself and determine whether I could replicate the results of their experiments. So, I looked up the professors in the parapsychology department that he'd been working with and asked them if they still had any of the mirrors out of which they'd been able to get results. Of course, they're all retired now, and the parapsychology program is mostly closed, but they still had access to the mirrors. All of them! After a little persuading, I got them to let me borrow several of the mirrors that had produced the best results. And it worked, just as Dad described it in his notes."

"What worked?"

"The mirrors! Some of them show the person or the scene just sort of moving along as if nothing had happened. With others, you have to say the name of the person who died in front of it. Regardless, whatever died or happened in front of these particular mirrors left some type of psychic imprint, I'm sure of it! These were the same findings that Dad and the others had come to right before he passed. Not long after that, the parapsychology lab was defunded, and the professors were let go, so they didn't manage to get any further. But they'd planned a lot more. To see if they could communicate with whatever was *inside* the mirrors as *intelligent spiritual entities*. Lately, I've been starting to take those extra steps, and I swear...I believe I've interacted with some of them! Do you know what this means?" Vicki asked.

In a flash, Nora put it all together. "It means that you're excited that you've found something new, and Mom's scared shitless that it will ruin your career because nobody believes in parapsychology as an academic discipline anymore."

"Well, yeah, that... *but...*" Vicki was rolling now. "It also means that there is a possibility of contact with human spiritual intelligence after death. Which in turn means that the dead aren't dead when their bodies stop functioning. They're just incorporeal. If I can keep pushing it further and actually record having sentient, responsive conversations with one of them..." Here, Vicki stopped abruptly. "Shit. I've got to get back to the lab now. The regular lab. I forgot that I have some new subjects coming for interview profiles from the incarceration project at two. We can finish this later, but remember, don't tell Mom! She knew that I was working on this, but I tried to distract her by saying I didn't find anything and gave up.

I didn't think she'd believe me, and she hasn't, because now she's nagging you to do something about it. Promise!"

"I promise," said Nora, wondering how in the world she was going to summon the acting skills to put that lie over.

"Okay, great. And hey... I can't wait to hear the whole scoop on that mirror you've sent me. You said it's old... what if it turns out to be the biggest find yet? Can you imagine?"

"It's completely beyond my wildest dreams," replied Nora, half sarcastically, as she and Vicki exchanged goodbyes.

After she hung up, Nora turned her chair around to face the old Blue Post mirror that hung over her office desk. Nothing. Pulling up the calendar app on her phone, Nora set a reminder for herself to stop by the street market on Saturday to try to meet up with Dean again. Based on what Vicki had told her, Nora planned on doing a little research of her own.

Chapter Seven

S hutting the front door and locking it at last with a decisive snap of the key, Nora flipped her slingback heel into the air and deftly caught it behind her back. *Still got it*, she thought, eyeing the refreshments table hungrily.

One sad little brisket slider was left on the tray, probably because it had been an end piece that was mostly bun. Still, Nora stuffed it into her mouth in two bites, washing it down with the remainder of her bottle of Diet Coke, which had grown hot after sitting forgotten on the windowsill for hours. It didn't matter. She was starving. Nora had nothing else to eat all day except a squished protein bar from the bottom of her purse.

After spending two hours on her hair and makeup that morning, Nora hadn't had time for her usual coffee. *Some soft opening*, she thought, brushing her side bangs off her forehead, which glistened slightly with sweat. *I'd hate to see a hard one*. The constant fanning of the door to allow the gaggles of curious customers in and out all afternoon hadn't left the air conditioning unit much time to catch up in Nora's high-ceilinged studio. Glancing around the room, she saw that *SOLD* tags already dangled from half of the pieces she'd staged for the first day. Nora was going to have to hire a refinishing assistant sooner than she thought. Otherwise, she'd be completely out of stock in a week.

The enthusiastic reception by customers, all of whom came brandishing cell phones with first purchase coupons from the social media pages that Nora had carefully curated for months, had been enough on its own. Following the whirlwind of that morning, however, which had included a ribbon cutting with the mayor and a storm of reporters all wanting photos, videos, and sound bites for their local business stories, Nora was completely exhausted.

Looking at her cell phone, Nora saw that it was not only after eight o'clock, but that she had three missed calls from her mother. She'd been putting Marjorie off all week, not wanting to get into the whole thing about Vicki with the opening coming up. Plus, her mother had an annoying habit of referring to Nora's design career as a "hobby," rather than a real job. For Marjorie, any occupation that did not require at least a doctorate and a significant amount of scientific research for entry was merely something to pass the time, no matter how successful the endeavor might be.

Deciding that she needed real food before dealing with her mother's condescension, Nora ordered *pad see ew* and *tom kha* delivered from the Thai place nearby. Slipping into a pair of retro sneakers, which looked oddly out of place with the sleek white sheath that she'd worn all day, Nora dropped the slingbacks in her tote bag and headed home.

Nora was about halfway through her soup and a glass of Sauvignon blanc when her cell rang again. *Mother.* Knowing that the *tom kha* would likely get cold before she had a chance at another bite, Nora slurped down the rest of its coconutty goodness before she hit *Answer.*

"My God, I thought you'd died or were in jail or something."

"Hey, Mom. Great to hear from you too."

"Oh yes, yes... you too and all that. Have you spoken to Vicki about what we discussed?" The usual impatience. Nora decided to wait until the very end of the conversation before saying anything about it being the opening day of her studio, just to see if Marjorie remembered.

"Yes," replied Nora, taking a sip of wine and deciding to lead with the good news first. "Vicki's leaving Pierce."

"Oh, wonderful! That will do *so much* to improve her chances of promotion to Chair. No committee respects a woman who can't run her own family."

"I wouldn't know, Mom. Not an academic." Nora looked longingly at the *pad see ew* and wondered if her mother could hear her chew on speakerphone. She decided to chance it.

"Well, let me just tell you..." and Marjorie was off. Nora had finished half of the noodles and already put the rest away in the fridge for later by the time that her mother noticed her only response for at least fifteen minutes had been *mmm hmm.*

"Nora, are you listening? Did you hear me? What about the other thing?"

Pouring herself another glass of wine, Nora decided to play dumb. "What other thing?"

"About her *work*, or rather, the work she's neglecting for that mirror nonsense."

"Oh, yeah, thaaaat..." Nora drew out the word. "It must have blown over. You know how Vicki gets obsessed with a new project and then sometimes loses interest after a while? Well, that must be the case with this mirror thing. When I spoke to her, she hardly mentioned it. Eager to get back to the lab and work on that stuff she's been at for years. You know, for the grant working with inmates and how their early childhood experiences set patterns of behavior that..." Here, Marjorie cut Nora off.

"And you last spoke to Vicki when?"

Nora breathed out heavily, blowing her side bangs over. She decided to offer her mother a small clue that she also had a life. "Gosh, I've been so busy with the studio opening all week. It must have been Monday. Right after I spoke with you, I think."

"Well, I hope that's the last of it." Marjorie snapped, completely missing the hint. "She's not answering the phone to me, as usual. I've been thinking about going over to her lab to see for myself."

"Oh, I don't think that's necessary," said Nora, gulping down the remainder of glass number two and pouring herself a third. The last thing either of them needed was an impromptu visit from Marjorie. Vicki left Nora a voicemail the day before saying her mirror had arrived and that she loved it. She was ashamed about forgetting to call back and planned on hanging the mirror in her lab to see what she might be able to get out of it for her experiments.

"Well, that's for me to decide. A mother *knows*, you understand, when a daughter is concealing something from her. Anytime one of you ever hid something from me, I *knew*."

"Of course, you did, Mom," Nora replied, rolling her eyes.

"*Hmpf*," snuffled Marjorie from the other end. "So, what's new with you? Anything happening out there in the coastal villages?"

Nora looked at the call timer on her phone, somewhat stunned. Forty-five minutes in, and her mother was already bored enough with gossiping about her older sister to ask about her life. "Today was the opening of..." Nora heard a beep on the other end of the line and a series of rapid clicks as her mother texted a response.

"Sorry, dear. Have to go. One of the guys on the memory and cognition team. You can tell me all about your little adventures over there by the seashore later."

Condescending as usual. Although Nora attempted to say goodbye, her mother was already off the line. She hadn't expected Marjorie to care about the success or failure of her studio opening. The only mention Marjorie had ever made of the entire enterprise was when she'd mistakenly introduced Nora to one of her colleagues in the Psychiatry Department over the holidays as "my daughter who's opening the little curiosity shop on the coast this summer." Marjorie made the entire enterprise sound more like Nora was a minor character who had escaped from a Dickens novel and not a designer who felt that she was taking the first steps toward launching her custom brand.

Nora had let it slide, though. She'd long since given up trying to explain to Marjorie that interior design was more than just someone paying her to pick out a sofa. Just as her youngest sister Calista had given up trying to explain that being a dancer was also a legitimate career path. Throughout her younger sister's career, Marjorie had perpetually referred to Calista as a "teacher," mumbling under her breath, "of dance" afterward. Even though Calista had danced with several prestigious New York companies and only taught dance to underprivileged urban youth for free in her spare time. At least now Marjorie was closer to correct, Nora thought, swallowing the last of her third glass of wine thoughtfully as she wandered into the living room. For the first time since high school, Calista was once again teaching dance lessons for money. After years of their mother explaining Calista's work as such. Marjorie claimed that she "couldn't very well tell people that her daughter was *just* a dancer" because "it sounded too lewd."

Having almost finished everything for the parlor in a style she jokingly referred to as "posh urban gypsy," Nora surveyed the contents. Handmade rugs, wrought iron lamps, carefully disheveled velvet window scarves, and vintage bookcases that still needed to be refinished into what she was working into her signature style of highly saturated, matte jewel tones painted over intricate woodwork. "Yep, yep, yep," Nora muttered softly to herself as she paced off the square footage once more. Only in her personal space was she ever so indecisive. *Chaise lounge and oversized side chairs.*

No sofa. Final answer. Remembering that tomorrow was Saturday, Nora made a note to go back to the street market. She had a hunch that Dean, the street merchant whom she'd scarcely thought of again all week, in the rush of opening day prep, would likely have something suitable squirreled away in the endless depths of that warehouse.

Weighing whether or not to finish off the bottle of wine, Nora toddled into the kitchen. Leaning face toward the wall by the bottom of the stairs was the mirror from the basement, right where Nora had left it, the first day after she'd arrived. For some reason that she couldn't quite put her finger on, Nora had deliberately walked around the mirror without moving it all week. Examining the reverse and noting again that it was backed in solid silver, Nora saw the place on the wall in the entryway that she'd intentionally left blank in which to hang it.

Why haven't I gotten around to it, Nora wondered, setting her wine down on the floor so that she could pick the glass up around the outside of the frame with both hands. It was tremendously heavy. As she grasped the edges, it felt searingly hot to the touch. A blue arc of electricity sprang from each hand. Nora jumped back but managed to shock herself anyway. Shaking her hands, Nora felt the tingle travel up to her elbows as her arms prickled in gooseflesh, making the tiny blonde hairs stand up. Even more curiously, a couple of her fingertips on each hand were singed bright red, as if she'd touched a hot kitchen pan.

Damn static, she thought, putting the smarting fingertips into her mouth like a child. Nora stared accusingly down at her sock-covered feet, which ached with blisters from standing in heels all day. *The friction in the rug must have caused it,* she rationalized. *Still, why would it burn?*

When she returned from the kitchen with the remainder of the bottle of wine, Nora sat in the middle of the rug on the parlor floor. She also brought back a pair of oven mitts. Shuffling her feet on the rug, she worked up a bit of static and then purposefully discharged it onto the knob for the front door. She'd left it open to allow the evening breeze to blow in through the screen. Mostly satisfied that she was now free of static, Nora nevertheless put on the oven mitts before she picked up the mirror again. As she did, Nora could feel the heat radiating from the surface of the glass, as if she were facing an old wall heater.

Looking down, Nora was shocked to see a slight scorched streak on the carefully refinished wooden floor, where the mirror had been, along with a similar mark on the shiplap wall. Scooting one of the small, flame-retardant kitchen throw rugs along with her as she moved into the parlor, Nora made sure that the edge of the frame rested on it before she set the mirror down on the spot that she'd selected. Removing one oven mitt, Nora extended a cautious finger out to touch the silver back of the glass. Surprisingly, it was cool. However, spreading her fingers wide in front of the surface of the mirror and then cupping her palm over the edge of the frame from an inch away, Nora could sense its heat. Feeling somewhat secure that the back wasn't hot enough to leave a burn mark on the wall through the oven mitt, Nora leaned the mirror back with its surface facing her and the mitt propped behind. She settled down on the rug cross-legged and reached for wine she'd brought from the kitchen. Nora took a sip directly from the bottle.

Almost instantly, the water stain at the bottom of the glass shifted and reformed, like clouds moving on a windy day. Gray shapes began to emerge, similar to those she'd seen on the first night, until Nora could see the form of a man lying in bed. However, the slow rise and fall of his chest that she noticed before had ceased. Nora realized the man must be dead.

Another figure emerged, followed by two more. In the smoky swirls beneath the surface of the glass, these too began to coalesce into human figures. Dimly at first, and then distinctly, Nora could see that one man was a doctor. He stood beside the man in bed with one hand on his wrist and the other holding a pocket watch. After a minute or two, the doctor shook his head and leaned down, his ear close to the man's mouth. Taking a deep breath, the doctor reached up and gently closed the man's eyes before turning and motioning to the other two. The doctor put a hand on each man's shoulder, and Nora strained to read his lips. The doctor seemed to be saying that he was sorry. The man on the left reached out to shake the doctor's hand and pulled him closer, as he whispered something else unintelligible into his ear. The man on the right simply took a step back and covered his face with his hands. Turning toward the corner, he seemed to shake a bit, and Nora could tell he was crying but trying not to allow the other men to see.

A few moments later, the doctor appeared to be giving directions to the two men, who nodded in understanding. The man who had shaken hands with the doctor pulled back the sheet covering the dead man and took a firm hold on his legs, just below the calf. The man who had been crying moved to the head of the bed and gathered the dead man's upper body into his arms, holding him so that the man's head rested against his stomach. The dead man's facial features were soft and boyish, his long, wispy hair straggling limply over his forehead still wet from his final fever.

As Nora watched, the doctor opened the door to the bedroom, and the men began to carry the body out. Nora was so engrossed in the scene, they were halfway down the stairs before she noticed that the shadowy image had sound in real time. With a shock Nora realized that the bedroom was *her* bedroom. The scene appeared to be a continuation of one she'd watched on her first night in the house. Nora could hear the same heavy footfalls coming down the stairs by the kitchen as she saw the men disappear from view in the glass, leaving only the image of the doctor behind, writing something into a notebook.

Nora scrambled backward, knocking over the remainder of her bottle of wine onto the rug, and sliding around the corner behind a bookcase. The labored, dragging steps continued to the screen door and came to a stop on the front porch. Suddenly, the main door slammed shut with a definitive *whack*. Trembling behind the bookcase, Nora peeped around the corner but saw nothing. In the world of the looking glass, the ephemeral doctor continued writing in his notebook.

This must be a dream, Nora thought. *I drank too much, and I'm dreaming*. She scurried on her hands and knees around the corner to retrieve a towel from the downstairs bathroom to clean up the spilled wine before it soaked into the rug. As she blotted, thankful that it had been white and would not stain, Nora was careful to keep her back to the glass. She purposefully lingered in the laundry room off the kitchen, placing the now empty bottle deep down into the trash can, all the time repeating, *You're drunk. This can't be real.* However, as she stood in the laundry room repeating this mantra, she heard the front door creak open again.

Returning to the parlor, Nora couldn't help herself. Looking into the glass, she saw the man who had tried to hide his tears and the doctor talking as they pulled the sheets from the bed. The man's hair was darker than the others, and he had deep rings beneath his eyes. His face looked haggard but seemed as if he understood everything that the doctor was saying. However, as the darker man moved out of the entryway, Nora could see a reflection in the glass of another figure. At first, she thought the other man who helped carry the body downstairs had also returned, but after a moment she recognized that man had curly hair and a beard, while this man was more youthful, with wispy long hair that straggled about his round face.

It's him, Nora realized in shock. *The dead man. Or his... spirit?*

The doctor exited the room with his arms full of linens, leaving only the dark man and the other behind. The pale figure slowly moved to the other end of the bed and came to rest beside the mirror on the wall. Nora recognized it as the very glass into which she'd been staring.

Thinking that he was alone, the dark man collapsed down onto the bed, burying his face once again into his hands. The ghostly figure's lips moved as if he were speaking, but his friend did not stir. The pale man seemed to grow impatient and repeated the same two-syllable word over and over, his mouth growing wider and his gestures more emphatic. *He's shouting his friend's name*, Nora thought, *but for some reason, his friend can't hear him.*

Finally, the dark man looked up, his face streaked with tears. The pale shape advanced toward him and reached as if to place a hand on the other man's shoulder. The dark man jumped back, and the entire image shifted, seeming to bend and twist as Nora watched the ethereal figure being pulled back into the glass, as if into a vacuum. Recovering from his start, Nora watched the dark man, now completely alone in the room, seem to catch a reflection in the looking glass.

He can see what I'm seeing, Nora thought, as she watched the dark man observe the curiously calm face of the pale man in the glass peering back out at him. He crossed the room halfway and then stopped, still staring into the glass for at least a full minute. The ashen face stared back at him with an expression that was a mix of anxiety and an attempt to appear friendly. At last, the dark man ran his hands through his hair and turned away. As his friend paced the bedroom several rounds, the pale man in the reflection again began to look apprehensive. When the dark man picked up a quilt and advanced toward the glass, the pale man became frantic, shouting his friend's name.

However, the dark man closed his eyes and shook his head in disbelief as he covered the glass with the quilt and removed it from where it hung. Setting the glass down on the floor, he wrapped the quilt around the back of it and leaned it against the wall. A strange look crossed his face, and he extended the palm of his right hand out toward the covered surface of the mirror. Pulling back, he stopped to examine his hand, and Nora had a flash of empathy. *It's hot*, she thought. *He can't understand why the glass would be hot.* Once more shaking his head in bewilderment, the dark man backed out of the room, his eyes still locked on the quilt-covered looking glass.

The moment that Nora lost sight of him, a strong rush of cold wind blew past her, across the parlor from upstairs. The front door slammed shut. She stood blinking at it in disbelief. Finally, Nora walked over and twisted the lock with a trembling hand. Turning, she once again saw her reflection in the looking glass, above the water spot. Placing her palm over the surface of the glass, as she had seen the dark man do in the image, Nora felt nothing. She reached out timidly and touched the wrought iron frame. It was room temperature.

Unsure of what she had seen, Nora did the only thing that she could think of. She quietly went to the linen closet and retrieved a blanket. Wrapping the looking glass carefully lengthwise, she folded the ends over the top and under the bottom. As if in a daze, she started to go upstairs to her bedroom to change but thought better of it.

That was his room, Nora thought. *The room that the pale man died in.*

Gathering boxers and a tank top from the chest of drawers, Nora felt uncomfortable changing in there. She'd already outfitted the other two bedrooms upstairs. The front one was a guest room, and the back was her study. Preferring the solid comfort of being surrounded by tangible items she used every day, Nora stretched out on the sofa in her study with a fuzzy throw. It just didn't feel right sleeping in the room of the scene that she had watched.

She thought about calling someone, but it was long past midnight. However, who would believe her? *Calista would*, Nora thought. Her youngest sister believed in all sorts of things that some people called *woo-woo stuff*—crystals, tarot, the whole nine. But Calista was an early riser, getting up with the sun for a morning jog for as long as Nora could remember. Not to mention, Nora felt certain that, in her current state of inebriation, if she opened with, *Hey Lis, sorry I haven't been in touch this week. By the way, there is a haunted looking glass in my house. Just thought you should know* that even her spiritually inclined baby sister would likely tell her she was drunk and to get off the phone.

Instead, Nora just lay there watching the eyes of her kitschy tuxedo cat clock shift back and forth, searching randomly on her phone for any information that she could find about what had happened in the parlor, until at last, she fell asleep.

Chapter Eight

The next morning, Nora woke up stiff and dry-mouthed on the sofa in her study. Padding downstairs for a bottle of electrolyte water, she carefully avoided going near the looking glass. Even wrapped securely in a blanket, what she thought she'd seen was not something Nora relished the thought of witnessing again in broad daylight. She hoped that further research would later remove the notion that there was a haunted looking glass in her parlor, rather than reinforce it.

Having intentionally set the hours of her shop from ten to six so that she would have time for breakfast every morning, Nora congratulated herself once again on the decision. She shared with Calista the tendency to wake with the sun, but having naturally low blood sugar, it usually took her longer to get going. Regardless, Nora was out the door and on her way to the coffee shop by eight o'clock.

Snarfing down the last bite of a bagel with her latte as she walked toward the design studio, Nora checked her phone and realized she still had a whole hour before opening. Marveling about the amount of free time that she had, now that she wasn't spending at least an hour and a half of her morning in the car crawling along a lethargic commute through throngs of tourists from East Nashville to downtown, Nora decided there was time for a quick swoop by the street market before opening her doors.

At the same stall where Nora found her the previous week, but now surrounded by an entirely different array of small antiques, Dean Goodnight called to her. "Well, well, if it ain't Nora Hewitt of Nora Hewitt Designs." Dean's call was followed by a raucous cackle mixed with coughing as she rose from a Victorian chaise lounge, cigarette in hand.

"Delightful, Dean, simply delightful!" Nora returned, heading over to meet her.

"Saw your opening in the news. Don't ya feel bad about yourself, now?" Dean pointed at Nora with her long cigarette holder, spilling a column of ash onto the ground.

Nora was puzzled but decided to play along. "Bad for what reason?"

"Why, 'cause ya gonna put a poor old lady out of business, that's why!" Another cackle, followed by a round of coughing, which subsided after Dean took a draw from the cigarette.

"B to the S, Dean. You know there's room for both of us."

"Eh, you're right. You're right." Dean replied, picking up her cane and waddling over to Nora. "What ya on the lookout for today? Maybe I can lighten the load o'cash ya got on ya."

"Actually," said Nora, walking over to the chaise lounge on which Dean had been reclining, "I think you might. How much for this falling down old thing?"

"Har, har, har," Dean laughed through another cough. "She ain't fallin' down. What'll ya give?"

"I know better than to make the first offer, Dean. You name a price."

"I would pay *you* just to not have to put it back on the truck. Heavy as lead." A woman with green eyes and shaggy brown hair emerged from behind the booth, carrying an old tea set.

"Hush your mouth! Can't ya see we's dealin'?" Dean scolded.

"Gramma, you know that came from the old Blue Post stuff that no one else wanted. You've already doubled your money on that lot, and half the warehouse is still full of it," the younger woman replied. Then to Nora, "What do *you* think it's worth?"

Nora paused, mulling over the possibility. She hated to lowball anyone as a matter of principle, but she would have to reupholster and refinish the chaise lounge. Still, the woodwork on it was very unique. Upon closer inspection, Nora could see that it was carved not with the usual flowers and vines, but instead with what appeared to be two mermaids across the top. "I'll give you a thousand for it."

"Naw," coughed Dean, waving a wrinkled claw at her dismissively and walking away. "Fifteen hundred, or I make *her* put it back on the truck."

Nora saw the woman frown and step back. "Let's split the difference at twelve-fifty," the other woman countered. Dean gave her a sharp look.

"A grand is all I have on me," said Nora, calculating in her mind how many hours it would take to remove all the old varnish from the woodwork. And there was no telling what kind of bugs might be living in the ratty cushions.

"Humpf," Dean snuffled. "Guessin' if ya want it then, you'll have to go find some more."

Her sharp blue eyes challenged Nora from behind thick black horn-rimmed spectacles.

"I suppose I could," said Nora, thinking about the money stacked up in her safe at the studio from her opening the day before. "Would you take thirteen hundred even? All I have are hundreds."

"Oh, is that all?" mocked Dean. "Thought ya just said all ya had was a grand. But if ya got another roll in your shoe or summers, I'll take..."

The younger woman interrupted her, "She'll take twelve-fifty. I can give you the other fifty back in change. And we're here until noon if you need to go get the rest from an ATM or something."

"I have it at my studio." Nora glanced at the clock on her phone. "And I think that I have just enough time to get down there and back before I open at ten. Or I could just take lunch early and come back to get it at noon as you're packing up. Whichever is easiest."

"No need to make two trips," said the woman. "I'll just put a *sold* tag on it and help you load it when you return."

Dean looked huffy at having her transaction interfered with. "She can leave the thousand with me now if she likes."

"Or she can just give us the whole amount when she comes back," the green-eyed woman added. "I trust her."

Nora smiled. "Thanks."

"Don't mention it," replied the woman, extending her hand. "I'm Hazel Goodnight. Dean's granddaughter."

Nora turned her head slightly to the side. She knew she'd heard the name before but couldn't quite place where.

"She's famous," Dean interjected, having recovered from her slight long enough to tap another cigarette out of the pack from the shirt pocket of her navy polo. "On the TV an' everythin'."

"Oh?"

"Not really. Gramma's just exaggerating. I have a podcast on the supernatural and paranormal, and I've been on local television a couple of times. But I'm a folklorist. I teach in the English department at UC Wilmington."

"Ya always make it sound like you're the marm at a grammar school," Dean cawed, lighting her cigarette and blowing a perfectly executed ring of smoke. "She's a doctor. Not the sawbones kind, but the college professor kind."

"No kidding?" Nora asked, slightly surprised. "So are my mom and older sister. My dad was too, but he passed away."

"What kind are they?" Dean said, skipping over the condolences.

"Gramma!" Hazel said sharply.

"It's okay. That was a long time ago. My mom and sister are both research psychiatrists. They work at Duke. Mom specializes in memory and cognition, and Vicki is a behavioralist. Right now she's working with inmates on a long-term study regarding repeat offenders and the looking glass theory. You know, where a person is expected to behave in ways that conform with what they see in their environment combined with what is expected of them."

"Makes sense," said Hazel, nodding. "A lot of people get caught in the difficult circumstances that they grew up in, not just because they don't have good examples, but because people stereotype and anticipate that they can only do wrong, given their situation."

"Or if ya was to put it *meta-for-ic-lee*," said Dean, "You can only be great if ya rubbin' shoulders with greatness, an' you're willin' to allow some of it to rub off on ya." She winked at her granddaughter and poked her lightly in the side with her chubby elbow. "Like this one here. I knew she'd grow up to be somethin' great if she hung 'round me long enough!" Dean chortled, erupting into another fit of coughing as Hazel rolled her eyes.

"So, I'll see you again around noon?" Hazel asked.

"Definitely." Nora dug around in her tote bag and pulled out a business card, which she handed to Hazel along with a thousand dollars, as she smiled at Dean. Seeing the money, Dean blew another perfect smoke ring of approval at her.

After a morning of casual browsers, in which she sold not a thing, Nora put up her *Closed for Lunch* sign and walked back over to the street market. Once again, she marveled at the new life of ease she lived. At her old job with the firm in Nashville, she had never gone out for lunch once in over a decade. If she had time to eat at all, it had been at her desk.

Hazel was waiting, with an old blue Ford 150 pickup backed into the stall. After a bit of a struggle, they had the chaise securely roped in. They drove the eight blocks or so to Nora's studio and then around back to unload at the dock. Scooting it to the area that Nora designated for refinishing, Hazel read the sign overhead. It said, *Where the Magic Happens*, surrounded by sparkles. Seeing her looking at it, Nora shrugged, "Eh, I try. Would you like a tour?"

As Nora was showing her around the studio, Hazel stopped in front of the large mirror that hung behind Nora's desk. She pulled a pair of gold wire-rimmed glasses from her shirt pocket and peered closely at the frame.

"You bought this from Gramma. It's one of the Blue Post mirrors."

"Good eye, and yes, I did."

"There were four of them once. Did you get them all?"

"Well, I got three of them. I sent the other two to my sisters." Hoping for further information, Nora decided to play dumb. "Was there a fourth one?"

"Yes," Hazel replied slowly, backing away from the mirror. Nora could sense that she was troubled by something.

"Well, I've been wondering about that. There was another mirror that used to hang in my late husband's recording studio, behind the console." *Looked just like these*, Nora thought, *which was why I bought them.* "I got it at a flea mall in Nashville. Do you think it could be the fourth one?"

"That depends," Hazel said, sitting down on a deep purple velvet chair. "Did he ever notice anything unusual about it?"

"If he did, he never said anything," Nora replied. "Although Jasper never really talked about what went on in his studio. Said it ruined the creative process for him or something."

Hazel continued to sit tensely in the plush chair. She squinted at the mirror, then removed her glasses and began to polish them nervously on her shirt. "If it were one of the four, and he was around it for a long time, especially playing music, he would have noticed something." She put her glasses back on and turned to Nora. "Have *you* noticed anything strange with this one?"

Nora felt herself stop breathing. *How would she know?* "Well, it *is* the weirdest thing," she said, forcing a laugh as she sat down in the other purple chair facing Hazel. "And you're going to think I'm kind of crazy, but the first night after I bought it, I was about to lock up the studio when I thought I saw something in it. Startled me a little."

"Let me guess," Hazel said, leaning forward. "It was a broad-faced woman with red hair."

"Oh my God, yes!" Nora exclaimed, clenching the arms of her chair, unable to feign disinterest any longer. "How did you know?"

"Because I've seen her too," Hazel replied, easing back into her chair. "It's Meg."

Nora paused for a moment. It was as if puzzle pieces clicked together in her brain. "Wait, wait, wait...Meg? As in Gallows Meg? From the Blue Post?"

"You've got it," Hazel answered, in a voice that Nora felt certain she normally reserved for students.

"But that's crazy! That would mean..."

"That she's a ghost. What you saw was a ghost."

"How can you be so sure?"

Hazel laughed. "I guess you've not listened to my podcast, then." She reached into the slim crossbody bag that she still had on and pulled out a card. "I should have given this to you when you gave me yours. Never quick enough on the draw for networking. Sorry."

Nora read the face of the card: *Hazel Goodnight's Haunting Grounds. A weekly podcast exploring the facts, fiction, and folklore surrounding tales of the supernatural, the paranormal, and the otherwise unexplained.* She flipped the card over. The back had a slogan, which Nora was sure was the tagline for the show, written in old-fashioned Blackadder font: *Good Night, Godspeed, and Good Luck.*

Pointing the card at her, Nora said quizzically, "So... you're a ghost hunter?"

"Emphasis on the *hunter* part," Hazel said, smiling. "Very few actual ghosts are found. As I said back over at Gramma's, I'm a folklorist. I study local legends and how or why they may have arisen. Since many of those stories often involve some sort of supernatural phenomenon, though, I suppose the simplest thing is to call me a ghost hunter. I often use paranormal investigation equipment to discern whether or not there is some sort of entity present. 99% of the time, there isn't. You'd be surprised at how many tales of alleged hauntings turn out to have begun with some kind of tragic personal story that has woven its way into the fabric of generalized cultural guilt. Why do you think that there are so many stories of haunted prisons, asylums, abused women, and so on? Because those are the people whom society gave up on, and now we're collectively ashamed. Or to use a different terminology—we're haunted by them."

Nora stood up from her chair. "But that other one percent... you're saying that this mirror could be one of those? That it's different?"

"Yes. All four of them were different. Which isn't surprising. The Blue Post has been authenticated many times as a place of paranormal activity."

"Okay, slow down," Nora said, waving both palms face up at Hazel. "You're going to have to take me step by step through this whole thing. Last weekend, I went on one of those local ghost tours, and..."

Hazel interrupted her, "Was your guide's name Scarlett? Did she have that new bluish-red hair that kids have nowadays? Sort of steampunk-looking?"

"I don't remember her name, but yes, she did have hair like that and looked steampunky. What is this, the Kevin Bacon game?" joked Nora. "Do you know everyone in town?"

"Almost. Scarlett was one of my former students. Continue."

However, just as Hazel began to speak again, there was a rapping on the beveled glass of the studio's front door. They both jumped and then looked at each other, bursting into a fit of giggles. Two bespectacled faces peered through the door like a pair of owls.

"Can't you read the sign, Estelle? It says they're out to lunch!" The man said, in a whisper that could have been overheard in a sawmill.

"Well, I can *see* two people in there! Maybe they're back early! I want to get another look at that handmade wallpaper. They say it's coming back in style," replied the woman, escalating in volume.

Hazel rose to leave. "I'll let you get back to business. As a matter of fact," she checked her watch. Nora noticed it was rose gold and had one of those tiny Victorian faces. "I need to get back to help Gramma load up. She doesn't need to be carrying heavy things out in this heat, but if I leave her alone for a second, that's exactly what she does."

Nora led her to the door. "If you're not doing anything for Sunday dinner, you should come over so we can finish up our discussion. I need to hear more about what I've gotten myself into."

Hazel turned back to face Nora from the sidewalk as the older couple scuttled in. "Plenty. If you've started having the same types of experiences that I had with those mirrors, you're in for *plenty*."

Chapter Nine

Sunday evening found Nora in her kitchen, having prepared her first actual meal in the new house. She'd decided to go with the tried and true, a lasagna and salad. Setting the table with her chicly asymmetrical sculptured white dinnerware and a burst of fresh lilies, she stepped back to admire the effect of their contrast against the dark wooden table as the doorbell rang.

"As Time Goes By," said Hazel, recognizing the tune of the chimes as Nora let her in. "*Casablanca* reference, nice." She handed Nora a bottle of wine but stopped when she entered the dining room to stare at the chandelier. "Is that..."

"Yep," said Nora, gesturing to the vintage black-and-white poster on the wall. "I made it myself from an old twin-engine airplane propeller. Same model as in the poster. Notice how the length of it parallels the dining table? I was quite proud of that happy little accident."

Hazel flinched, as a thoughtful expression clouded her face, then cleared into a forced smile. "If they paid college professors more, I'd have to pay you to redesign my place. That's pretty genius. And also the last thing I expected to see in the dining room of the old Hostler house."

"You haven't even sat down yet, and already you're telling me things that I don't know about my own home." Nora motioned for Hazel to sit and began to uncork the bottle of wine.

"I can't believe that you're as into antiques as you are and haven't already ferreted out that piece of information," replied Hazel, reaching for the salad tongs. "Any realtor with half a brain should have made that a big selling point for someone like you."

"Ah, that explains why I remain in the dark," said Nora, successfully extracting the cork and reaching for Hazel's glass to fill. "My soon-to-be ex-brother-in-law Pierce was the real estate agent in question. He must have been too busy entertaining his side piece secretary to share any of that important information. Enlighten me."

"Gotcha," said Hazel. She left an appropriate beat of comprehending silence before continuing.

"This house should be eligible for one of those historic preservation plaques if you're interested. Although, I probably wouldn't, if you plan on continuing to modernize," Hazel said, gesturing around. "A lot of the powers that be in that arena can get pretty picky on what you're allowed to do and not do. My own house could be declared historic too, but I don't want to put up with the hassle. Pure nosiness, if you ask me. I love what you've done with this place so far. Old homes shouldn't be allowed to become mausoleums. But I digress..."

Hazel took a sip of wine. "Before it was divided up into apartments for college kids a couple of decades ago, this house was originally owned by Mr. Alexander Hostler. Sound familiar?"

Nora took a sip and swirled the remainder in her glass as she pondered. "I feel like it should be, but I'm not great with names."

"Well, this one you should have heard on the tour that you took with Scarlett if she's visiting all the usual places. Hostler was the guy whose friend was buried alive."

"Shut up!" Nora sat her wine glass down and picked up her phone, scrolling through the notes she'd taken after the tour. "Samuel Jocelyn! That was the fellow who died, right?"

"As rain," replied Hazel. "Since you missed out on that little tidbit, I suppose you're not aware that Jocelyn died in this house either? Or rather, that the doctor *thought* he died."

"Wait, wait..." Nora scanned her notes again. "Scarlett said that Samuel lived out on a plantation near the swamp. Wouldn't it be more logical for him to have died at his own house? Or at the hospital?"

"It would have, but that's not what happened. Wilmington didn't have a hospital until 1890, and it was too far for them to have transported Samuel back home. Given the swelling on his brain, most likely the doctor decided that it wouldn't be prudent to move him. Since his best friend lived right next door to the doctor, the easiest thing would have been to put him up here."

"In my bedroom," Nora said, thinking aloud before finishing up the rest of her glass in one large gulp. "Samuel Jocelyn died in my bedroom."

"Hey, we'll never make it to the pasta if you don't pace yourself," joked Hazel. "We haven't even gotten to the part about the mirrors yet."

"We have." Nora stood up and went over to the blanket-covered object still leaning against the wall. Unlike the rest of the house, it was the only thing left untouched as she prepared for her friend's arrival. "I'd like to show you something."

"Let... me... guess," said Hazel, rising from the table and going over to stand next to Nora. "Another mirror."

Nora nodded at her. "Yep." They exchanged glances, and then Nora put her hand out toward the edge of the wrought iron frame. She frowned. "I don't know why it's not doing it right now, but sometimes, it's hot. The two times that I've seen it..." she trailed off.

"It's a surge in energy just before the spirits materialize," Hazel responded. "Different objects manifest in different ways. Sometimes, a room will have a cold spot. In other cases, an object will emit heat."

"So, it's real. What I saw in this looking glass was... a ghost?"

"Likely, if you've experienced it more than once under similar conditions. Objects can hold spiritual energy just like houses. As I mentioned yesterday, there are all sorts of folktales about being able to see a person who died in front of a mirror long after their death. For example, people of the Jewish faith have covered mirrors in the houses of their dead for centuries because they believe that a person's spirit can become trapped in there."

"And I suppose you've encountered this sort of thing before?"

"Once for sure, although I've heard of others," replied Hazel. "Not every mirror seems to catch spiritual energy equally. Or perhaps not everyone who passes on while in front of one still has anything that they want to say. No one really knows. However, with the one that I feel most assuredly was the case, and the same with others who have shared similar experiences, there seems to be something about mirrors backed in silver as being especially receptive to it. As best as I can determine, silver acts like a sort of spiritual battery, storing up energy until it's ready to be released. All true hauntings are merely a release of pent-up energy. It's the reason that a place that claims to be haunted initially seems to disappoint so many wannabe ghost hunters as it becomes more famous. A spirit needing to be heard expends all its energy for the first few visitors, but if too many come, it gets exhausted and needs time to recharge. I also believe that if the entity's goal is simply to be heard and it tries several times but receives no release or whatever other results that it is seeking, it seems to become disappointed in the fact that no one is listening. So, it goes silent for a while."

"Charging up for the next round of people to try again. Like a battery," Nora summarized, letting the information sink in. Then thinking to herself, *this must have been what Vicki was working on, revisiting Dad's experiments. She must have access to mirrors that emit paranormal energy.*

"Or an introverted person who becomes exhausted by intense social situations, yes." Hazel gestured at the table. "We should have dinner before the pasta gets cold. I can talk and eat at the same time. This is going to be a pretty extended discussion, and I should start from the beginning. I think it's easier to take in the details that way."

As they sat down at the dining table again, Hazel explained. "Just before my freshman year of college, my parents passed away in a small plane crash."

"Oh, I'm so sorry!" apologized Nora, looking up guiltily at the propeller light fixture. "I had no idea."

"Don't worry. It's okay now. I've had a long time to work through it. They owned a construction company that specialized in building beach condos around the Southeast. One day, they were on their way up the East Coast back to Wilmington when they ran into the front edge of a tropical storm. They had been trying to get ahead of it and land in time to check in on a new development their company was working on, but they never made it. Authorities picked up many pieces of the wreckage, but their bodies were never recovered. Lost in the storm surge that followed."

Hazel paused here to take a bite of her food and then continued. "I was an only child, so I inherited everything. But, being only nineteen, I didn't exactly know what to do with it or whom to trust. Gramma Dean helped me through it. She lost her husband in a truck-driving accident while my father was still a baby, so she was used to picking up the pieces."

"That's a lot for one family to go through," Nora said, trying to chew quietly in deference to the story. "But I have a feeling that Dean's the sort of person who could handle it."

"Old lady is tough as nails. Smart too, even though she quit school in 10th grade. She had to be. Those kinds of things seem to follow the Goodnight family, but that's another story for another time." Hazel glanced downward at her plate before going on.

"Anyway, Gramma Dean and I decided the best thing was for us to sell all the projects that were in progress to a larger company and then put the rest away in trust, which we did. Since I had plenty of money but needed something to occupy my mind, I stayed in school. Way better than therapy, in my opinion, and far more interesting. Finished up with undergrad in three years because I didn't take summers off, went to Chapel Hill through the PhD, and then came here to teach. I was almost thirty by the time I'd finished. Just after that, Gramma Dean broke an ankle falling down the stairs while carrying a box of books that was too heavy for her. I convinced her to sell her bookshop down in Alabama and move in with me, hoping she'd retire. However, as you saw on Saturday, she couldn't sit still. As soon as her ankle healed, she was out roaming the streets of Wilmington for something to do. That's when she got the idea to start salvaging antiques to sell to tourists at the market. We bought that warehouse you've been to down by the wharf, and she started filling it with all kinds of estate and bankruptcy sale deals that she'd find, combing the listings every day. It was during the height of the Great Recession around 2008-2009, so a lot of things were going for cheap, and she had an eye for a bargain."

Here, Hazel stopped, having finished her lasagna, and motioned toward the kitchen, meaning to put her plate away. Nora waved her off, took the dish, and returned with a tiramisu from a local bakery. She sat down in the middle of the table with a couple of dessert plates. They each cut off a piece as Hazel finished her story.

"A few months into Gramma's quest to buy what seemed to be every piece of antique furniture in Wilmington, she came upon this quick sale auction online of all the stuff remaining in the old Blue Post building. Some developers had bought it for a song and planned to gut the structure to turn it into some kind of hipster gastropub concept. When I got home from class, she nagged me to go check it out that night, since bidding on the lot started early the next morning. She doesn't drive by herself anymore. At least she's not supposed to, because her vision isn't very good, so if you see her out, tell me. I agreed to run over there and scope it out. When I arrived, I went around peering in the windows but couldn't see that much because the panes were so dirty. But I could tell that people had already been working in the building recently, from the tools left lying on the floor. So, I thought I'd see if anyone was still around to let me walk through."

Hazel finished her wine and poured another glass. Nora sat on the edge of her seat, leaning forward, her tiramisu untouched. "When I tried the door, it was open, so I went in. I called out for anyone who might be in the building, but there was no answer. I'd been inside for a minute or two, poking around, when the door slammed shut behind me. Thinking it must just be an old door frame out of alignment, I flipped on the flashlight on my cell phone and kept looking around. That's when I first saw her."

"Who?"

"Who do you think? The point of this whole long-winded story. Gallows Meg! In the mirror. Or rather, mirrors plural, since there were four of them lining the walls of the whole front room. The same mirrors you own now."

"How did you know it was her?"

"I didn't at the time. I had to look it up the next day. But as I stood there, I could see a scene unfolding, like out of a mist from within the mirror. Apparently, from the moment the door closed, it started playing out the night in which she was killed. Later, I figured out from the angle of the side panel windows next to the door that the whole scene would have been reflected in the mirror over the bar facing the door and then refracted again in all the mirrors surrounding the room, creating a sort of hall of mirrors view of her murder."

"Jesus, how awful!"

"It was gruesome. In every reflective surface of the barroom, I could see Meg standing there, done up in all of her madam's finest, tall powdered wig, breasts pushed up high in her corset, and dripping with jewelry. Meg was holding the bag of money in one hand and locking the door with the other. Then, from alleyways on two sides, there came this mob of men. I have no idea how many of them there were, at least a dozen that I could see. They looked like they might have been sailors, but they were so ragged, I couldn't tell. One of them tried to stab her in the chest, but she dodged it and grabbed his hand. Took the knife away and stabbed him with it instead! Meg was crazy strong and taller than all the men who descended on her, but there were just too many of them. She pulled a pistol out from among her skirts and shot one, but another made a running tackle into her back and shoved her to the ground. They tore her dress and wig off, and still, she wrestled and fought with them there in just her corset in the street, yelling for help. Finally, they got her arms and legs pinned down, a man on each limb, and the last sat on her chest while he slit her throat. As she lay bleeding out in the street and gasping for air, some of them stomped on her body while others tore apart her money sack, kicking and gouging at each other for every gold coin that spilled out. Once they had gotten it all, they left in a swarm, dragging the two that Meg had killed along with them on a bloody trail. Meg lay splayed out on the ground, her nose broken and cheeks smashed in. Her jewelry was gone, and her ears were half ripped off as they snatched her earrings. She was stripped almost naked by their grabbing hands as they ransacked her body trying to find any more cash left on her."

Here, Hazel paused to shake her head. "One thing you have to remember about dealing with spirits from the past. Most people who become ghosts don't die peacefully. In fact, they often had quite brutal deaths. Nowadays, we tend to romanticize the past. What we forget is that women alone back then especially were extremely vulnerable, regardless of their wealth or social standing."

Nora remained silent for a moment, before asking, "What happened then?"

"Well, I froze. It was like watching a car wreck, only worse. I couldn't take my eyes off the reflection of her mangled corpse. Then, ever so slowly, a sort of mist began to form. At first, I thought it was smoke, but then, as it began to coalesce over the body, I could see that it was *her*. Meg. Or rather, her spirit. The door creaked back open, and I finally turned away from the mirrors to see her float in. I could see right through her and out into the street. Only, it wasn't the street that I had left before. It was the street as it looked when it had been *her* street, but it too was like a fog, the edges of shapes blurring and churning. She came toward me and reached out a ghostly hand as if to take mine. I don't know why, but I reached out to her instinctively too. Instead of our hands meeting as they normally would palm to palm, hers passed through mine. It felt so cold, like putting my hand in a bucket of ice, so I withdrew quickly. Meg stared at me as if she didn't know what was going on. Then, as it dawned on her, she began to scream, the most piercing, otherworldly shriek you've ever heard. I felt a force like walking into the headwinds of a hurricane, pushing me backward toward one of the mirrors. It grew stronger so that I couldn't stand in the place where I was. I kept having to retreat further until my back was pressed into the mirror. Meg's ruined face was now inches from mine, still screaming, with that icy wind pressing me back. However, I could feel that the surface of the mirror was growing hotter behind me until it felt as if my back were on fire. Also, I could feel the surface bend inward as if it were melting. Suddenly, I realized what was happening, and I panicked. Meg was trying to push me *into* the mirror! And it was working!"

"Oh my God, how did you get away?"

"I did the only thing that I could think of. I dropped straight to the floor and curled up against the wall in a fetal position. As I did so, I felt a huge rush of cold air meet a wall of heat above me, like a winter firehose turned on a burning building. Then, Meg fell into the mirror. It happened in just a fraction of a second, and she was gone. I lay there on the floor for several minutes, listening to the surface of the mirror sizzle like a hot pan doused in water, praying that it was over. Finally, when I felt it was safe to stand up, I got out of there as quickly as I could."

"So, did you tell Dean what happened? Why in the world would she ever buy the mirrors after that?"

"Oh, I told her," Hazel said, this time beating Nora to the kitchen to put away her dessert plate. "Gramma Dean claims to be Catholic, but she believes in all kinds of stuff. And she didn't buy them intentionally. No one did. Turns out, not a single person bid on the auction. The whole lot went to scrap in some warehouse somewhere, and the idea of turning the place into a gastropub never panned out. But Gramma Dean accidentally ended up with them anyway in another auction lot she bought a few months after. Of course, she had no way of knowing that *those* mirrors were among the lot, sight unseen. However, I recognized them instantly one day as we were moving things around in the warehouse. We argued about it. I told her it was irresponsible to sell them, but she said that no one who bought them would ever know, and perhaps since they came to her for free, it was meant for her to get rid of them. Also, she brought up a pretty good point, which was that the mirrors might not work anymore if they were taken outside of the Blue Post. That they might have to be grounded in the location where the events took place for Meg's energy to come through."

"Do you believe that?" asked Nora, at last taking a bite of her tiramisu. "I mean, one of those mirrors is now hanging in my office, and both of my sisters have the others. Then, there was that moment when I thought I saw her face. Could Meg still be in there, just *waiting*? Should we be worried?"

"I don't know," Hazel shrugged. "Maybe not. Nothing strange ever happened with them for the decade they were in the warehouse that I know of, and I'm in there at least every week, often alone. But they've been wrapped up, so that could be a contributing factor. Perhaps what you saw was just a leftover bit of residual energy. A spiritual impression, if you will, but not with enough force to act as before. The thing I find more reassuring is that you thought you'd seen the fourth one before, in your husband's studio, where it would doubtlessly have hung in plain view of people alone many times, and nothing happened. Maybe that was all the charge that Meg's spiritual battery had left, and it all blew out at once. It's possible. I've since heard and investigated various stories many times about allegedly haunted mirrors and other objects but never found anything else that I'd call *conclusive*. Some had shadow figures, which might have been explained by other things. A few had strong EMF ratings and were hot or cold to the touch outside of normal temperatures, but nothing like that. A full-body apparition of not just a ghost or a shadow figure, but an actual poltergeist that could move a person with physical force. Perhaps Gramma Dean is right... that these mirrors are more of a conduit. They have to be in the place where the death occurred for the apparition to fully manifest."

Nora finished off her tiramisu and took her plate to the kitchen. "Okay, that makes me feel a little better. But what about this one? It was covered and left unattended in the basement for a very long time, and I've seen, or thought I saw, things in it twice already."

"That *is* very unusual," said Hazel, walking back over to the wrought iron-framed mirror and holding her palm over the surface. "Nothing. *And* it's still in the home where the actual death occurred," she shrugged. "You say that both times it happened late at night?"

"Yes, why?"

"Occasionally, apparitions are time-sensitive or date-sensitive. They move at the time something significant in their corporeal lives occurred." Hazel paused, thinking, and looked at the tiny face of her Victorian rose gold wristwatch. "It's not even nine o'clock yet. We have plenty of time for me to run back home and get my equipment. Set it up as a real investigation right here in the living room."

"I'm game if you are," replied Nora. She pointed to the half-empty bottle of wine. "But if we're going to be up late, I'm putting a cork in this and starting some caffeine."

"Are you kidding? This is what I live for! Who knows, if we get anything good, it might make a great podcast episode. Could be good for your business too, you know. A local designer who lives in a house with haunted looking glass? Kind of a press machine gold mine."

"Let's hit the pause button on press for now," said Nora, as Hazel picked up her purse to leave. "But I'll start the coffee."

Chapter Ten

Hazel returned with her paranormal investigation equipment around 10 o'clock. Nora helped her set up, asking questions along the way. Although Hazel referred to it as her "portable" outfit, Nora wondered what else there could be to capture evidence of a haunting. There were three microphones and a low-light infrared camcorder with a wide-angle lens hooked up to a small multi-channel mixer that was in turn plugged into Hazel's laptop, plus a light grid that cast a bright green web over the room. The checkered pattern made Nora feel as if they were in some sort of 80s sci-fi movie. Also, Hazel went upstairs to place something she called a REM pod, along with a GoPro that she positioned on the window seat in the far corner of the room.

"The placement sort of allows us to be in two locations at once," Hazel explained. "The frequency field emitted by the REM pod can be interacted with by any spirits that happen to be present, and it will cause the lights on top to flash. We can ask it questions to try to provoke a reaction, and the GoPro will hopefully catch it on film."

After leaving those tools upstairs, Hazel came back down and handed Nora a clipboard with a chart on it. "Here. Record what I tell you. We want to get a baseline reading of the house for temperature and electromagnetic frequencies so we don't misinterpret any findings that later turn out to be false."

Last, they made the rounds of the house with Hazel using an infrared handheld thermometer and an EMF meter, while Nora took notes of any anomalies. "You have excellent wiring here," Hazel mentioned offhand as they finished up. "Not a lot of radiation escaping from random electrical outlets and such like most old houses."

"Thanks, I guess," replied Nora. "It was old, and I had it rewired because I wanted it to be safer and easier to work with on my new handmade fixtures."

Hazel gestured to Nora for the clipboard and studied the almost completed page of their readings. "I don't remember seeing a wireless hub anywhere. Do you have one?"

"Oh, no. I was trying to see whether I could get by without having one at home since the office is so close and my connection is super-fast there. I don't know why, but I'm just generally able to relax and rest better in rooms without everything so wired."

Hazel looked at her strangely. "Me too. Do you have any idea by chance whether or not you might be clairvoyant?"

"Not that I'm aware of," said Nora, surprised at the question, considering everything they had done so far appeared to be so precise and scientific.

"Just wondering. That's often the case with people who are WiFi-sensitive. We can talk about it later if you like. Have a seat. We're about to get started. Oh, and…" Hazel gestured to the phone clipped onto Nora's pocket. "Turn off your cell. Power it down. I will too. Those sometimes give off false signals."

They both turned off their phones completely. For some reason, Nora felt a small wave of panic wash over her as the screen went blank, but she dismissed it.

They sat down in the two dining room chairs that they had brought in, with their backs to the empty fireplace. The looking glass itself was placed against a tufted ottoman about ten feet in front of the small pop-up table for Hazel's mixer and laptop, with a camera on a tripod beside it. It was angled in such a way so that they could both see and the camera record what was happening in the glass. Plus, the viewpoint would be able to catch anything that crossed from the kitchen toward the front door, where Nora had felt the rush of cold wind before.

"All right, that looks like everything," said Hazel, surveying the room. "Just a few last directions before I flip off the lights. First, paranormal investigation is a lot like fishing. You often have to be very quiet but remain attentive for a long time before anything happens. Second, if you need to make a sound that we can't see the source of on one of the cameras, even if it's just your stomach growling or a sneeze, you should announce that it was you by saying your name and briefly stating what the sound was. I will do most of the initial questioning to try to see if I can provoke a response, but if you feel moved to ask them something else after we get going, feel free."

"Ask who something?"

"The entities," Hazel said, as she flipped off the lights and settled into her chair behind the camera tripod. "Hit record for me, please. I can't reach that far." Nora did so, and immediately Hazel began to speak. To Nora, it sounded as if they were about to perform an autopsy on television.

"This is Dr. Hazel Goodnight. It is currently 11:05 pm, Eastern Standard Time, on Sunday, June 7, in Wilmington, North Carolina. This is an investigation of the house formerly owned by Mr. Alexander Hostler, now owned by Ms. Nora Hewitt. It is believed that Hostler's friend, Mr. Samuel Jocelyn, was pronounced dead in the house. I am accompanied this evening by Ms. Hewitt herself, who has on two occasions witnessed possible paranormal activity associated with a silver-backed looking glass found in the basement of the home. It was most likely left by a previous owner. We are seated in the downstairs parlor, facing the dining room, with the front door of the home to our left and the entrance to the kitchen, which also leads to the stairs going up to the master bedroom, on our right. The looking glass is placed directly in front of us. Some degree of activity has been observed by Ms. Hewitt in each of these locations recently. Readings have been taken around the home, with nothing unusual to report, and will continue to be taken periodically throughout the night. A REM pod and camera have been placed in the upstairs master bedroom, and a second camera, recording equipment, and a light grid are down here with us. We will now pause for a few minutes before attempting to begin questioning."

Here, Hazel stopped and put her finger to her lips silently, like a librarian. "Now, we wait," she mouthed to Nora, who nodded soundlessly. They sat in silence, listening to the sound of each other's breathing before Hazel began speaking again.

"Is there anyone here with us tonight who would like to say something?" They waited. Nothing.

After a few more minutes passed, Hazel tried again. "Alexander, are you here?" Again, nothing. Followed by, "Samuel, if you are present, can you make some sort of sound so that we know you are here?" The minutes crept past as they watched the digital clock. Over the next quarter hour,

Hazel tried various other questions, each to no avail, before stating for the record, "Well, that's all from me then. Nora, would you like to give it a go?"

Nora sat up straighter in her chair, blinking her eyes. The dark room and heavy meal were making her sleepy, despite the two cups of coffee that had followed.

"What do I say?"

"Anything you like, and that you think will encourage it to interact with us. Don't be shy. If there's something here, it's been watching you for a week already. It probably knows you."

Nora could feel her pulse quicken as she considered the implications, and then she began.

"Hello, Alexander? This is Nora. Nora Hewitt. You have a lovely home. I like the little cupola. I've always wanted a house with one." Here Nora stopped and glanced at Hazel, who urged her to proceed. "I've enjoyed bringing it back to life, so to speak. Was it you whom I saw in the mirror upstairs?" Here, Nora stopped again. Nothing. She went on. "If it was you, are you still here? Could you make some kind of noise to let me know?"

"Nora, look!" whispered Hazel, pointing at the mirror. Then, for the record, she stated, "A cloud-like shape appears to be forming behind the surface of the glass." Hazel peered at the mirror through the camera lens. "However, it is not visible through what I'm seeing in the camera itself or," she leaned over to look at the laptop, "via the live feed. I'm going to take an infrared measurement of both the surface and frame of the mirror. You should be able to see the beam on camera."

Hazel flipped on the infrared and directed the beam at the mirror. Nora watched the laptop feed. She could see the beam clearly, and she could also see the swirls that Hazel called to her attention. They were forming exactly as they had before, starting at the bottom of the glass around the water stain. However, Nora couldn't see them at all through the feed.

"The temperature of both the glass surface and the wrought iron frame is 124 degrees Fahrenheit. That's a significant increase from the original at 74 degrees. Ambient room temperature remains at," Hazel flicked the beam on and off, then pointed to the wall behind her, "the same 74 degrees as previously recorded. That's a 50-degree increase throughout the last"—she looked at the clock on the laptop—"half an hour or so, since we've begun the investigation." Like a mom speaking on the phone while talking to her kids in the room, Hazel said aside. "Continue, Nora."

"Alex, may I call you Alex?" Nora began again. "I feel like we should get to know each other a bit if we're going to be sharing this house. Could you give me some kind of sign that you can hear me? Was it you that I saw in the mirror last night? I am very sorry about your friend, Alex. You must have cared for him very much."

As Nora spoke, the mists within the mirror continued to move until they coalesced into the same image that she had seen twice before. "That's it," she whispered to Hazel. "That's the man who I saw die, and they carried him out."

"Say it louder for the recording, please," Hazel said, pausing for Nora to repeat her statement and then continuing on her own. "Taking a second temperature check on the glass versus the room." Hazel flicked the beam over the surface and back to the corner twice, mentally noting the numbers. "Surface and frame temperature of the mirror are now at 160 degrees and still climbing. The ambient temperature of the room is 72 degrees. A slight drop from less than two minutes ago. It is approximately 11:40 pm and..."

Nora jumped as the REM pod upstairs went off in a flurry of beeps. Hazel didn't move. She merely squinted into the viewfinder before her and then craned over to see what might be visible from the GoPro. "The REM pod just went off. Lights of the REM pod are visible via the GoPro live feed, but no apparitions are visually recorded either there or in the tripod camera downstairs. However, Hewitt and I both confirm by personal witness that a moving grayscale scene is progressing in real-time before us on the glass itself. There appear to be three subjects in the scene. A man in bed who does not seem to be breathing, another man standing to his right dressed as a doctor, and a third with long dark sideburns, whose purpose is unknown. My suspicion is that the bedridden man is Jocelyn, and the third man is Hostler."

To Nora, Hazel explained. "I'm going to continue to narrate the scene as it unfolds and request confirmation from you, since we aren't picking it up on the cameras. When it gets to a point near the end of what you saw before, start asking the spirit to make its presence known by making a physical demonstration." Nora nodded.

Over the next twenty minutes or so, the scene in the glass played out just as it had on the night that Nora witnessed it alone. Hazel announced various events as they happened. As it came to the part in which the curly-haired man with the goatee entered, they heard footsteps come down the stairs in real time, crossing the floor. Then, the front door swung open. Nora grabbed Hazel's arm.

"Oh God," Nora whispered. "I thought I locked that door!"

"I unlocked it," said Hazel, making note of the fact, along with the opening of the door by itself for the record. "I didn't want to do anything that might make it too difficult for the flow of energy to continue."

They watched in silence as they heard the sounds of the body being carried out, followed by the doctor and the man with the goatee leaving, after which the door closed of its own accord. They watched as Hostler sat alone in the upstairs bedroom, sobbing with his head in his hands. "Now," breathed Hazel to Nora. "Ask him again now."

"Alexander," Nora said. "I am so sorry about your friend. Do you want to come down here and talk about it?" Here, the figure in the glass stopped and looked up. Only this time, it was different. The image shifted instantly. Nora found herself not merely watching a scene of the man getting up to go stare in the mirror, as if he had heard something strange. Instead, as Hostler approached the glass, it was as if a panoramic camera swung around. Now, he was looking through the mirror, directly at her.

Hazel could tell something had changed from the shocked look on Nora's face. "Nora, what's happening? How is this different from before? What's changed?" Into the air, Hazel called for the recorder. "Hewitt is observing a different sequence of events from previous encounters. Subject may be about to respond to her inquiry intelligently."

"Who are you?" A low, masculine voice echoed from upstairs. The image in the glass churned and dissolved as the man turned his back. The women once again began to hear heavy footfalls as if he were pacing back and forth above them. Hazel reached for the temperature gun and EMF meter with both hands, narrating faster as Nora spoke, her voice trembling.

"I'm Nora Hewitt. I live here now. Who are *you*?"

Suddenly, the door of the upstairs bedroom burst open, slamming against the wall. Heavy bootsteps banged down the stairs as the entity ran down to meet them. The steps stopped at the entryway to the kitchen.

"Oh my God!" Nora gasped.

"Yesssss!" Hazel exhaled, gaping wide-eyed back and forth from the cameras to the apparition shimmering before them. A dark, muscular young man in his late twenties, in his shirtsleeves and vest, tie undone.

"My *name*," he boomed, "is Alexander Hostler." Flickering, he stopped short. Slowly, he floated out into the parlor, eyes burning with a cold, white-hot light as he scanned the room. Nora sat breathless as she watched him survey her work.

He stopped next to the dining table and looked up, studying the propeller light fixture curiously and frowning. He floated back into the parlor and surveyed the room again before reaching up and rubbing his eyes. Putting his hands down, he blinked hard several times and shook his head. Looking up, he appeared to see them clearly for the first time.

Hostler's voice reverberated around the room in booming echoes as he pointed at Nora. "What in Hell's blazes *is* this? *What have you done to my house?*"

At that moment, there was a huge flash of light. The front door flew open, and with a blast of freezing air, the light collapsed into a ball and sailed out. The door slammed shut again behind it.

Nora turned to Hazel, her mouth agape.

"Guess he didn't like the remodel," Hazel quipped.

Chapter Eleven

Nora and Hazel spent the rest of the night reviewing the footage taken by the cameras and recorders. They had clear EVPs of Hostler's ghost both walking and speaking, but the visuals were decidedly sketchy. The GoPro picked up nothing but sound, and the low-light HD camera downstairs, which had been pointed directly at the apparition, merely showed a blaze of white light moving around the room. In the end, it swiftly exited the front door with a whoosh. Hazel was not surprised by the results.

"I've never been able to record a full-bodied apparition visually," Hazel explained. "Even with a full-spectrum camera, for some reason, it just doesn't pick up. Although I had high hopes for this one because he was so clear. But it's a great orb, and the EVP is one of the sharpest I've heard."

"Well, that's wonderful for you, Hazel. Great podcast fodder. But this is *my house!*" Nora exclaimed. "How am I supposed to keep living here knowing that there's a pissed-off ghost watching my every move?"

"The same way you've *been* living here so far," said Hazel, seeing that her friend was not as excited as she was over discovering the presence. "Hostler seems to be triggered by the unveiling of the glass, so just leave it covered. That's probably why it was in the basement in the first place. Still, I can see both sides. I understand that the thought of some unknown man, dead or alive, wandering around your residence is disturbing. Judging from his response, though, he was more surprised at how the house had changed than angry at you, even if his voice was very loud. Perhaps over time, you two could learn to coexist. After all, it *was* his house before it was yours."

"And how do you propose I do that? Draw up some kind of roommate agreement, like we're Sheldon and Leonard from *The Big Bang Theory?*" Nora sniped.

"Not exactly, but you're on the right track," replied Hazel, taking off her headphones and getting up to pace around the room. "Hostler always seems to enter here, coming down from upstairs," she said, pointing to the open doorway leading from the kitchen into the parlor, "and exit there." Hazel stepped over and put her hand on the front door. "What if you were to put up signs explaining who you are and what we think is happening? Then, leave the cover off the mirror for a few nights so that he has the opportunity to read and understand what's going on. Then try to address him again. He seems to be able to see and respond to things in this world. Perhaps it would work."

"But what would I say?" asked Nora sarcastically. "Telling the guy, *'Hate to be the bearer of bad news, but you're dead. Now, I own your house. Sorry you don't like my decorating style, but maybe it will grow on you.'* That probably won't go over well."

"True," answered Hazel, as she continued pacing. "Tone is important, and I like that you mentioned style because style is key to ensuring that the communication is well-received."

Hazel's gaze shifted around the room and came to rest on the pile of unread mail stacked on the kitchen counter. "We have to communicate with him in a way that he's used to. Considering he died in the 19th century, that would most likely be a handwritten letter. Perhaps you could write a letter that explained what we think has happened to him in the gentlest way possible and then tape it up where he'd be sure to see it."

Nora accepted the idea, her enthusiasm for the approach building despite her exhaustion. "That sounds logical. What if it weren't just one letter, but a series of letters and notes? You know, sort of like a little verbal map of the house. We could hang the looking glass back in the upstairs bedroom, where we know he becomes aware of it initially, and place the first note in an obvious spot next to it. Then, have a series of additional notes that lead him down the stairs and around the house. That way, he'd have multiple spots to stop and read, digest the information, and wouldn't think that he was hallucinating with grief or something."

"That sounds like an excellent plan," agreed Hazel. "You should include some sort of explanation about that propeller for sure. The Wright Brothers were probably still children around the time Hostler would have died, so human flight would have been just a dream. It caught his attention, probably by instinct. He was a transportation man, so that might create a conversation point."

"Yes, I can see myself sitting down to a nightcap and having a stimulating discussion with a ghost about the improvements that flight has made over shipping cargo on actual boats. *Not!*" said Nora, rolling her eyes.

"Oh, come on. It could be fun!" Hazel replied playfully. "I mean, you've built a business out of making old things new. Hostler could be a resource. Plus, he seemed to like you."

"Why do you say that?" Nora asked.

"Because he answered when *you* spoke to him, but not *me*. Spirits do that sometimes. They become attracted to one certain person or another if they remind them of someone in their life."

"Wonderful. We've gone from basic communication to attraction in one conversation. Next thing, you'll be saying we're soul mates." Nora made air quotes with her fingers.

"I see what you did there," sputtered Hazel, repeating the words. "Soul mates. Ha, ha. Maybe you are, and this is your first domestic spat. He doesn't like your decorating style."

"He'll get over it," replied Nora, as she glanced at the clock. "This is going to sound weird since we just ate dinner together last night too, but are you hungry?"

"Starved. Staring anxiously into a screen all night burns a surprising amount of calories."

"True story. Why don't you go home and shower, and I'll do the same here? We can meet at The George down on the riverwalk for brunch around ten. I've been dying to try that place, but I hate eating out at a restaurant alone. Makes me feel like a friendless old woman."

"Me too. I always prefer to eat with another person. And you'll love The George. Been there many times. See you at 10." Hazel let herself out and then turned back to peep in again, grinning mischievously. "We can work on a love letter to your ghostly boyfriend then."

"Hush your mouth!" laughed Nora, shooing her out. As she locked the door before heading upstairs to the shower, she thought about how she'd described her reluctance to dine alone.

After graduating from Belmont and seeing all her sorority sisters marry off one by one, Nora didn't have many friends left in Nashville. No one in her design firm ever hung out together after work. Socializing between junior designers and clients was highly discouraged. The view was that such interaction was a "privilege" reserved only for senior management, who were allowed to entertain on the company credit card. Nora had come to think of those coveted cards as little plastic lines of demarcation separating the upper caste shareholders in the firm from the untouchables who did most of the work. Every time she and Jasper went out, it was always with Jasper's friends, talking about Jasper's music. Nora thought it was interesting at the time. She loved music, and she found observing the blatant social climbing in Nashville's music business circles somewhat amusing. However, as she reflected on those circumstances, they seemed shallow. Not a single person from Nashville had called Nora to see how she was doing during her first weeks in Wilmington.

"So," Nora said to the covered and now-silent mirror as she passed it on the way upstairs to the shower. "This is what it feels like to have a real friend as a grown-up. Pretty sweet."

A couple of hours later, Nora, wearing a yellow sundress, walked down to the waterfront. Immediately, she spotted Hazel in a similar bright turquoise sundress, waving her down to the patio from behind an enormous Bloody Mary pitcher. "Well, don't you look like a little ray of sunshine," Hazel said, reaching for Nora's glass. "I hope you like Bloody Marys. Forgot how big this thing was. I need help!"

However, Hazel's invitation fell on deaf ears as Nora caught a glimpse of a couple canoodling on the other side of the patio. "Swap seats with me. I don't want to look at those two."

Hazel got up and slid over to the other chair, straining to see. "Those who?"

"That's Pierce, my sister's soon-to-be ex-husband who sold me the house," Nora whispered venomously, "and his assistant, Harper."

"Ooooh," replied Hazel, drawing out the word comprehendingly. "Gotcha. Bet she assists him with a lot of things. Looks about the right age for a daughter, not a girlfriend."

"Close," replied Nora, flicking the white linen napkin into her lap with a snap. "His sons with Vicki are nineteen. College freshmen. Harper will be twenty-three, I think, in December."

"Hmm..." said Hazel, carefully choosing to avoid Nora's ill mood by studying the menu. "Sagittarius. Pretty fickle as a general rule. Maybe you'll all get lucky and she'll dump him."

"Let's hope so," said Nora. "It's embarrassing." The waiter came and went, refilling glasses and taking their orders for omelets. Hazel took out a notepad, and they began to brainstorm ideas for what to say in the notes to Hostler. Just as they were finishing their food, Nora's cell rang. It was her younger sister Calista.

"Have you heard from Vicki in the past couple of days?" Nora noticed that both her sisters and mother always began phone conversations in the same narcissistic way, by launching immediately into whatever question inspired their call.

Am I the only one in my family who ever says hello? Nora thought to herself before responding. "No, but I'm sitting here trying not to see her husband feeding his assistant brunch. Perhaps I should ask him. Why? Is something the matter?"

Calista skipped right over Nora's extra details, continuing in a panicked tone. "Well, I don't know, but Vicki isn't answering her phone." Calista said the last word as a sort of cry. Nora could sense the tension in her sister's voice.

"How long have you been trying?" Nora asked.

"Since Friday night. I was going to see if we could meet up sometime soon for dinner, now that I've gotten everything rolling at the studio. It went straight to voicemail, but her mailbox was full, so I couldn't leave a message. Then, Saturday night, when I couldn't get an answer, I tried calling the 'Munks, but they hadn't heard from her either. Vicki was supposed to get back to them to set a date to fly up for a visit, but she never called *them* back either."

"That sounds more serious," Nora said, forcing herself to glance over her shoulder at Pierce and Harper. The pair were drinking from a fishbowl cocktail with two straws, completely oblivious to the world around them. "She's been working hard on trying to connect more with the 'Munks this year."

The 'Munks were what the three sisters collectively called Vicki's twins, Chip and Brad. The name began with Nora, and then it stuck. As children, they tended to use their cute, chubby-cheeked faces to squirm out of whatever mischief they'd gotten into. It invariably worked well for them, since they continued to be able to do little wrong in Vicki's eyes, even though they were grown. Like their father Pierce, they had learned to trade on good looks and charisma, rather than intellect, in almost every aspect of their lives. In Nora's opinion, her sister indulged them far too often, probably out of guilt for being an absentee mother. The result was that both boys had become mediocre college athletes with undeclared majors, already precariously close to flunking out of college after the end of their first year.

"I know," Calista said with a sniff. Nora could tell that she was trying not to cry. Calista rarely cried unless she was frustrated. "I'm thinking about just hopping a bus to Durham and then Ubering over to her lab. I mean, maybe I'm overreacting and she just slept over there or something."

"There's no need to do that. But I don't think she'd work into a third day without even looking at her phone to check for missed calls. She's not *that* disconnected," reasoned Nora. She added silently to herself, *Vicki's not like Mom.*

"I know it seems like a terrible imposition, but could you drive over there and check?"

"To Durham? Today?"

"Yes, I just have this awful feeling that something's wrong."

Nora considered the situation for a moment. Her little sister's "feelings" were well-known in the family. Over the years, Calista's "feelings" had predicted many things. She'd had nightmares for weeks before their father had died. Although she didn't like to admit it to herself, especially when her stomach was starting to sink too, Nora knew that her baby sister's "feelings" were usually right.

"I'm guessing you still haven't bought a car yet?"

"No," Calista sniffed. "I'm trying to continue living a car-free life even though..."

Nora stopped her. "Yes, yes, I know. Even though you now have money for a car but are still an advocate of transit, yada, yada, yada. Save the lecture on the evils of carbon emissions for later. I'll go."

"Oh, thank you!" Calista said, emitting her biggest sniff of the conversation. "I know it's a burden, and I hope it's just me being stupid, but I need to know. And the boys..."

"Need to know too," finished Nora, although in the back of her mind, she was thinking that the 'Munks might not care, so long as their allowance continued to arrive at regular intervals. "I'll call back tonight as soon as I know something."

"What was all that?" Hazel asked, draining the last of her Bloody Mary glass.

"Unnecessary family drama as usual," replied Nora, downing her final sip. "My younger sister Calista, current Asheville dance teacher and former car-hating New Yorker, wants me to drive to Durham today to check on my older sister, Vicki, who is probably just behind a cinder block wall in her lab and not answering her cell phone. Calista's worried about her."

"Yeah, I heard the part about her having bad feelings. Do you think she's right?"

"Unfortunately, she usually is. Otherwise, I wouldn't be going. When Calista's worried, it worries *me*."

"Well, it's sort of a long way, and we've been up all night. Do you want a ride-along to take turns driving? It's Sunday in the summertime, so as a college professor, I don't have anything else going on until Wednesday. That's Gramma Dean's night to prove to me once again that she's a superior bowler. Plus," Hazel continued, "I would like to get a look at those other mirrors that we talked about. Your father's and the one that you sent to Vicki. If it turns out to be nothing, and she's there, I'd like to speak with Vicki about whether she's found out anything else that's interesting with her experiments."

Surprised by the offer, Nora agreed. "Sure, that would be sweet of you, if you don't mind. However," she motioned at Hazel's notebook. "It's still not even noon. We need to let this alcohol digest, then go ahead and put up those letters before we leave."

"True," replied Hazel, "I should stop by your place and pack up my equipment too. Bring it along, in case we can see something more. Who knows? While we're off comparing notes, maybe our ghostly friend will leave us one here in return."

"Sounds like a plan," said Nora. Turning with a scowl toward Pierce and Harper's table, she added, "Regardless, I think I'm going to try to enlist one more soldier in the Find Vicki Army before we go."

Nora marched over to their table, where the couple sat waiting for the server to return Pierce's credit card. He looked surprised to see Nora but did not drop Harper's hand.

"Just FYI Pierce, your *wife* is missing. Not that you'd care. I can see that you've been... occupied." Nora made sure that she directed the word *wife* loudly at Harper, who squinted at her with an annoyed look in her little hooded eyes. Nora noticed that the liner previously drawn to make a cute little winged shape had smudged in the heat so that the corners no longer turned up. With her pointed face, Harper looked like an angry kitten. *Hope Pierce has the foresight to save up for a lid tuck in a few years,* Nora thought, *or maybe he'll just continue to trade up for newer models.*

"What? Who told you that? I haven't heard anything." Pierce seemed truly startled. Nora wondered briefly why he appeared concerned before continuing.

"Calista just called, and she's worried. She wants someone to drive back to Durham to check since the 'Munks can't reach her either."

Pierce turned toward Harper, who looked away, pouting. "It's not like Vicki to not answer the boys. I should probably go too."

"Whatever," Nora responded. "I have no expectations one way or another. I'm leaving this afternoon. I have to run by the house and wrap up a few things first, but then I'll be off." Nora headed back to the table, picked up her bag, and started for the gate. However, she couldn't resist getting in one more jab as she walked away. "Harper, take notes. If you stay with Pierce, you'll have to get used to doing a lot of things *by yourself.*"

As she followed Nora out of the restaurant, Hazel pulled her tortoise-shell sunglasses out of her purse, put them on, then removed them as they stepped into the blinding light. Still peeved from her encounter with Pierce and Harper, Nora shot her a look. "Why in the world would you take your glasses *off* in the sun? I wish I'd thought to bring mine!"

"No need," said Hazel. "You're throwing more shade than an eclipse today." She made a little drum roll and cymbal crash motion with her hands.

"Ha, ha," Nora mocked, although she was happy to have some levity. It would be good to have a funny friend, she thought. She'd always been considered the serious sister among the trio of Hewitt girls. Even Vicki, who'd always been the most intellectual, was droller.

"If we're going to leave the notes first and pack up all that equipment, there's no way we're going to be on the road before 2 pm," Nora explained. "It'll take us two hours to get there, and who knows how long before we can head back. Do you think we should each pack a bag? We can stay overnight at Vicki's. I have a key, and she has plenty of rooms."

"Probably," replied Hazel. "You work on the notes first and then get your bag packed. I'll run home and get a change of clothes and the larger paranormal investigation rig too. We'll pack up what I've left at your place and head out from there."

"Sounds like a plan," said Nora. "Give me your notebook, and I'll get it done."

Chapter Twelve

An hour later, Nora walked through her house, turning this way and that to check the logic of her trail of notes. She left the longest one, explaining the general nature of what they had witnessed and the reason for her presence, upstairs next to the looking glass. Nora rehung the glass in its former spot on the bedroom wall. Then, a series of shorter notes, intended to create a sort of guided path, explained various things around the house that had changed due to her renovations and the existence of modern technology.

Last, Nora set out a legal pad and several sharpened pencils on the entry table next to the final note on the door. It read: *We will be back soon. Please feel free to leave us a message. We would love to speak with you further. Sincerely, Nora and Hazel.*

Hazel pulled up in the driveway just as she was setting out the pencils. "Wow, that's pretty thorough," she said, as Nora showed her around. "It's like some sort of museum tour. Should get his attention."

"Do you think he'll answer?" asked Nora as they loaded bags into the Tahoe.

"If he's able, yes," answered Hazel. "Some spirits are capable of transcription. Let's just hope he's one of those who hasn't already blown out all his energy and needs to take a long time to recharge."

"I *guess* I hope so," returned Nora, uncertainly. Although she didn't like to entertain the possibility of further irritating an angry ghost in her house, she found her curiosity about Hostler growing as she wrote the notes.

Changing the subject as she pulled onto Interstate 40, Nora informed Hazel, "Just so you know... I am *not* responsible for the decor in my sister's house."

"That bad, huh?"

"Not bad… it's just," Nora found herself at a loss for words to describe it without sounding too harsh. "Very bland. My sister loves minimalism, which I detest. Everything is white and sterile, like a lab. But it's all very expensive."

"Almost like she's trying to bring her work home," Hazel returned.

"That's exactly my thought. My mother is the same way. Only at Vicki's, there are more places to sit or lie down because of the twins, whereas at Mom's there is only one. One chair, one table, one bed, and so on, even though both have huge houses."

"So, if there's barely any decoration, what's in them?"

"Art, mostly at Vicki's," said Nora. "But that's Pierce's doing. He's an art collector. It's what he invests in, allegedly. However, I guess all of that will be going with him. Now that Pierce is moving out, Vicki's walls will be as blank as Mom's."

"How awful!" exclaimed Hazel. "I can't stand an empty wall. Makes me feel like I'm in a hospital. And full disclosure—I'm scared to death of doctors. Is Vicki's lab in a hospital?"

"Afraid so, but it's fairly innocuous. It looks like a regular academic building," said Nora. "I'm surprised you're afraid of anything, though. You seem completely at ease around any kind of ghosts, which would scare the crap out of most people."

"Strangely, I've never had the slightest fear of the dead," replied Hazel, polishing her sunglasses. "In my life, I've found it's only the living that you have to worry about."

Nora nodded but said nothing, pulling a couple of energy drinks out of her bag. Hazel plugged her iPhone into the Tahoe's sound system, and the two of them sat in comfortable silence as Ed Sheeran's voice filled the car.

The relative peacefulness of their drive was broken as they turned onto Vicki's street in Durham. Several police cars were parked outside. Dozens of attractive blonde women, most with strollers for toddlers in tow, and all clad in expensive workout clothes, milled about, whispering to one another. Three news vans were at the curb directly in front of the house, their reporting teams already chattering away on the lawn.

"Jesus, this place looks like *The Stepford Wives* took a wrong turn and ended up on an episode of *Unsolved Mysteries*!" remarked Hazel as they passed through the neighborhood of McMansions.

"There's Pierce," said Nora glumly, as she maneuvered the car deftly around the hordes of gawking onlookers to pull into the driveway and park. However, before Nora even had time to fully get out of the car, a short, fat cop with bulldog jowls ran up and began yelling at her.

"Ma'am, you can't park here! It's a crime scene."

In no mood for being bossed around, Nora went on the defensive. "Well, this is my sister's house, so until you tell me what in hell is going on, I'm not going anywhere."

The cop gave her a snotty look. "Your brother-in-law probably killed her; that's what's going on." Into his radio, the cop barked. "Get a tow truck to get this car out of here."

Nora stood looking stunned, but Hazel intervened. "There's no use for the tow truck, Baby Stalin. We'll move the car if you can part the Stepford Sea behind us here." Hazel gestured at the growing crowd of curiously wrinkle-free women blocking the exit to the driveway. The fat cop ran over and began herding them away, blowing his whistle unnecessarily. As he approached, they retreated swiftly as if from a leper.

After parking the car several blocks away, next to one of the numerous neighborhood watch signs, each of which she noticed was accompanied by a multidirectional camera on a pole, Hazel rejoined Nora at the front door of Vicki's house, handing over her car keys. Nora was engaged in a second heated debate with another cop and a tall, stony-faced blonde woman in a severely cut skirt suit, whom Hazel knew without asking must be Nora's mother.

"Well, she's already filed the divorce papers; I can tell you that," Marjorie snapped. "So even though we're waiting on all of the formalities," Marjorie waved her long fingers in the air dismissively, "They're separated. Pierce should be arrested *immediately*, and he should *not* be allowed into this house. Who knows what that *beast* has done to my daughter!"

"Mom, calm down," Nora pleaded. "I just saw Pierce in Wilmington not two hours ago. We were in the same restaurant. He's been over there with Harper all weekend. I'm not his biggest fan either, but do you really think that he has anything to do with this?"

"I most *certainly* do! He *had* to get her out of the way because, in a fault-based divorce, she would take *everything* from him! Just *look* at this petition! It has every motive in the *world!*" Marjorie thrust a thick sheaf of legal documents at Nora.

"Ladies, we're going to have to move this discussion out of the way," said the older second cop, plainly exasperated. Having dealt with her mother's temper for years, Nora knew *that* look. Total resignation, after having been verbally whipped into submission. "We're going to have to bring the suspect out this door," the tall cop explained.

Just then, the beveled glass door swung open, and a group of four more cops emerged with Pierce, wild-eyed and in handcuffs. Nora noticed that he was still wearing the same outfit that she'd last seen him in at brunch a few hours before. A previously crisp white linen shirt, now soaked with sweat, slim-cut Nantucket reds that clearly showed the definition of his muscular thighs, and expensive calfskin leather driving mocs without socks. Pierce looked like what he was, she thought. A very scared little rich boy. Without wanting to, Nora felt sorry for him.

The fat-faced cop blared commands into his electronic megaphone to clear the area, while two others held Pierce firmly by the arm on each side. Yet another cop followed behind, brandishing a revolver. The sea of Stepford blondes continued to recede, but a wave of reporters surged forward in their wake.

"Why did you do it, Mr. Eichhorn? Was it for the money? Was your wife taking it all?"

"I didn't do anything," Pierce cried back. "I just heard that my wife was missing, and I came home to all of this. Ask her if you want proof!" Pierce inclined his head toward Nora.

"Shit!" Nora breathed out as all three news teams turned on her in unison. They descended like vultures, demanding to know who she was and how she knew of her sister's disappearance. Although she tried to answer as quickly and succinctly as possible, Nora could tell they were not getting the responses that they wanted to hear. The fact that Calista had been trying to reach Vicki on the phone for three days but had gotten no response, so she sent Nora to check on their sister was not sensational enough.

Fortunately, Marjorie pushed her way in. Nora's mother was more than willing to supply the reporters with every possible gory detail of the devolution of Vicki's marriage to Pierce, along with her wild speculation about his motivations for her disappearance. As the circle of reporters reformed surrounding Marjorie in the yard, Nora and Hazel were able to sneak past them and into the house. Despite the police and media circus going on outside, they were surprised to find the house empty of investigators.

"If you had asked me this morning, I never in a million years thought I'd be saying this, but poor Pierce!" Nora said, shaking her head and glancing around. "Also, why are there so many police out there, but none inside? Shouldn't they be looking for clues or something?"

"It does seem suspicious," Hazel agreed. "As for Pierce, he seems like your basic country club douchebag, but not the murdering type."

"He's not. Pierce can't even go to the dentist without someone holding his hand. I mean, he played college football, but he's super squeamish about blood and any kind of confrontation. That's how I think he ended up married to my sister in the first place. Vicki always said that she wanted to get married and start a family right after graduate school. Pierce was just the first genetically suitable guy she could snap up. She badgered him into it."

"Sounds like it runs in the family," said Hazel. "Your mom was certainly pushing those reporters and cops in all the ways that she wanted them to go. She must hate Pierce."

"She used to love him," Nora mused. "He was completely non-threatening but genetically ideal. Mom knew that between her and Vicki, they could spend a lifetime bossing Pierce around. It was only after he became so blatant with all the affairs, which in turn became the talk of campus, that he fell out of Mom's graces. In her opinion, he'd made his sperm donation, so he was supposed to sit quietly basking in the glow of my sister's brilliance for the rest of his life."

"So that's why she wants Pierce gone? Because he's an embarrassment?" Hazel asked, scowling. "Quite a petty reason to accuse someone of murder, unless she's trying to set him up for some reason."

"Not that petty when you factor in that I'm sure Mom's super-micro-managing my sister's divorce to make sure she wrings every possible dime from the marriage and leaves Pierce broke. I mean, look at this place," Nora gestured around the room at the dozens of pieces of modern art displayed against stark white walls like a gallery. "My sister has zero interest in modern art. She hated most of it and wouldn't have wanted anything to do with it. All these pieces were selected by Pierce. Vicki's money was more than enough to run the household, so every time he sold a house and got a commission off it, he bought more. Vicki can be bossy, but she's not vindictive. She'd have given him all of it in the divorce, I'm sure. But Mom knows it could be sold for a lot of money, so she would push Vicki to make a play for it out of spite. Check out the estimated price list attached to this thing." Nora picked up the industrial-strength stapled inventory packet lying on the entry table and handed it to Hazel, who scanned the pages.

Nora continued. "I know you don't know her, but Vicki wasn't about money. She'd have never gone to the trouble to make this list. Mom made it, I'm sure. Now that I think about it, Vicki probably didn't even decorate this house, if you can call it that. Mom did, which is why it looks so much like hers. White and empty. Vicki's all about science and research. It's been her way to escape ever since Dad died. It was the way she kept him alive."

Drifting off into a world of her thoughts, Nora began to wander around her sister's house. The last time she'd been there was over Christmas, but it looked the same. Eventually, she found herself in Vicki's study. All the walls were lined floor to ceiling with bookcases, their spines one of the few things of color in the sterile entirety of the house. Even the worktable and chairs in the center of the floor were clear plexiglass sitting on top of a pale gray rug, with a steel gray laptop perched on top of it.

What a cold room. Nora mused, glancing around her sister's study for anything remotely interesting. Suddenly, she spotted a large, flat, white cardboard box propped up against one of the bookcases. *Pierce must have ordered another painting*, Nora thought. However, there were no shipping labels on the box, and the flaps were partially open. Curious, Nora turned the box on its side and reached in.

"Nora, where are you?" called Hazel, coming up the stairs, but Nora didn't hear her. Feeling the frame of the object and deciding that it must be a piece of art, Nora pulled it out. As she flipped it over and propped it up against the bookcase, Hazel popped into the room.

"Found you!" Hazel said, slightly breathless. "Everybody's starting to leave out there." She moved closer to Nora. "Is that another mirror?"

"Yeah," said Nora. "It's the one that used to hang in my dad's office at Duke. I thought Mom had gotten rid of all his stuff from there though. It was always super cluttered, and she couldn't stand it. Hold on just a sec..." Nora reached back into the box and pulled out an expandable file folder filled about an inch thick with papers. On it were written the words *LGE Subject 153.*

Hazel peered over her shoulder. "What's that?"

"I think it's one of my dad's experiments," Nora said, looking at the date on the outside as she unwound the string that held the file securely closed. "Maybe his last."

Chapter Thirteen

Nora opened the file, pulling out a sheaf of documents, several color photographs, an old VHS tape, and an audiocassette. Handwritten on stickers on the sides of the tapes read *Recordings of Subject 153 - Fall 1992.*

"That was the semester my dad died," breathed Nora slowly. "This must have been one of his experimental recordings. I remember hearing them playing in the background late at night in his office at home while he took notes. But I was ten, so I never really paid much attention. I thought Mom must have gotten rid of all of them when he passed away."

"I'm sorry," said Hazel, putting a hand on Nora's shoulder. "I know it must be difficult. To listen to him talk. Do you... do you want me to go over them and tell you if there's anything important?"

"No," Nora shook her head quickly. "If Vicki's been listening to these, then I can too. Besides, it might jog my memory to hear him."

"Okay," said Hazel. "If you think so. But we still have the problem of finding a VHS player."

"True," replied Nora, mulling it over for a moment. "Wait... the 'Munks used to have an entire collection of old Disney tapes they used to watch together. When they got too old for them, I remember Vicki saying that she wouldn't let Mom throw them away after they remodeled their room. They might be upstairs in the attic with the player."

Nora trekked up the wide staircase that curved around the chandelier in the foyer, trying not to think about all the wasted space, as she made it to the spot underneath the attic door. Pushing the button, the pneumatic pump let down the ladder-like staircase. Flicking the flashlight app on her phone, Nora went up.

The evening sun slanted hotly through the windows as Nora looked around. True to form, everything in Vicki's attic was meticulously cataloged along rows of white shelves that lined the perimeter. On the shelf above a large, clear Tupperware bin marked *Videos,* was a VHS player. Nora plugged it into a nearby socket and wasn't surprised that it worked. A dead player wouldn't have survived to be in the attic storage of any house Vicki lived in.

Scanning along the shelves, Nora was struck with an odd observation. The entire right side of the attic was filled with shelves of things that belonged to the 'Munks, and the entire left side was filled with things that were Pierce's. However, there wasn't a single bin or shelf that had anything to do with Vicki. Up in the attic, it was as if her sister had never lived in the house, even though now with Pierce moving out and the 'Munks off at college, Vicki was the only one ever really there.

On Pierce's side of the attic, Nora found an old boombox that she'd remembered seeing on some of their mutual trips to the beach years before Vicki and Pierce married. *And before we all knew he wasn't just a dumb jock but a careless douchebag*, Nora mused. There was a tape still in it. She pushed the *Eject* button, and a cassette of Journey's *Frontiers* album popped out. Closing it back, Nora plugged it into the second outlet on the wall and hit *Play*. The opening chords of "Faithfully" filled the room. It had been Vicki and Pierce's first dance song at their wedding.

God, what a cliché, Nora thought. Her husband Jasper would have been mortified. Jasper made a point of listening only to vintage vinyl and underground artists that Nora had never heard of. The memory of it made her wince, and she pulled the cord from the wall.

"Got them both!" Nora called down to Hazel, handing her the player and boombox before starting down the ladder. She pushed the button, and the long pneumatic sigh of the attic door pulled the ladder back up into the ceiling.

Down in the office, Nora plugged in the VHS player first, hooking it up to the TV that, even though it was a flat screen, still surprisingly had the triple cord input they needed. She switched it on, selected the correct output, and hit *Play*. There was a bit of static, and then...

"Dad," Nora squeaked, her voice unexpectedly hoarse for being caught off-guard at the abrupt beginning of the video. She suspected it would be Henry speaking but hadn't mentally readied herself for the initial shock of seeing his face again all these years later. Nora slapped the *Stop* button and sat for a few seconds, looking at her father's face on the screen.

"Are you sure you don't want me to watch it for you?" Hazel asked gently.

"No... no, I'm okay. I've got this. It's just..." Nora struggled for the most believable lie which wouldn't involve her admitting that seeing her dad again made her feel like a little girl. "I've never seen him talk about these experiments before. I heard Mom allude to them. Always in the negative, of course. But *he* never spoke about them. Only his regular work with the inmates and behaviorism and all that boring stuff." It was a logical explanation for her reaction, she thought. Still, Nora felt her chest tighten as she hit *Play* again.

The camera focused on her father standing in a white button-down shirt and slacks, with a gray shawl collar cardigan that she recognized instantly. He half-smiled pleasantly at the person behind the camera and nodded, showing his assent to begin.

"Good afternoon! My name is Dr. Henry Hewitt, and this is my examination of Subject 153. It is part of an ongoing series of experiments into what my colleague Dr. Bill Yates and I refer to as the Troxler Fading Effect. Once again briefly for the record, the Troxler Effect is a possible explanation for the Bloody Mary phenomenon, in which people stare into a mirror in a darkened room and chant a name, allegedly causing a spiritual presence to emerge. What we are attempting to prove is that Troxler's Fading Effect is the cause of this phenomenon. An optical illusion affects visual perception when a person fixates on a particular point for even a few seconds, causing an unchanging stimulus away from the fixation point to seem to fade away and disappear. This particular mirror," Henry motioned to the mirror behind him, "was sent to us by a family in Rhode Island. It was purchased at a local flea market for possible use in their living room. After refinishing the wooden frame to cover old marks, which may have been burned, with new varnish, they hung it on the aforementioned living room wall. That very evening, they began to notice strange images appearing in the mirror. This phenomenon recurred numerous times until they felt too disturbed to leave it hanging in their home. After inquiring about the mirror with a professor at Brown, the professor wrote to us. He asked if we would like to include the mirror in our experiments, which were known to him. Thus, he shipped it to us, and we presented it for examination here. Nothing further about its origins is known at present, other than the fact that the owners revarnished the frame once to conceal the scorch marks. Yet, as you can see," Henry picked up the mirror and carried it close to the camera. The image bobbed slightly as the person on the other side of the tripod brought the lens into closer focus. "The inner edges of the frame touching the glass appear to be singed black."

Here, Henry ran his index finger around the inner perimeter of the frame. The camera closed in even further to show the burn marks more clearly. "Also," Henry moved back a step and turned the mirror over so that its back was facing the camera, which zoomed out and then back in again to refocus once more. "This mirror, as with all the others in this series that have tested positive for irregularities beyond the expected Troxler Effect, has a full silver back. Not paint, but actual silver, behind the surface of the glass."

Taking a few more steps away, Henry flipped the mirror over again so that its face was back to the camera and set it onto the wooden easel from which he had taken it originally. "We will now begin the experiment with all the lights off, save for the single dimmable picture light above it that you can see affixed to the top of the easel here. The intention of using this small, low-level light only is so we can see what is happening with the mirror once the lights are off, and all other possible sources of light are eliminated."

Henry paused for a moment to demonstrate the picture light and its levels of illumination. "I am putting the light on a setting of 3 with a possible high of 10. Next, I will turn out all the other lights and take a seat with Dr. Yates. You will be able to hear my voice asking questions from the left side of the area off-camera, but no other voices or auditory phenomena should be discernible unless vocally checked. You may also hear Dr. Yates moving about as he adjusts the camera to follow any movement that might be observed." Shutting off the lights, Henry took his place and began questioning, like what Hazel performed the night before.

After a few moments, the familiar misty vapor began to swirl on the surface of the mirror. Yates zoomed in for a closer look, leaving just a foot or so around the perimeter.

"No, no, no, no, no," a woman's voice could be heard pleading, faintly at first and then gradually louder and faster, rising in pitch as she continued. When the swirls coalesced into an image, it was clear to see that the woman was wearing a long dress with a tight bodice and a full skirt. The fabric had a pattern of rosettes on it, and her hair was in a chignon that was coming undone. Limp strands of hair straggled down across her sweaty face.

"Please Joe, don't," she begged, her hands clasped together against her forehead. She fell forward onto the floor as if in prayer.

"Don't what? This is the last damn time I'll come back from camp to an empty house." Joe jerked the woman up to her feet and bent her back roughly by the remains of her chignon. She yelped once in pain but otherwise made no sound. Joe's back was to the mirror, but it was easy to see how far the woman's back was arched and that she was shaking from the strain of it. Joe yanked her hair again, and the woman slipped and fell with a thud flat on her back to the floor. Gasping as she tried in vain to catch her breath again, Joe kicked her hard in the ribs with the toe of his heavy boot. Unable to hold back any longer, she curled up into a ball and screamed. Joe pounced upon her, and she fought against him as he pushed her arms back, pinning her hands above her head with one meaty paw as he pushed her skirts up with the other.

"How many times have I told you that I expect you to be waiting to give me this when I get home, but then when I do, you're not there? *How many times!!!*" he yelled.

Joe paused for an answer. The woman stammered, her chin quivering, "I... I don't know, Joe. I'm sorry. I... I told you I was sorry. I wasn't doing anything; I was just..."

"You were just what?" Joe prodded, astride her now. "What kind of excuse do you have for me? To not be here where you're *supposed to be. What excuse do you have, when I own everything about you!!!*"

The woman said nothing but continued to whimper. "That's what I thought," mocked Joe again. "Crying your goddamned guilty tears. You're just a damn liar. You know what you've done. Now you *owe* me. And I will *take* what I am *owed*. Do you hear?" Joe slapped her hard across the face. He pulled both of the woman's hands back down to her sides, setting a thick knee down hard on each of them. The crack of the wooden floor, or maybe the bones of her hands, was audible. Her screams were abruptly stifled as Joe clapped a heavy palm over her small face and held it there. Their eyes locked.

"Let me look at you closer," Joe said, putting his heavy jowled face nose-to-nose with hers. Nora could see that the woman's eyes were beginning to swell shut, her nose likely broken. Joe sat back up and moved his hand down around her throat. "Just like I thought. Already getting old and wrinkled anyhow. And fat." He bounced up and down on her solar plexus. She started to scream again, but Joe slapped it out of her so that the scream ended in a choking sound. Then, Joe leaned back and studied the woman. An evil grin spread across his face, as he cocked his head to the side.

"On second thought, no. I don't think I want anything from you after all. No. What I think is that it's about time for the two of us to part ways, my old, old, old girl," Joe said, wrapping both hands around her neck. Sensing even greater danger, the woman struggled harder. She bit at him, but Joe laughed. His hands were so tight around her throat that she could no longer scream but made hard wheezing sounds, beating her heels against the floor. After a surprisingly short amount of time, her struggles began to cease. Joe closed his grip even tighter until finally, she lay still.

Shrugging, Joe struggled to his feet, wiping his bloody hands on the woman's wadded-up skirts. The sound of his heavy boots echoed across the floor as the door slammed shut from somewhere outside. From the corner of the woman's parted lips, a small trickle of blood dropped to the floor. Her lifeless eyes stared blankly out of the mirror as the scene once again faded into a swirl and was gone.

"What you have just witnessed here," said Henry, rising from the chair off camera and crossing the room to switch on the lights. "Is the tragic assault and murder of a young woman at the hands of her husband or possibly her boyfriend. We are not quite certain. Efforts will of course be made to look into the crime that was committed. You can see from the nature of their clothing that it happened a long time ago, and they appear to have been working class. Therefore, there may be no record of her death, especially if the body was later disposed of." Visibly disturbed by what he had witnessed, Henry wiped his glasses and cleared his throat several times before addressing the camera again directly.

"Dr. Yates and I have now observed this same phenomenon three times together and once each separately. The scene is always the same, and it does not change course. Once it starts, it plays out completely, regardless of any type of questioning or visual or verbal stimuli. Whatever spiritual phenomenon is occurring here, it is not what one might call intelligent, meaning that it does not seem to be aware of our world and our attempts to communicate with it or to stop the violence. Simply, it continues to play on a loop from the beginning when summoned and then ends, just as you have seen here. In this way, it differs from some of the other mirrors that we have recorded, a few of which have intelligent spiritual presences that can be provoked into responsive action. Thus, Subject 153 has become the latest in our series to be confirmed as housing an actual spiritual presence and not merely exhibiting the Troxler Effect."

To the man off camera, Henry asked, "Dr. Bill Yates, do you confirm that what we have just filmed here, and that I have witnessed, you have witnessed also?"

There was a shuffling noise as Yates came out from behind the camera and stood next to Henry on the other side of the mirror. He was wearing a pair of shiny, medical-grade, heat-resistant gloves. "Yes, I confirm that everything filmed today has been accurate and that I have witnessed it. Also, I would like to add that the evidence of extreme heat, leaving burn marks on the wood of the easel against which the mirror was resting, is visible." Yates took a step backward and gingerly took the mirror by its frame off the easel. Holding it with one gloved hand, Yates pointed at the scorch marks on the easel with the other.

Henry nodded and spoke into the camera again. "Yes, thank you for remembering to note that, Bill. Once again, as we noted before in the previous 152 subjects that we've tested and found positive for paranormal activity, the scorch marks indicating extremely high temperature during the occurrence of the phenomenon are consistently present. Anything further to add, Bill?"

"Nothing at this time, thanks, Henry." Yates gave a quick half-wave goodbye at the camera before settling down behind the tripod again off-scene.

"Okay, then that concludes our film of Subject 153. Thank you for reviewing this tape. The notes will be in the folder as usual." Again, Henry smiled his familiarly official, yet still pleasant, half-smile directly into the camera as the tape went to static.

Hazel reached forward and hit *Stop,* then looked at Nora. "Are you sure you're okay?"

Nora sat motionless and leaned in toward the screen as far as her chair would allow on its two front legs without tumbling her onto the floor. Snapping back to awareness, she pushed the chair back to its correct position. "I'm... fine." Nora began slowly. "Yes, I'm as good as I can be, considering," she gestured toward the television with a shaking hand.

"That was horrible to watch," Hazel agreed. "However, it helps me understand more about how souls become trapped behind the mirrors. Think about the amount of human trauma it would take to make such a lasting spiritual impression. Remember the attack that killed Gallows Meg? Restless spirits are rarely made by peaceful deaths."

"Yes," replied Nora, pulling the stack of papers into her lap so that her trembling hands were occupied. "That's true. But also, I think we've received a few important bits of information on several fronts. For starters, we've got to find this Dr. Yates, if he's still alive. Next, we have to ask him if what we've already uncovered is accurate. That different spirits in different mirrors behave in different ways."

"Oh, absolutely!" returned Hazel, standing up and beginning to pace. "I mean, these were on a 'loop,' as he called it. Not responsive to stimuli at all. Whereas Hostler's spirit was willing and able to engage intelligently in his environment and ours. Then, what I saw before with Meg..."

Nora interrupted her. "Yes, but what does it all mean? And more relevant to the reason we're here, what, if any of it, has to do with Vicki's disappearance?"

"I haven't the foggiest idea," said Hazel, reaching for the papers in Nora's hands and flipping through them to the last page. "But I know who might." Hazel pointed at an address and phone number. "Dr. Yates."

Chapter Fourteen

When Nora called Dr. Yates's office using the number in her father's report, she was disheartened to find it reassigned to the Office of Student Success. However, Hazel had another idea. She called the number again. After being routed through the university phone tree finally to the Office of Faculty Services, she learned that Dr. Yates had retired but still lived in the area. A quick internet search revealed that Dr. Bill Yates still lived on the other side of Durham, only a half hour away.

"Is there anything else that's left to do here? Related to Vicki, I mean, before we try to reach out to Yates?" Hazel glanced at her watch. "If we call and he's not busy, we might be able to see him tonight."

Nora considered the question for a moment. She'd been so startled by seeing the tape of her father that she was still processing it. "I'll take a look around the house. See if anything is unusual or missing. But if anything happened to Vicki, I don't think it happened here." Nora paused, knowing that it sounded illogical. Hazel studied her intently. "It's just a feeling, I guess."

"Feelings," said Hazel, "if we take the time to listen to them, are usually right." She reached over to the desk for the audiocassette. "We still haven't listened to this yet. Or read through all the papers."

"That's your job in the car on the way over to see Dr. Yates," said Nora. "You'd know better than I do what to pay attention to anyway." She motioned to the boombox. "I don't have a tape player in the car, but we can use that to listen. Check it for batteries. Hopefully, they're not corroded. But if it doesn't, Vicki used to keep multiple sizes in the kitchen drawer farthest away from the fridge. When you're done," Nora tossed Hazel the keys to the Tahoe, "I'll meet you in the car. Won't be long."

Walking through her sister's house, Nora felt uneasy. Strangely, it wasn't just her sister's disappearance, but the look of the house itself. Everything inside was expensive, immaculate, and extremely uncomfortable looking. The sculptural white leather chairs in the living room were perhaps the most disturbing thing of all. Although Nora knew that her sister had owned them for at least a decade, they looked as if they'd rarely been sat in. Upstairs, the bedroom was almost as eerie. All of Pierce's clothes were conspicuously missing from the "his" side of the master bedroom's Jack and Jill custom closets, but Vicki's side was sadder. Dozens of meticulously pressed lab coats hanging side by side, fresh from the cleaners, appearing sterile, as if they were in body bags. Identifying the work immediately as having been a California Closets design, Nora couldn't help but poke around in the drawers. Inside were enough of her sister's precisely folded shirts, tees, and underwear to make Marie Kondo proud. However, it only made Nora sad as she left the closet and glanced around the bedroom. The whole thing sparkled with quiet luxury in a dimmed plexiglass prism of clear, white, and gray.

"Where are your other clothes? Is there anything to keep this from looking like a real estate staging?" Nora wondered aloud. Even the book on the bedside table was a generic collection of black and white Ansel Adams photographs. The last time she'd been at her sister's house, it was Christmas. Nora remembered being slightly drunk as she'd carelessly tossed her coat in the pile upstairs, on this very bed. At the time, she'd never stopped to consider whether her sister or Pierce ever slept there at all.

Heading back downstairs, Nora admired the vintage white subway tile in the kitchen, along with the thirsty slate countertops and Bosch appliances. Still bland, but at least in the current style. Glancing inside the fridge, Nora was met with another mild shock. Only boxed water, not even any condiments. Opening the cupboard doors revealed a few packages of granola bars and individual mixed nuts, along with a vast array of black enameled Le Creuset cookware, but otherwise, nothing. Stepping back through the study, Nora saw that Hazel must have packed up the mirror and other things back into the box already. Nora locked the front door and joined Hazel, who waited in the Tahoe.

"Find anything important?" Hazel asked.

"Yes and no," answered Nora. "My sister's always been a big neat freak and somewhat compulsive when it comes to order, but..." She shook her head as she started the car and pulled out of the driveway. "The whole house looks like a hotel. Everything is so perfect, it's like no one even lives there. It's not a home really; it's just a property."

"Maybe they don't," said Hazel, pulling the boombox out of the back seat. "But Vicki certainly made it easier to listen to the tape by keeping this old thing equipped with fresh batteries. Should we listen to this, or do you want me to hit the highlights of the report?"

"Go ahead with the tape first," Nora said, tightening her grip on the steering wheel. "If there's time while we're waiting, you can fill me in on the rest."

To Nora's disappointment, the remaining materials gave her no further insights regarding Vicki. Regardless, Nora saw out of the corner of her eye as she drove that Hazel's attention was devoted completely to it. She even pulled a small pad out of her purse and took notes. After about twenty minutes, the tape finished. "Wow, that was something!" Hazel breathed, continuing to annotate.

"What?" Nora asked. Her interest had begun to wane once she could tell the tape held little relevance to her present mission of finding her sister.

"So, apparently there are over 150 of these mirrors in storage somewhere. They each have some kind of legitimate paranormal activity going on. Only a very small fraction is what I might call intelligent or responsive, like what we've witnessed with Hostler's looking glass. The rest are just loops of deathbed scenes." Hazel flipped through the notes in the folder and pulled out a few pages, stapled at the corner. "The rarest of all are instances in which the world behind the mirror flexes."

"What do you mean by that?" Nora asked, turning off the interstate to follow the insistent chirping of the Tahoe's GPS.

Hazel placed the papers back in her lap and ran a hand through her hair. "It means that in some very rare cases, a spirit can not only enter and exit the mirror itself but can also bring a living soul back into the world of the mirror with it."

"You can't mean..." Nora began.

"I absolutely can!" Hazel exclaimed. "That time years ago, when Meg appeared and she was pushing me. I felt the mirror bend behind me if I hadn't ducked and fallen..."

Nora interrupted her, "You'd have gone through the mirror." Nora took a deep breath of recognition and shuddered. "Do you think that could happen to anyone?"

"By anyone, do you mean Vicki?" Hazel asked. "Because if so, my answer would have to be I don't know, but it's possible."

"Well, if it's true, does it say anything about how to get her back?"

Hazel fanned the pages. "Not in this particular report, but," she nodded at the mailbox they'd pulled up in front of, which said *Yates* in bold, script-style letters. "Perhaps he can."

Ten minutes later, a slight, gray-haired gentleman with a long, fuzzy beard answered the door. He wore a very wrinkled white Oxford shirt, rolled up to the elbows, jeans, and a pair of navy-blue New Balance sneakers. "Can I help you two ladies?"

"Are you Mr. Yates?"

"Doctor Yates, yes," the man replied, stiffening slightly. "What is the purpose of the inquiry?"

"My name is Nora Hewitt," the man cocked his head to the side as she continued. "And I believe that you worked with my father, Henry. I have some questions for you."

"I'm sure you do," replied the man, relaxing as he gestured toward the living room. "Please, have a seat. Henry spoke of his girls constantly. Can I get you anything? Iced tea? Water?"

"No thanks," said Nora, sitting down quickly. "Did we catch you at a good time?"

"Young lady, I'm a retired professor. I have all the time in the world. Only appointments that I keep these days are with him." A chubby ginger tabby cat swirled around Yates's feet and immediately leaped into his lap as he sat down. The cat rolled over, expecting a belly rub. Yates obliged.

Nora took the folder from Hazel and held it in front of her. "Great. I guess I'll just get right to the point then. We were wondering if you could tell us anything about this."

Yates's pale blue eyes grew large as he took the folder. "Where did you get this?" His tone was unexpectedly stern.

"It was in my sister's study," Nora explained, somewhat intimidated by the sudden change in Yates's demeanor. "She's gone missing, and..."

Yates broke in. "Was it in a white cardboard box, by chance? With a mirror?" The ginger cat in Yates's lap rolled back over on its stomach, casting Nora an irritated look.

"Yes, but why? What's wrong?"

Yates shifted around in his seat, crossing his legs. The cat leapt down. Yates examined the large expandable folder in his hands. "153. That was the last one. Before poor Henry..." Yates shook his head. "It didn't have anything to do with this, you know? Henry's suicide. We were making real progress, it seemed. Although he wasn't happy at home, I could tell he was pleased with what we were doing in the lab. Still, I couldn't believe that he'd ever have done such a thing. We'd known each other since," again Yates shook his head. "Since we were freshmen. Long before he met your mother, Marjorie."

This wasn't the response that Nora had mentally prepared herself for, but fortunately, Yates continued unbidden. "Henry always believed in the paranormal. Long before I did. He was the one who introduced me to it. What was ironic, though, was that about the time Henry brought me around to his way of thinking, he stopped. Of course, she had a lot to do with it. Marjorie, your mother."

Nora looked frustrated, so Yates qualified. "There was never anything wrong with Marjorie, except that she lacked imagination. Beautiful girl, highly intelligent, and very driven to succeed. Perhaps too much. Zero ability, though, to believe in anything intangible. If she couldn't physically sense it, Marjorie never believed it existed. We tried to convince her way back in the early days, but it was useless. Her mind was just made up."

"Could you tell us a little about these experiments in general?" Nora attempted to steer Yates back from his trip down memory lane. "Or 153 specifically? I'm wondering why my sister Vicki might have had it in her study when she went missing."

"Vicki's missing?" Yates appeared genuinely disturbed. "I'm so sorry! I hadn't heard. Such a sweet girl! Brilliant, but she never let on. Henry was so proud of her. He just knew she'd follow in his footsteps. What happened?"

"That's what we're trying to find out too," replied Nora, leading the conversation. "You see, our youngest sister, Calista, called me out of the blue. She was worried sick about Vicki because she hadn't heard from her in a couple of days. So, I said I'd go over to her house and check it out. When I got there, police were in the middle of arresting her husband, Pierce. After they left, I went into Vicki's study. I found a white cardboard box with a mirror inside of it and this file."

Nora motioned to Yates, indicating that he should open the file. "We watched the video and listened to the tape. Hazel looked over the report."

Yates looked at Hazel. "Hazel Goodnight? From *Haunting Grounds*? Well, I'll be!" Yates reached out to shake Hazel's hand and nodded in approval. "I wondered what you looked like. I listen all the time. Great podcast! Sometimes I think our work was just ahead of its time. If we'd have done it now, with all the self-publishing platforms out there, who knows?" Yates opened his arms broadly.

"Hey, it was guys like you who paved the way," Hazel said. "Without places like the Parapsychology Lab, there wouldn't be people like me. Speaking of which, you wouldn't happen to have access to..."

"Yes, I'm sure the two of you will have plenty to talk about," interjected Nora, trying to stay patient as the conversation once again veered off-topic. "Did you know that Vicki was going over some of your old experiments? Would anyone else have known?"

"Oh, no, I didn't know," replied Yates, settling back in his chair. "But that doesn't surprise me in the least. None of the psychiatrists or psychologists in the other *legitimate fields*," Yeats paused briefly to emphasize the phrase with air quotes, "Would have been caught dead doing anything with the Parapsychology Lab. It was a sure detour off the tenure track. Henry already had tenure, and he was interested, so he didn't care at all. Vicki must not have cared either. I heard some rumors at the faculty dinner that Vicki was working with something unusual, but you know how academic rumors get started. I figured it was just someone gunning for her position. And trying to suggest a scandal to discredit her."

"Would you know who that might be? Was anyone especially jealous of her?"

Yates paused for a moment as the ginger cat once again shoaled about his legs, searching for the right angle at which to regain the lap position that he'd previously enjoyed.

"Not that I can think of. Vicki got along with all her colleagues. Her work was considered top-notch by everyone too. Except, perhaps..." Here, Yates stopped for a second, as if he didn't want to admit as much to Nora, "Your mother. But then that's Marjorie. She's like that Prince song. Never satisfied."

"Oh, how well I know," said Nora, lost for a moment in her reflection. "Still, would it be too much to ask if I wanted to see Vicki's lab? We've just come from her house. We haven't found evidence to suggest anything there, other than she was working on this." Nora gestured again toward the folder in Bill's hand. "Since Vicki spent so much of her time at work, I'm hoping that her lab will yield better clues."

Yates nodded and rose to head into the kitchen. Nora could hear him rummaging around in a drawer for a second, then he returned. "When I retired last year, they let me keep my campus key card for building access. I suppose they were thinking that I might come back to teach a class or two part-time as an emeritus. Then when all that pandemic mess hit, no one thought it was prudent to have seventy-year-olds wandering around campus randomly. Regardless, I'd be happy to escort you and show you around. Also, I'm kind of curious. If Vicki was dabbling in our old experiments, I'd like to know if she found anything new."

"So would I!" Hazel burst out, more excited than she'd meant to sound. Nora shot her a look. She added sheepishly, "It might help us find out more about Vicki too."

Fifteen minutes later, the three of them pulled up into the parking space next to the Rhine Center marked *Emeritus*. "Best parking spot I've had in my whole career," Yates joked, as he slid out of the Tahoe. "Now that I'm not even here anymore."

Yates swiped them in with his key card and held the door so that they could follow. Walking through the upstairs of the building, past a hallway of glass-fronted conference rooms and faculty offices with their witty door signs, Yates took them downstairs into the basement. There, he swiped his access card again by a door marked *Lab Storage*. He clicked on the lights and ushered them inside.

Quickly, Nora saw that it wasn't just one small storage room, but rather a catacomb of many different rooms, each with a professor's name on the door. "We moved all the mirror experiment documentation into my space after Henry passed," Yates explained. "Be careful where you step. It's pretty crowded."

Yates's warning was an understatement. The room was filled, floor to ceiling, with row upon row of extremely dusty, yet carefully labeled, flat white cardboard boxes of various sizes. Only a narrow pathway about a foot wide allowed entry or exit. Heading immediately for the back row nearest the far wall, Yates called, "A ha!" and motioned for the ladies to come over.

"Look," Yates said, pointing to a low shelf with a long row of boxes. Each was identical to the one that Nora and Hazel found at Vicki's house. They strained over to see through the narrow aisle. Unlike the rest of the room, which was thick with dust, the last row looked as if it had been used recently by someone in a hurry. The corners of some of the boxes were bent and torn, obviously from someone wrestling them in and out of their tight squeeze.

"Here's the real mystery, though," said Yates, pointing to a box marked *Specimen 154* in a style of large, rounded handwriting much different from the others. Nora recognized it as Vicki's. "I stopped the mirror experiments after Henry's death. Our last one was 153."

"So, what's 154 then?" Hazel asked, craning over Nora's shoulder for a better look.

"I haven't the foggiest idea," answered Yates, as he began to struggle with pulling the box out from its space. "But we're about to go upstairs and find out!"

Back up in one of the lab rooms on the second floor, Yates pulled out another folder from the box and peered inside. "Holy shit!" he exclaimed, momentarily losing his composure as he slid the mirror out of the box. It was smaller than the large, wood-framed mirror that they had seen in box 153. This one had an ornate brass frame and a little stand on the back of it so that it could easily be set up on top of a dresser.

"This mirror," Yates said, "used to sit on Henry's desk next to the computer. He often ate lunch in the lab while he was working. I used to tease him about being vain and whether he used it to check for spinach in his teeth because it was so feminine. Henry claimed that he kept it for sentimental reasons because it was his mother's. I wonder if she's..." Yates drew a square shape with his hands in the air to suggest the obvious.

"In the mirror," Nora finished, as she unwound the string from the folder that was also inside the box. "Only one way to find out. We should watch the tape. Although, full disclosure: my grandmother died when my dad was still young. Cancer. He rarely spoke of her. I think it hurt too much. So, I wouldn't know if it's her or not. We'll have to find a picture."

"I don't think it's just her," said Hazel, looking up from the stack of papers that she'd taken from the folder after Nora set it down. Hazel held up the report so they could see the cover page. "Specimen 154: Henry Hewitt."

Chapter Fifteen

"Oh, my Lord, why didn't I think of that!" Yates exclaimed, snatching up the mirror and grasping it tightly in both hands. "It was right there!" He shook the mirror at Nora. "This was on his desk when Henry died. All those years of wondering why I couldn't see it, why I couldn't understand what he had done. All I had to do was think and ask. Oh, Henry, I am so sorry. I failed you!"

Yates laid the mirror down on the worktable, surprisingly softly, and turned his back to Nora. He took a deep, ragged breath as he turned back to face her. "I failed you too. I'm sure you wanted answers. You deserved them. But for some reason, I just didn't think." Yates inhaled deeply again and rolled his eyes to the ceiling. When he looked back at Nora, his eyes were rimmed with red, but his gaze was steadier. "Or perhaps it was that I just didn't think fast enough. Henry's office was cleared out the next day. The police took everything because at the time they were still trying to determine if foul play was involved. I was so overwhelmed that it never occurred to me that there might be another way to find out what went wrong that night."

"You're going to have to slow down," said Nora. Her head was swimming so that the room had begun to tilt sideways, as it did when she had a severe migraine coming on. She reached out to the table to steady herself as Yates continued.

"Yes, yes, you're right. I should begin at the beginning. Right, okay." Yates was nervous, pressing his hands against the sides of his face beneath his beard.

"I think I get it," said Hazel. "If Henry died in front of the mirror, then whatever he said or did in the moments just beforehand would have been imprinted on it. You're sorry that you didn't think of it before now, because Henry might have left some kind of final message behind that would have allowed them closure."

"Yes, of course, that!" snapped Yates testily, still visibly angry with himself. "But also, Henry was clairvoyant. Extremely so, though very few people knew. Thus, if his spirit had become trapped in the mirror, it would have remained responsive. Then, we might have learned..."

"So that's the difference!" Hazel interjected. "It all makes sense now! If the person who died in front of the mirror had psychic abilities, then he or she would have been accustomed to moving between worlds. Astral projecting and who knows what else, even after death."

"Precisely," said Yates, sinking back down into the chair again. "I could have communicated with Henry directly. You and your sisters could have spoken to him. It wouldn't have brought him back, but you would have been able to continue interacting with him. Forever."

"But perhaps," said Nora, in a hoarse whisper, from behind the hand that covered her mouth, "it was best that you didn't. Because after that, we would have had to watch him die." Her voice began to quiver as her hand moved to her chin in an almost unconscious effort to stop it. "That time, and then every time we missed him after. Over and over and over again."

Nora stopped and looked straight at Yates. "You didn't miss anything. It was better not to know. To keep going, I chose to think that maybe something just snapped one day. That was better than the speculation of what could have happened, what Dad might have been hiding. How he might not have been the father we knew. It was easier just to grieve and then go on."

The three of them were silent for a long time.

"I can understand how you feel," said Yates. "Everyone grieves differently. But your sister, Vicki. She devoted her whole career, her entire life, to continuing with Henry's work. We may never know how she came by this mirror and got the initial idea to test it using our experiments. Regardless," Yates reached again for the papers. "Vicki found something very important that has to do with your father. It may very well be the best piece of evidence we're going to find as to the reason for her disappearance also."

Hazel reached back into the folder and held up a flash drive. "And then, there's this." Nora stared at it, knowing full well what it would most likely contain. She sighed heavily to Hazel. "As I said this morning. If Vicki can stand it, I can. Especially if it's the best chance we've got at helping get her back."

Yates took the flash drive gently from Hazel and plugged it in. He turned on the laptop and logged into the media player. Nora and Hazel pulled up their chairs around the screen. "Are you both ready?"

They nodded to Yates. "Then, let's begin."

After Yates pressed *Play*, a title screen displayed the subject number and date. Then, Vicki appeared. "Hello, my name is Dr. Victoria Hewitt, and what you are about to see is both very disturbing and intriguing. It is also deeply personal, although I will attempt to compartmentalize."

That certainly runs in the family, Nora thought to herself, but she said nothing as the video continued.

"When I was a young girl, I often used to spend my after-school hours with my father in his lab. One day, as I sat on the floor coloring, I witnessed something very unusual. Dad was talking to a mirror." She gestured to her left. Nora could see Vicki was indicating the mirror sitting on the table beside the computer station. "*Would you like to come and see your grandmother?* Dad asked me. I agreed, although I was hesitant. You see, my grandmother died many years before I was born, while my father was still a boy.

Next, my father took me on his knee, and we both looked into the mirror. There, I could see a woman, quite lovely, although I remember she seemed extremely tired. She was dressed in a long nightgown and had her hair cut to shoulder length in one of those late fifties-style bobs. Father introduced me to the woman as her granddaughter. I remember exchanging pleasantries. She smiled at me and told me I was very pretty, but that was about all. Moments afterward, the woman sat down in the chair and appeared to fall asleep. The image of her went away. Being only five, I did not fully comprehend then what had happened. Later that night at dinner, I brought up what I called the *magic talking mirror*. My mother seemed concerned at this statement, and she began scolding my father, which confused me. They went outside, and I could hear them arguing. Afterward, my father returned to tell me that what he had shown me that afternoon was just a magic trick and that I shouldn't mention it again."

Here, Vicki walked over to the table and picked up the mirror, holding it in front of her. "I did not see this mirror again for over thirty years. During that time, my father passed away. Although I was led to believe that he committed suicide, I learned that was not true after I rediscovered this mirror."

Hazel clicked the mouse to pause the video. "Nora, here." She reached into her purse and pulled out a small packet of Kleenex to hand to her. Saying nothing, Nora held the packet without removing a tissue as her eyes began to water. Hazel hit *Play*, and the video began again.

"After my father's death, I became more determined than ever to follow in his footsteps and to also become a psychiatrist. For many years, I studied the long-term effects of depression on the brain for obvious reasons. Although I still feel that work is very important, and I plan to continue it, this will be the first in a new line of experiments, which are a continuation of my father's work. That is the personal portion of this record."

Vicki paused to take a sip of water and continued. "Here is the objective portion. Last year, I had a chance meeting with a former colleague who is now retired. His name is Dr. Bill Yates. We spoke very briefly at a faculty banquet. He mentioned that he had worked with my father on some experiments. Since I remembered most of my father's colleagues from dinners at our house, but not Dr. Yates, I looked him up. I found that they had worked together, but for some reason Dr. Yates's position was reduced from tenured to adjunct status after the Parapsychology Lab was largely defunded. This led me to dig deeper and go into the department archives, where I uncovered many records, 153 to be exact, of their work together. Watching the videotape of one of them jogged my memory of the *magic talking mirror* that I had seen in my father's office as a child. By pure coincidence, I was cleaning out my attic of some boxes one afternoon when I found this mirror again among some of my father's personal effects that my mother had put away after he passed. When I set it up, the mirror began to perform in the manner that I have described already. I had to reintroduce myself to my grandmother as I am now much older than when I first saw her in the mirror. Yet, she informed me of something shocking. Eleanor, my paternal grandmother, told me my father's spirit is now inside the mirror as well and he did not commit suicide. He was murdered. Eleanor did not know who the murderer was, only that she had seen the shot. However, she'd been unable to do anything, as her spirit was locked inside the mirror. Eleanor further informed me that, if I would wait until 11:11 pm, I would be able to witness it for myself and perhaps begin to figure out who was responsible. Therefore, since it is currently 11 o'clock, I will now step behind the camera to allow the scene to unfold undisturbed for preservation as a part of this record."

Nora leaped forward to hit *Pause* and sank back into her chair. Although she had managed to avoid tears, her face was red and blotchy from the effort. She removed a tissue from the packet and pressed it to her lips. "We don't need to watch that part right now," Nora said quietly into the tissue.

"I agree," echoed Yates. "I think we know most of everything that this video is going to tell us from Vicki's narration. She survived long enough to make this detailed report afterward, so I don't think there's any benefit to watching Henry be..." Yates couldn't say the word. "Hazel, since you're more removed from the situation, could you glance through the remainder of the record and tell us if there's anything else we should know?"

Hazel quickly skimmed the brief. "Nothing besides what's already been described, then the *other* part. But it doesn't name a suspect. It says the killer was not visible in the reflection."

"Weird as it seems, that's kind of a relief at this point," said Nora, recomposing herself. "I don't think I could take another revelation. We already have more questions than we began with. Yet, we have no better idea what happened to Vicki. And I've just found out that our father didn't kill himself, but that he was murdered."

"I have a strong theory," said Yates. "That we've just learned more than we realize, if we put the pieces together. Your father was killed in his lab, late at night, while working on these experiments mostly in secret. Your sister has now disappeared only a few weeks after restarting this same series of experiments. I had no hand in either of these incidents. If you don't believe me, which is your every right, I will be happy to submit to any type of truth-finding test you require to prove my innocence. Neither your father nor Vicki had any professional enemies I know of who would do such things, which leaves me with only one question."

"What's that?" said Nora.

"For *that*," Yates replied, "I think you should ask your mother."

Chapter Sixteen

J ust then, Nora's phone rang. When she answered, an automated voice
asked whether she would accept a collect call from an inmate named
Pierce Eichhorn. Nora agreed as a breathless Pierce came on the line. His
panicked voice sounded hollow, as if from inside a cave.

"Nora, thank God you answered! Please don't hang up!"

"Why would I hang up? Where are you?"

"Because everyone else has. I'm still in jail, unable to post bond. Nora,
my attorney won't speak to me. No lawyer I know will. The cops are acting
strange too. I believe your mother has gotten to them somehow. I need
your help. Didn't you say that your attorney in Nashville is also licensed in
North Carolina? Do you think that you could get him to take my case? I
have plenty of money, but I'm just…" Here Pierce's voice suddenly became
a whisper, "I'm afraid, Nora. I have to bond out of here. Something's weird
about this, and I'm scared. Really scared. I thought they'd just question me
and then let me go because everyone always suspects the husband in things
like this, but I think they're trying to railroad me."

"Whoa, Pierce. Slow down. Yes, I can call Cliff for you. I can't guarantee
he'll come right away, though. Have you been charged with anything?
How much is your bond?"

Pierce's answer was louder and full of false confidence, like a man making a point to be overheard. "I've been charged with murder. The bond is
one million dollars."

"Christ!"

"I know," said Pierce, getting softer again. "Listen, if you're willing to
help me get out of here, we can figure out how to get a meeting with your
attorney. I always keep half a million in cash in the safe at my office. I can
give you the combination. That is if you're willing to sign my bond and

bring the other half of the money for my bail. I promise I will pay you back."

Nora sat quietly thinking. Although she felt fairly certain that Pierce had nothing to do with her sister's disappearance, she still had some reservations about helping him.

"Nora, will you do it?" Pierce begged.

"Yes," Nora finally replied. "Yes, I'll do it. Give me an hour or so to get down there and to call Cliff to see what we'll need to do afterward."

Pierce took a deep breath. "Thank you, Nora. You've always been much better to me than I deserved."

You've got that right, thought Nora, but instead she replied, "I'm only doing this because I don't think that you're responsible for whatever has happened to Vicki. However, I'm going to need all the help I can get to find her. Will you help us?"

"Of course! Our divorce is amicable. We'd just grown apart. I mean, if we ever were *together*, together, you know? With Vicki, it was always so hard to tell. She was so unreachable most of the time. But I'm just as upset as you are to think that anything bad has happened to her."

"I doubt that," said Nora. "Regardless, count on me being there tonight."

"I can't believe that you're going to help him. You should let him sit in there for a while," said Hazel as Nora ended the call with Pierce and scrolled through her contacts for Cliff's number.

Nora waited for Cliff to answer the phone, then hit mute. "I couldn't care less about what happens to Pierce. What I'm worried about is why they're trying to stick him with a murder charge so quickly. If he's not guilty, that's a big fat lawsuit waiting to happen. My worry is who would risk whatever is happening to Vicki while they're putting Pierce through this whole little charade."

When Cliff picked up, he listened to Nora explain the situation. He agreed to accept the case only after Nora told him fees were no object. "He won't be able to leave the state on a bond like that, most likely," Cliff cautioned. "And I can't take more than a day or so away from my other clients. Is there somewhere closer to the state line that we could meet?"

"My sister Calista lives in Asheville. We could meet there."

"That's a good idea. It might be better if Pierce stayed there and out of town for a while. If this case has some ulterior motive like you're suggesting, it might not be safe for him in Durham. Let alone the media circus that'll follow. I mean, the disappearance of a wealthy Duke professor whose husband has been charged with her murder would be a pretty juicy tale for any reporter hungry for a story," replied Cliff.

"I hadn't thought of that, but you're right. I'll call Calista as soon as I get off the phone with you. Anything else?"

"Just one more thing. I hate to have to bring it up with everything else going on, but Julia's been driving me crazy to contact you. Something about Jasper's studio, but she's being intentionally vague. It could just be about royalties or equipment. I don't know why she's acting so cagey, though. Regardless, Julia seems to want you over here ASAP. I've been trying to hold her off until you had time to get settled in."

"Why can't Julia call me herself?"

"Because she's Julia," answered Cliff. Nora could almost see the lawyer rolling his eyes. "Why else?"

"Gotcha," nodded Nora. "Well, I might as well come on over to Nashville after I drop Pierce off in Asheville anyway. It's only a few hours more. Then, we can both ride back to Asheville together. Save you part of the trip."

"Sounds good to me." They exchanged goodbyes, and Cliff hung up.

"No rest for the weary, it appears," said Nora to Hazel. "Now I have to drop Pierce off in Asheville on my way to Nashville because Jasper's mother wants me for something."

"Speaking of mothers," interjected Yates, "did I happen to overhear Pierce say that your mother may be the reason why he hasn't been able to find legal representation on his own?"

Nora nodded.

"Well, as I was just about to say before this new wrinkle, and please forgive me for potentially piling on to what I am certain is an already stressful situation, I'd always thought it was Marjorie's disdain for Henry's experiments that may have pushed him over the edge. Now that we've seen this new video that Vicki has made, though, I'm not so certain... again, please forgive me for the insinuation... that there might not be even more to it."

"I'm not following, Dr. Yates," said Nora. "And I don't fault you for insinuating anything at this point, so please be frank."

"I'm saying that Marjorie, as I am sure you know, is a woman desperately concerned with achievement, reputation, and prestige. If she saw there was potential for your father's experiments to cause the family shame or even embarrassment, and/or possibly damage either his career or her career also by association, then I'm not sure what she would have been willing to do to stop that from happening."

Nora said nothing as Yates watched her anxiously. She knew all too well Marjorie's character flaws as he described them. The old professor wasn't wrong. Still, the thought that her mother was capable of what Yates suggested was simply too much to comprehend.

"Have I offended you? If so, I'm sorry." Yates apologized.

"No, it's just..." Nora trailed off, trying to refocus her thoughts on the most urgent matter at hand. "I have so many things on my mind. Right now, I have to focus on doing what I can to help the living. Since I believe my oldest sister is still among us, I'm afraid we'll have to table discussion about my father until another time."

"I understand completely," said Yates. "Nothing we can do at this point will bring Henry back."

"Actually, in the physical sense, that's true," said Hazel, thoughtfully. "But in the spiritual sense, as we have already seen here, it might be possible. Bill, have you ever tried to communicate directly with Henry? Since his death, I mean."

"No. For a couple of reasons," said Yates. "First, because I didn't know there was even the remotest possibility that Henry might have become trapped in his mother's mirror when he passed. And second..." Yates paused, choosing his words carefully. "Sometimes just because a scientist *can* do a thing doesn't mean he *should*. Do you follow me?"

"All the way," said Hazel, glancing at Nora, who echoed her response.

"All the way."

***

By midnight, Nora, Hazel, and Pierce were pulling up in front of Calista's dance studio in Asheville. The bonding process had been relatively hassle-free, all things considered. The police seemed surprised that Pierce was able to come up with such a large sum on short notice but otherwise hadn't shown any special interest in his case.

Calista was awake and waiting anxiously for her three guests, having set up air beds on the broad expanse of the dance floor downstairs. Sheridan had the presence of mind to order Chinese takeaway for everyone. They all sat down at the table in the conference room immediately upon arrival.

After they'd finished dinner, Hazel excused herself to the bathroom. Upon her return, she glanced back and forth between Nora and Calista with a strange sort of smile. "So, I know the large mirror on the far end of the practice floor is one of *the* mirrors."

A sleepy-looking Calista brightened, "Oh, yes! That's the one Nora sent me last week. Everyone who comes in comments on it. It's quite the conversation piece."

Hazel looked at Nora, though her question was directed at Calista. "Yes, it is. I was wondering whether you'd noticed anything unusual about it."

"Unusual how?" asked Calista, her blue eyes blank and flat.

"Well, Calista keeps telling me I'm crazy, but I keep telling her it makes me feel funny," said Sheridan. "Like someone is watching me or something. So much so that I try to avoid being in the room with it late at night by myself." He laughed nervously. "Glad you guys are here with me tonight. More wine? We need to finish off this bottle."

Sheridan motioned toward their glasses. Nora, Pierce, and Hazel all leaned forward eagerly. Sheridan squinted at the barely half glass left before setting the bottle down on the table. "Demand remains high. That's not a surprise after the day you've had. On second thought, let me run upstairs and get another." He rose, but Calista stopped him, insisting that she go instead, since they were *her* guests. Once Calista was gone upstairs, Sheridan motioned for the other three to come closer.

"Cali claims there's nothing unusual about the mirror, but that girl's got to be lying. I've heard noises downstairs late at night several times now. When I go down to check, she's just standing there staring at it. Me, I can't get away from it fast enough, but her," Sheridan flapped his hands like wings. "Like a moth to a flame. It's crazy."

Hazel studied Sheridan with a concerned expression. "Does she speak to it?"

Sheridan drained the remnants of his glass and rolled the stem thoughtfully between his thumb and forefinger. "No, not really. It's more like she's listening to it, but she says nothing. Like she's sleepwalking. Why?"

Hazel shot Nora a knowing look before proceeding. "She probably is. Sheridan, how late do you usually stay up?"

Sheridan looked at his watch. "Lord, not until this late even these days. We're doing a summer dance camp that runs ten to six five days a week. I need my beauty sleep to be able to keep up with all those kids. Why? What do you have in mind?"

"I'd like to sit up with you to observe what's happening with the mirror. How Calista's interacting with it when she isn't aware we're watching. Not tonight though, I agree it's too late. We'll try it tomorrow," said Hazel, as Calista returned with a fresh bottle.

"Try what?" asked Calista, using a corkscrew to pop open the chardonnay.

"Dancing," replied Hazel hastily, before anyone else had the chance to react. "I was just asking Sheridan if he could show me some ballroom moves." Hazel caught Sheridan's eye. He winked and played along.

"Oh, yes, honey. I said it was too late tonight, but if she stays here while Nora goes on to Nashville to meet up with the ex-monster-in-law, we could give it a whirl after the girls leave tomorrow."

"That sounds like fun," Calista yawned and stretched. "But it's fun that will have to wait until tomorrow for me. Are you three okay if I leave you with Sher and go on to bed?"

Sheridan exchanged a look with Nora this time. Both mentally noted how unusual it was that Calista, renowned for her ability to operate on little sleep, was throwing in the towel so early, while a house full of guests with an exciting story still half-told waited downstairs. Even Pierce picked up on the skepticism going around the room and said, "It's okay with me, doll."

Calista's tired eyes went cold as she looked at her soon-to-be ex-brother-in-law. "I'm so glad *you're* okay with it." Feeling the verbal sting, Pierce stared down at his empty plate.

"Go ahead, sugar," Sheridan said. "I know this summer camp has worn you out lately. I'll make sure everything is cleaned up and the kids are tucked in." At this, Calista's smile changed from sarcastic to sincere. Calista walked over, ruffled Sheridan's hair, and returned upstairs.

Once she was out of earshot, Sheridan beckoned for the others to move closer again. "That's the other thing. Little Miss Dynamite is tired *all* the time now. At first, I thought it was stress, what with the move and opening the new studio. Then I began to notice she only seemed awake when she was working."

"It's not like her, I know," seconded Nora.

"I like the sound of this less and less," said Hazel, reaching forward to refill her glass. "Nora, if you're okay with what we said before, I'd like you to go and handle whatever is happening with Julia alone. I'll stay here. If my suspicion is correct, Calista may be in just as much danger as Vicki right now. Possibly more."

"Well, I'm glad you're willing to take care of it," said Nora, slumping back in her chair. "I don't think that I can take one more mystery."

"Life is an eternal series of mysteries," quipped Hazel. "We have to keep solving them every day."

Chapter Seventeen

Pulling up to her former mother-in-law's house in Brentwood, Nora couldn't help but marvel at the wasteful splendor of it all. A long, curved driveway took her over forty acres of rolling pasture that contained only two elderly horses. However, it was a hot day, so they were snug and cool inside the air-conditioned barn. Nora knew their routine. They would soon be fed organic oats and apples, taken for their late afternoon exercise by a hired groom, brushed thoroughly, and then prepared for bed like the well-cared-for, yet otherwise ignored, children they were. No one had ridden them, or even mentioned them really, since Jasper died. Nora had never ridden a horse at all. Those two had been a special mother-and-son hobby.

The main house itself was massive. Built to look like a simplified storybook castle, the exterior was covered in pale grayish-pink Tennessee limestone, the two stories culminating in large round turrets at either end. Each turret was built to somewhat resemble a lighthouse, the symbol of Jubal Chandler Music Ministries. A large Roman archway surrounded the heavy, medieval-looking double doors in the center. In front of the house was a large white marble cross, at least twenty feet high, which was encircled by an enormous white marble fountain and a rounded drive. In the center of the fountain was a lighthouse-shaped pillar, which sprayed a backlit rainbow cascade of water. Hovering over it was a shimmering hologram of the initials *J.C.* spinning into infinity. The driveway itself was white pea gravel, the kind that most people reserve for flower gardens. Limestone statues of winged lions and carefully sculpted topiaries of angels lined the walkway leading up to the house. Nora chuckled to herself, as she could not help but do every time she'd visited the house during her relationship with Jasper. Though the estate was allegedly a farm, the boxwood angels were the wildest things there, and even they had been tamed into topiaries.

Leaving her Tahoe in the driveway, Nora scanned the compound for Julia's car, a Tesla Roadster, or Jasper's older black Hummer. Neither were to be seen, so she rang the doorbell. Nora was not surprised to hear the chimes echoing through the expansive marble hallways to the old hymn, "Holy, Holy, Holy." After several rounds of the tune, Nora could hear the sharp clip-clap of Julia's high heels trotting across the marble floor and the much softer beeps as she entered the security code, allowing the door to swing open untouched by human hands.

"Finally, you're here!" said Julia, snapping up the remote to dim the lights and lower the curtains from a nearby antique, whitewashed sideboard.

"Nice to see you too," replied Nora, stepping out of the foyer and into the main hall, taking in how little anything had changed since she'd last visited Julia over a year ago. The white lacquered Steinway grand piano, upon which Jasper had taken his boyhood piano lessons, was still stationed opposite the double-beveled glass doors at the other end of a room roughly the size of a basketball court. On top of the piano was the urn that Nora knew contained Jasper's ashes. His mother insisted on keeping them after his death.

In the center was yet another fountain, an ascending cluster of white marble angels trailing ribbons of gilded musical staves into the water. Arranged around it were half a dozen custom-made puffy white leather loveseats, in a style that Nora was certain had not been popular since the late nineties, but were nevertheless spotless and expensive. Seeing them again reminded her of what Jasper told her the first time she'd visited the mansion many years ago, at the beginning of their relationship. "Whatever you do, don't sit on Mother's clouds."

Julia ignored Nora's half-hearted attempt at pleasantries. "Don't just stand there. Come upstairs with me. I have something to show you." Julia stood tapping her foot impatiently as Nora followed her up the sweeping, hand-carved white oak staircase that covered most of the right side of the room. Once upstairs, Nora continued to follow Julia into the suite of rooms that had been Jasper's. Even well into his adult years, Julia maintained them as such. Partly for Jasper's visits, which she shamed him into almost every Sunday, and Nora suspected, partly as a museum of the promise Jasper had shown as a boy, yet never fulfilled to his mother's satisfaction as a man.

"There," Julia said, extending a bony finger toward a wall, curiously empty save for the object of her attention. "I've hesitated to contact you directly because I know that you already think I'm crazy, but that's it. What do you know about it?"

Nora recognized it instantly. It was the mirror that used to hang behind the mixing console in Jasper's studio. The one that had caused her to buy the three others exactly like it from Dean Goodnight. The fourth that had hung on the walls of the Blue Post, as she now knew. Nora hadn't seen it since the day after Jasper's death, when it must have been taken away and put into storage by Julia. Nora assumed it had later been sold, like most of his musical equipment and the furnishings of the studio. However, wanting to draw out Julia's reasoning for summoning her urgently from nine hours away to see it once more, Nora decided to feign ignorance.

"Wasn't it in Jasper's old studio?"

Julia instantly rejected Nora's attempt at guilelessness. "Don't act like you don't know. Of course, it was there for years. What I want to know is where it came from. I paid for everything else in that studio. Neither Jasper nor his father would have had two dimes to rub together if it weren't for me. And I didn't buy this mirror. I assumed that someone must have given it to him since he would never have spent so much on anything decorative. It certainly looks expensive. My son used all his money for *other things*."

By this time, Nora was used to Julia's incessant referral to Jasper's addiction problem with passive euphemisms, as if it had been an unspeakable personal offense to her. Even during Jasper's seven years of sobriety, Julia could only shut up about it if sidetracked onto her other favorite derogatory theme—his father Jubal's drinking problem. Julia always claimed that she had personally "saved the family" and the Chandler Music Ministries empire from it.

Nora weighed whether or not to tell Julia the truth. Finally, she decided it was the easiest option that would get her out of the house quickly. "I bought it years ago and gave it to Jasper. I didn't think that much about it. But, the weekend I moved to Wilmington, I met a woman in the market on Front Street who had three more of them."

"And do the other three replay my son's death night after night?" Julia asked.

"No... no, they don't," Nora stammered, caught off-guard.

"Well, if you can take the time away from your little decorating hobby," Julia always referred to Nora's design career as a hobby, since in her opinion, the proper place for a woman who didn't have to work was hovering over her husband's every move. "I'd like for you to stay with me tonight and watch what happens. I guarantee you'll be shocked, as I was."

"Why would I ever want to watch Jasper overdose?"

"Because he *didn't* overdose, you idiot! Wake up! Jasper was poisoned!"

"Poisoned!" Nora exclaimed. "By whom?"

"That's what I needed you for! I don't know all his dirtbag friends!" Julia snapped. The older woman didn't like having to wait for Nora to absorb the emotional impact of her revelation before she could continue. Yet, something in Nora's pained expression and failure to respond provoked a softer reaction.

"Look, I know it's difficult for you. You were always so sensitive. But I'm not. Jasper was my son, but he caused me inexplicable pain in the years after his father's heart attack. Running wild, doing drugs, in and out of jail throughout his twenties. Whatever you had to endure, I assure you it was *far* less. He calmed down *significantly* after he met you. I loved Jasper too, but I learned that I had to keep my emotional distance from him so that I could preserve all of this." Julia swept her heavily ringed hands over the room.

Nora noticed that the rings spun around on her fingers. For a second, she speculated as to how in the world Julia could continue to lose weight. Julia was above average height, close to six feet, but couldn't weigh a hundred pounds soaking wet.

Nora swallowed hard. "Okay, okay. I can do that. I just... I've just had another shock yesterday, before I came here. I need a minute."

"What could be more shocking than finding out your husband was murdered?" Julia stared at Nora coldly.

It was something about being challenged, called out explicitly that her feelings didn't matter, that made Nora finally snap. She strode across the room and slapped Julia as hard as she could straight across the mouth. The force of it knocked Julia spinning onto the floor, where she lay with her skinny arms splayed out as if she'd been mortally wounded. Nora, in a rage, screamed at Julia, where she lay.

"How *dare* you! All you've ever done since the moment I met Jasper is rant and rave about how terrible he and his father were and try to lord over me with your fake Christian, condescending, skinny ass! You never offered Jasper any compassion after his father died, which was what he *needed*! Not you pushing him into maintaining your *empire*," Nora mocked Julia's earlier sweeping arm movements. "If you'd *ever* had the courage to go out and do anything for yourself for once in your *entire* life, rather than pushing men to do it for you, then maybe you wouldn't be such a bitter old hateful *bitch!*"

Julia rolled over on her side and glared spitefully at Nora. Nora felt her own eyes grow hot with tears of rage that she wished she could stop from falling but failed. "Even now, after Jasper's been dead a year, you can't let him rest. Or me either. You've got to dig up *this*!" Nora thrust her hand at the mirror "And punish me with it all over again. Well, today is *not* the day, Julia! *Goddamn it!* Do you even know what I've already been through just to get here? Do you even care?"

"What have you been through?" Julia sniped, her lips shriveled and tight, like a prune.

Nora dropped to her knees and jerked the older woman up face-to-face with her by the jacket collar of her Dior suit. For the first time, Julia looked genuinely scared.

"Yesterday, I went in search of my sister, who is missing, only to find the reason is somehow connected to her reopening my father's experiments with other mirrors just like *THAT* one." Nora tightened her grip on the collar of Julia's jacket, stood her up, and then shoved the older woman toward the mirror. "Turns out, he didn't kill himself. My dad was murdered *too*. Possibly because of *my* power-hungry bitch of a mother, if his old lab partner is to be believed. So, I've had about *enough*," Nora pushed Julia backward, putting her back squarely against the mirror, "from cold-raging bitches like *you!*"

Nora dropped her hands and stood panting from exertion. Julia straightened her suit and brushed off the carpet fuzz from her sleeve. Regaining her composure, and with eyes slightly curious rather than flat and cold, Julia said, "I see. Well, we will chalk that little outburst up to you being overwrought then."

Julia took several steps away from the mirror, wincing away from Nora like a cat who had been kicked. She turned to face the mirror. "So this is what I believed it to be then. I wasn't hallucinating." She put her hand out to touch the wide, gilded frame. "My son's spirit is trapped in here." At this, Julia let out a crazed, witch-like cackle. "All these years of denying the presence of ghosts in the church, only now to have peace because of one. Serves me goddamned right."

Nora swabbed at the sweat dripping from her face with the back of her hand. "Serves you right for what?"

"For being everything everyone says I am," replied Julia. "All these years, I knew it was all bullshit. But I kept it going until I believed it myself. Jubal and that whole charade. The church. The ministry. So now, finally, I have what I wanted. My name isn't even really Julia. Did you know that? I picked it to match Jubal's name. It's Wanda. Wanda Jean Hooten. From Lickskillet, Tennessee. Here in this big, fancy empty house, while my only son hangs up there. Dead on the wall. And while his wife slaps me back to my senses for being such a, what was it you called me? *A cold-raging bitch*?"

"You don't always rage," offered Nora. "Mostly you just stew and simmer." She couldn't resist adding, "So... Wanda Jean, huh? From Lickskillet. No, I never knew that. You don't sound like it."

"Took me years to lose that hick accent," Julia replied. "I'll never look like them either. One of those fat rednecks. My mother weighed over 300 pounds. Sisters too. All dead now. Diabetes. That's why I worked so hard to stay fit. I used to run ten miles a day."

I wouldn't exactly call it fit, Nora thought to herself. *More like skeletal*.

"Anyway, what the hell does any of it matter now? I'm dying. And you'll just lose it all. Any kind person who stays in this town long enough does. It's a den of thieves."

Having caught her breath again, Nora countered. "Julia, we're all dying. Don't be dramatic."

Julia cackled again. "Oh, what a tangled web, when I can't even weave a single thread of truth through it. No, I really *am dying*. Kidney failure. I'm already on dialysis now. Look!" Julia untucked the blouse from the skirt of her expensive suit and lifted it to reveal a port sticking out of the wrinkled, concave surface of her stomach. "Just barely holding myself together, *darlin'*. It appears staying thin hasn't saved me from diabetes at all. It's genetic. We are what our parents make of us, as much as we try to avoid it. We either fall in line or we rebel, but it's all the same. We are only who we're destined to be, and we have to make our peace with it." Julia retucked her blouse into the top of her size zero pencil skirt without the slightest struggle.

Nora noticed it was the second time Julia had said the word *peace*. In all her dealings with the woman, those were the only times she'd ever heard her mention it.

"Anyway, that's what this cold-hearted bitch wants you to watch with her in the mirror tonight. To try to see who killed Jasper. For both of us. Despite everything I've said, Jasper was my only son, and I loved him. I know you did too. You never gave up on him like I did when he relapsed. I'm sure it was your faith that kept him sober toward the end. That's why he gave you everything in his trust fund. Jasper trusted you. I do too." Julia paused, seeing the skeptical look that clouded Nora's face. "You don't have to *like* someone to trust them."

"Julia, I'm very sorry you're not well. And I'm sorry I slapped you, but I've never understood why you've never liked me. Even now."

"And I thought you were a smart one! Parents who were college professors and all. Ha! Shows how much that means." Julia crossed the room and cupped one long, bony hand around each of Nora's shoulders. "How could I *ever* have liked you? You reminded me so much of myself. Of what I *could* have been only without the kindness sucked out by the vacuum of poverty. You haven't the slightest idea what it's like, Nora Hewitt, to have to fake and fight your whole life just to survive. Compassion is a luxury affordable only for the rich."

"Then why haven't you acquired any?" Nora asked. "After all, you've been rich for a very long time."

Julia turned her back on the question and walked away from Nora as if to leave the room. At the door she stopped, her gaunt face almost cracking as she smiled. "Perhaps I'm just emotionally bankrupt."

"Would coming back tonight to see you through this thing with Jasper help settle any of that debt?" Nora asked.

Julia said nothing. She simply looked Nora squarely in the eye and nodded once.

Chapter Eighteen

Nora's meeting with her attorney Cliff that afternoon was blessedly brief. His assistant, Daphne, had prepared all the necessary documentation about fee arrangements.

The discussion of Pierce's alibi during the time of Vicki's disappearance was simple too. Nora had personally seen Pierce acting normally both before and afterward. Plus, they could count on Harper to testify that she was with Pierce at his condo in Wrightsville Beach the entire time. On the phone in the car from Durham to Asheville, Pierce had confirmed Harper would be more than willing to testify. He was surprised Harper had no qualms about appearing in public as a potential homewrecker at the tender age of twenty-four, but Nora was not. Although her interactions with Harper were minimal, she'd seen enough of the girl to know she had few reservations about anything, so long as the result was what she wanted. Agreeing to meet up with Cliff the next morning at ten for their return drive to Asheville, Nora headed back to her mother-in-law's compound.

On the way south out of town from Cliff's office, Nora couldn't help but drive down 17th Avenue toward Belmont. Indie Row, as it used to be called, was on the other side of the block from 16th Avenue, the famous Music Row. Jasper's old studio had been in one of the little brick Craftsman-style bungalows just past Ocean Way. It was now a cosmetic dental office specializing in custom veneers, according to the sign. Initially, Nora resisted selling the property to a Canadian investment firm, but once they'd offered her twice the price of any other local buyer, she relented. Like every other neighborhood in downtown Nashville, Indie Row was just another street of medical offices, juice bars, hot yoga studios, and overpriced, nondescript high-rise condo developments. Jasper's recording studio was one of the last independent studios remaining two years ago.

Now, there were none. Their absence reassured Nora that she'd made the right decision about Wilmington. Driving through New Nashville made her feel sad and old.

As she passed the ASCAP building, which faced the new super luxe Virgin Hotel instead of the small publishing houses that built the city, Nora marveled. Corporate America with a view of more corporate America. One of the ever-present, yet constantly changing, banners outside the PRO's offices caught her eye.

Congratulations to Buddy Conway on his number one single, "Lonely People." Then on the second line in a smaller font, *For Booking Contact Tommy Ponder Management Group."*

Nora blinked in disbelief. "Lonely People" was the title of one of the songs Jasper was working on during the weeks just before he died. Although Nora paid little attention to most of Jasper's commercial work—all modern country songs sounded the same to her—she'd been interested in that one because she'd inspired it.

Her whole life, when anyone heard her given name was Eleanor, they'd immediately start humming the Beatles tune, "Eleanor Rigby." The song had so haunted Nora that, not long after meeting Jasper and having the mayhem of the music business suddenly descend upon her otherwise peaceful life, she'd briefly attempted to take up guitar. Having only two main chords and an easy strumming pattern, "Rigby" was an easy first choice. Sadly, Nora's tiny hands ultimately proved an impediment to any hopes of guitar proficiency, and it remained the only song she'd ever learned to play. It became a running joke between Nora and Jasper for the rest of their relationship. If he were ever late for a gig, and in the early days they were together before he got sober, he often was, that Nora should go onstage and play the one song to stall the crowd. Jasper reasoned that "no one could stay mad watching a pretty girl play a Beatles tune." She'd never actually done it, though. After Jasper became sober a few years later, the time for their running joke expired.

Regardless, one afternoon they'd been standing on the rooftop at Acme Feed & Seed just after a sudden shower dispersed the usual throngs of tourists. As Nora watched them begin to reemerge into the street from the bars that lined Lower Broadway, which stank more than usual of stale beer and vomit after the downpour, she'd taken a sip of her Old Fashioned and, for no apparent reason, asked her favorite rhetorical questions from the song. *All the lonely people, where do they all come from? All the lonely people, where do they all belong?* That was all it took. Moments later, Jasper was scribbling on a napkin. In ten minutes, Jasper was begging Nora to hurry and finish her drink so that he could get down to the studio and try out a melody.

Who in the world is Buddy Conway? Nora thought, staring at the banner, as the memory subsided. The boy on the banner was young, possibly not over 21, with corn-colored curly blonde hair and a perfectly spray-tanned, unlined face. His western-style, snap-front shirt was half unbuttoned and intentionally two sizes too small to emphasize his well-developed pecs. Together with his cliché souvenir shop pukka shell necklace and silly, undersized straw cowboy hat, Buddy Conway looked like a kid who belonged in an old Abercrombie & Fitch catalog, rather than someone who would sing a mournful ballad about the fate of "Lonely People." Nora seriously doubted Buddy Conway had ever been lonely a single moment of his short life.

Nora pulled her car over, got out, and took a picture of the banner with her phone. From Jasper, she'd learned that the country stars of yesteryear normally got at least what was called a "3+2" contract, meaning a guarantee of an album release each year for three consecutive years, with a possibility for two more. Those two were usually a Christmas set and a greatest hits collection, which often signaled the end of an artist's initial contract and the beginning of a negotiation period for a new one. However, Nora also knew that any fresh face in this bold new era of digital singles had a much higher chance of being a one-hit wonder, so questions about royalty proceeds had to be acted upon quickly. She texted the picture to Cliff, along with the message, "Was this song one of Jasper's? He was working on one with that title. Didn't see it mentioned in the last royalty statement." Although Nora kept checking her phone on the return to Brentwood, no text came back.

Nora concluded her trip down memory lane with a swoop through Hillsboro Village. Once a hip neighborhood between Belmont and Vanderbilt, it had since been eclipsed in coolness by the New Nashville movement, which had refurbished rougher areas east of the city. Since it had always been overpriced due to its location between two privileged private universities, Hillsboro Village hadn't skyrocketed in value. Rather, it maintained a steady plateau of unaffordability, primarily as a neighborhood of Nashville's newly transplanted young elite professionals. The kinds who attempted to appear "authentic" with frequent trips to coffee and crystal shops, as well as dealers from poorer neighborhoods nearby, to procure liberal doses of weed and other drugs. Nora often joked that having lived in Hillsboro Village after college, she barely noticed the rising prices that frustrated everyone else. Hillsboro had always been high, in more ways than one.

On her way out of town, Nora passed by several packs of spray-tanned Vandy Candy girls sporting a spectrum of expensive balayage hair. They popped in and out of shops with armfuls of single-use plastic and paper bags, which ironically touted their sustainably sourced wares. Nora noted the block of older townhouses where she'd lived with two roommates many years ago after taking her first design job was now a parking garage for a much more expensive-looking high-rise condo development. A few streets over, she passed the first bungalow she'd shared with Jasper before they moved into his then-new tall-and-skinny condo in East Nashville, which was their last home together. No longer a private residence, a sign in front advertised something called *Naughty Girl Fitness—Perfect for Your Next Bachelorette Party!* Nora wondered in disgust how many naughty bachelorette parties one woman could attend in a lifetime as she drove out of the neighborhood and onto the ramp for 65 South to Brentwood, congratulating herself one final time for moving away.

To Nora's surprise, Julia greeted her cordially, if not warmly, upon her return. The furniture in Jasper's old room was moved up against the walls, and a couple of chairs were brought in for the two of them to sit. Except for the absence of paranormal investigation equipment, Jasper's boyhood room now reminded her very much of her living room, where she and Hazel first contacted Alexander Hostler. It was only two nights ago but seemed much longer.

"This is how I've been doing it," Julia said, gesturing to the chairs. Nora was surprised that Julia's voice was uncertain, almost nervous, as if she were asking for her approval.

"That's how these experiments *are done*, it seems," replied Nora. She scanned the room. "Except... you wouldn't happen to have any kind of recording device, would you? I mean, other than on your phone. Video, audio, anything?"

"No," Julia shook her head. "I don't think so. All the equipment from Jasper's studio was sold. I didn't think it was appropriate to keep any of it."

Then, Julia brightened. "Wait... I might have one of his father's old reel-to-reel recorders in the basement. I'm not sure if I have any tape for it, or if the tapes are still any good, but they might be. Jubal kept them in a climate-controlled vault. Come with me; I might need your help in moving some things around."

To say the basement was packed full was a complete understatement. In stark contrast to the pristine white orderliness of the mansion upstairs, the basement was a total mess. Rows and rows of record boxes from over five decades of Jubal Chandler Music Ministries swayed on sagging shelves. Pieces of discarded instruments, everything from drum kits to pipe organs, lay piled in heaps on the floor. Julia indicated for Nora to go ahead of her to help clear the pathway to the back corner where the vault was located. It was stacked randomly with old, heavy black road cases that threatened to topple over at any moment. Nora, who was always a little claustrophobic, felt as if she were in a game of human *Tetris*.

Once they'd made it through the jumble, they came to a heavy steel door with two combination locks. Julia pulled a small card out of her pocket and made no secret of wheeling the dials in plain view of Nora. As the tumblers clicked into place, Julia handed Nora the card.

"What do you want me to do with this?" Nora asked.

"Keep it," replied Julia, distractedly. "It will all be yours soon anyway. I don't need it anymore."

Nora put the card into her pocket and followed Julia into the vault.

The vault itself was a perfectly round room. Nora realized from the direction of the trail they'd made through the basement that they must be directly under the opposite turret from the one for Jasper's room. Free from the clutter in which the rest of the basement swam, the vault was encircled with neat metal shelves, each filled with meticulously marked white paper boxes. In the center of the room was a vintage, 60s-era RCA reel-to-reel magnetic tape recorder sitting atop a clear, square Plexiglass table on casters. Nora felt certain it was of the same vintage as the recorder, although the table had a more timelessly modern look.

"Will this do?" Julia asked. "I'm not certain it will work. It hasn't been used since Jubal died, that I know of. This was Jubal's original playback recorder from when he first started with the music ministry. He kept it in here with the tapes in hopes that it would make it to a museum someday." The machine still had a tape strung on it, which was surprisingly dust-free.

"Is this a completely airtight room?" Nora asked.

"Yes," Julia replied.

"Then it should work," said Nora. She walked over to the recorder and pressed *Play*.

After a few seconds of static, the deep, husky baritone of a man with a thick Southern accent filled the air. "Hello, Future World! This is Jubal Chandler of Jubal Chandler Music Ministries. If you're listening to this, it most likely means that I'm no longer among the livin'. But don't feel sorry for me, because I'm in a much better place. I've gone to be with my Lord and Savior at last. As the Bible says, *He has gone ahead and prepared a place for me at his table*, so you can rest assured that old Jubal is doin' just fine and eatin' well." Nora heard a sharp intake of breath behind her and turned to see Julia pressing the tips of her long, bony fingers over her lips. Nora reached to hit *Stop*, but Julia leaped forward and grabbed her hand. She shook her head. *No.*

The voice of Jubal Chandler continued. "'Round in here, you'll find copies of every single master recording ever made by me and by all the other artists at Jubal Chandler Music Ministries. As you can see, I've preserved them for posterity. They begin with 1967 right up front here," and without thinking, Julia and Nora turned in unison toward the front of the room, as if Jubal were there directing them, "and go *aaaaaawwwwwwllllll* the way around clockwise to end up in our current year of 1997 right there." Jubal's voice stretched out the word, which had the intended effect of making both women's gazes follow around the perimeter. "Now it may be 1997, or it may be 2097 when you're hearin' this; I don't know. My guess would be closer to 1997 if my beloved wife Julia had anything to do with it. She's always been the brains of this outfit. If I know her, she wouldn't let all these masterpieces lie down here lonesome for long." Though Nora had never met the man, in her mind's eye she could almost see Jubal wink at that statement, in the same way she'd seen Jasper wink so many times.

"Anyway, I hope you still enjoy good ole' time Christian music out there in Future Land, 'cause if you don't, my boy Jasper will probably have to get a real job, 'cause this is all the inheritance I've left him." Jubal laughed heartily. "Just kidding, folks, mostly. I love my boy. Hey out there, Jasper!

If you can hear me, I just want you to know that you have nothing to fear by dyin'. Just like I told you when you were a little boy and asked, it ain't possible to fall through them clouds." Here, Jubal laughed again. "Seriously though, folks, feel free to look around, put on a few tapes, and enjoy yourself. 'Cause that's what it's all about anyway. Good, heartfelt gospel music and the Spirit of Our Lord can make even the darkest day brighter. Praise be to Jesus; He is so good!" Suddenly, the voice stopped. All that could be heard was static. Julia let go of Nora's hand and pushed *Stop*.

"Well, I suppose it works," Julia said. "Unplug the cord while I look around for some blank tapes. Do you know how to set one of these up?"

Nora hesitated. "You're going to go right on and not even acknowledge the fact that your dead husband just spoke to you from the grave?"

Her initial shock at hearing his voice having subsided, Julia returned to her familiar bitterness. "I spent my entire life acknowledging Jubal Chandler. I began acknowledging him at Bible camp when I was 16. I kept acknowledging him through an abortion when I was seventeen so that he could keep up the facade of playing Mr. God Squad. Then I resigned myself to that acknowledgment permanently, through thirty years of loveless marriage, countless affairs, and *many* stints in rehab that I kept hidden from the press. The only thing that saved Jubal from going to prison for embezzlement and tax evasion was the heart attack that killed him. So yes, I am going to go *right on*. I'm going to wheel this machine upstairs to make a recording of the only real thing Jubal Chandler ever gave me except trouble in our entire life together." With that, Julia snatched the tape off the reel, wrapped both skinny hands around it, and whacked it hard against the edge of the table. The tape did not break.

Before she could slam the tape down again, Nora grabbed the older woman tightly around her upper arms. Julia struggled to free herself, but Nora was stronger.

"Wait, wait!!! Don't break it!" Nora exclaimed. "I have an idea."

"Yeah, what's that?"

"Did Jasper love his father?"

"Are you kidding? He worshiped the old windbag. Wanted to be just like him. Looked just like him too, when he was younger. It was pathetic. I did *everything* a mother could do for a son, and Jubal did *nothing*. Just ran in and out of the house to gigs and God knows where else, sending a trail of checks back that should have been made out to say, *Sorry, I don't want to be there, but here's the payoff*. Yet, Jubal hung the moon, as far as Jasper was concerned."

Nora ignored Julia's rant and loosened her hold. Julia recomposed herself.

"Then I say we *use* this tape to call Jasper out. Forget about recording just his voice; it will be better if we have a video anyway. My iPhone can probably hold it. You say you've been watching Jasper in the mirror every night, and he hasn't noticed you, right?"

"Yes." Julia hissed. "After all I did for him, all I'm *still* doing to find his murderer, he can't even say one word to me from..."

"From beyond the grave," Nora finished. "I know, I know. But if he responded to his father more in life, doesn't it make sense that he'd listen to him more now even after death?"

"I suppose so," Julia said grudgingly. "There was only one person who ever lived that Jasper paid more attention to than his father."

"Who was that?" asked Nora, scanning the names written on the spines of tape boxes around the room, looking for anyone else that she'd heard Jasper mention whose tape she could play that might prompt him to speak.

Julia barked back. "Idiot! It's you!"

Chapter Nineteen

B ack upstairs, Nora and Julia set up the recorder and positioned Nora's iPhone on a music stand with a clear view of the mirror. They still had an hour or so to kill before the appointed time of Jasper's appearance. To Nora's surprise, Julia offered her a drink. She had supposed that her mother-in-law did not drink at all, given the super-devout persona she portrayed. However, once that fact was acknowledged, Julia's preferred choice of cocktail was no shock at all. Vodka martini, extra dry. Or rather, as Nora noticed while Julia shook them up, just chilled vodka with no vermouth and a clean lemon twist.

While Julia prepared the cocktails, Nora told Julia everything she had learned so far about the spirits who lived beyond the mirrors.

"So, let me see if I have this correct," Julia said, swirling the last few drops of vodka in her glass swiftly around the lemon like a tiny hurricane, "How a spirit reacts to an external stimulus seems to depend on two factors: the level of clairvoyance of the spirit itself and its connection to whoever is attempting to initiate an interaction."

"Almost," replied Nora, taking her first sip of the vodka. It was as cold and bitter as a January morning. She swallowed it slowly, bit by bit. *Not pleasant.* "It seems to work best if the individual contacting the spirit is clairvoyant as well."

"Do you perceive yourself to be clairvoyant, Eleanor? Is that why this Mr. Hostler reached out to you, do you think? That the two of you have some sort of psychic connection?" Julia probed.

Nora flushed, "Not until recently. I mean, I'd had the everyday experience of thinking about someone, and then the phone would ring. I've always thought of myself as lucky, but beyond that, nothing truly significant. As for a connection with Mr. Hostler, I'd never heard of him in my life before I took that ghost tour in Wilmington. Hazel told me the rest of his story afterward."

"Well, perhaps it was in some sort of other life," Julia said wryly, raising a slender, penciled eyebrow as she leaned down to drain her second lemon vodka out of the shaker. "Hopefully, you'll have the same level of connection with my son."

Ignoring the insinuation, Nora checked the clock on her phone. "It's almost time." Needing no further prompting, Julia settled hastily into the other chair. They both sat side by side, staring into their perfectly normal reflections in the enormous mirror. For the first time, Nora noticed how similar they were. Same color eyes, hair, and face shape. They even held their glasses the same. The main thing truly different was that, in looking at Julia's emaciated face, Nora felt as if she were viewing her death mask.

Nora's reverie was interrupted by the familiar clouding around the edge of the mirror. As their image blurred away, Nora could see the shadow forms of the control room in Jasper's studio beginning to take shape. Nora realized that, given their viewpoint over Jasper's shoulder and into the sound booth, they were looking out of the mirror on the wall behind him. Jasper had on his noise-canceling studio headphones. He seemed to be working with the controls on the board. As the figures became clearer, Nora could make out who it was in the sound booth.

"Buddy Conway?" she whispered to herself.

"Who?" asked Julia, leaning forward for a closer look.

"He's a singer. I saw a banner outside ASCAP for his recent number one hit today. Took a picture on my phone. I think he's singing."

But Nora didn't have to think. As they watched, Buddy Conway began to croon the opening lyrics of "Lonely People."

Walking down the wrong Broadway, I'm just trying to find my way back home.

Nora gasped. "It *is* the song! My song! Ours!" She pointed at the mirror, tipping the rest of her drink over. "Jasper wrote that for me!"

"Quiet," Julia hissed. Another man with a long, chest-length hipster beard and a red and black flannel shirt entered the room from the right-hand side. His back was to Nora so that she could not see his face. He leaned in and motioned for Jasper to cut off the recording. Gesturing toward the phone and then to Buddy, Jasper nodded and hit the intercom button.

"Hey Buddy, you've got a call. Why don't you take ten, and we'll come back and do it again?"

Buddy looked more disturbed than Nora thought he'd be at getting cut off mid-verse. He seemed as if he were really into the lyrics, which was unusual since he hadn't written them. Regardless, Buddy took off his studio headphones and exited the booth. Although it was unintelligible what Jasper said to the bearded man, it was clear that he intended to take a break as well. As they spoke, Jasper smiled the warm, genuine smile that had always made Nora weak. After exchanging a three-pat bro hug with the man, who sat down in his engineer's chair and twisted casually back and forth, Jasper left the room.

"This!" Julia grabbed Nora's arm, sloshing half of her remaining vodka onto the floor. "Watch this carefully!" Nora jumped back, and Julia moved over to the table where they'd set up the recorder. "Get ready; this is the crucial moment!"

Just as Julia spoke, the bearded man, his face still in silhouette in the darkened studio, rose to peer out of the small arrow-slit window of the studio's sound booth. Seeing no one, he reached into his pocket and pulled out a folded piece of paper.

Although it looked like a headache powder, Nora knew that it was not. The man poured its contents into Jasper's glass, which was filled with what looked like a thick protein smoothie. Picking up a pencil lying on the desk, the man stirred the contents vigorously, wiped the pencil off with a handkerchief, and then slipped the pencil into the back pocket of his jeans. Although she still couldn't see his face, the light from the side window had fallen just right so that Nora could recognize the tattoos on his arms. It was Tommy Ponder, Jasper's manager. Nora turned quickly to tell Julia, but Jasper's mother waved for silence. She stood with her right hand on the *Play* button of the recorder.

"When he comes back, I'll start this," Julia whispered loudly. "If he doesn't respond, be ready for my signal to do anything you can to try to get his attention."

Jasper re-entered the room, and Tommy got up to leave. He and Jasper shook hands. Tommy left through the same side door. Nora heard a loud click as Julia pressed the button on the recorder. Jubal Chandler's jovial baritone filled the room.

After a few seconds, Jasper rose, cocking his head to the side inquisitive-ly. While the recording continued, he paced around the room, even open-ing the interior door and peering into the sound booth. "It's working!" Julia hissed. "Say something! Anything!"

Nora called out the only thing that she could think of to say. "Jasper! Jasper, it's me! Nora! Can you hear me?" For a second, he seemed to. Walking towards the mirror, Jasper put his hand on the surface. Nora rose to meet him.

"No!" screamed Julia, pushing past Nora. "That's *my* boy!" Julia hurled herself toward the mirror. Rebounding off, Julia staggered back, stunned by the impact. She sat down hard on the floor. On the other side, Jasper froze and looked strangely into the mirror. Nora continued forward, call-ing his name.

However, it was to no avail. Jasper shrugged and settled back down to the console. Nora watched in slow motion as Jasper reached to drink from the glass.

Julia was watching too, but she was quicker to react than Nora.

"No!" Julia screamed. "Nooooooo!!!"

Julia rushed toward the mirror, hitting it in full stride with the sharp edge of her shoulder. The mirror shattered on impact. Nora had just enough time to fall to the floor as she was showered with broken glass.

Moments later, Nora crawled over to Julia, who lay bleeding profusely on the floor. A large shard of mirror jutted out of her throat. Nora had seen enough movies to know not to remove it. Instead, she sprang as quickly as her spongy legs would allow to hit *Stop* on her phone's video recorder. Then, Nora called an ambulance. It was no use.

Julia Chandler died on the way to Vanderbilt Hospital.

Nora rode the rest of the way in the ambulance with Julia's body. She completed all the attendant paperwork. Not knowing what else to do or where to go, she started walking in the general direction of the riverfront. By the time Nora reached it, it was daybreak.

Nora stayed down by the riverfront for several hours. She strolled aim-lessly past old Fort Nashboro and saw a homeless man sleeping on a piece of cardboard under the dog trot. *Mama Tried* was heavily scrolled in green tattoo ink across his back. As she rustled about in her purse for a few dollars, the man awakened, saw her, and fled. Nora put the money back in her pocket.

As soon as she saw the clock on her phone click over to 10 am, Nora called her attorney Cliff with the bad news. He took it as all attorneys did, with professional courtesy somehow inexplicably short of sympathy. Cliff said that he was sorry for not replying to her text the day before and asked her when she would be available to come in. Nora told him an hour. For once, she was glad that many of the cheesy tourist bars on Lower Broadway opened early. Cleaning up her dripping mascara in the bathroom of a nondescript honkytonk, Nora mentally prepared herself to explain what had happened to Julia. Nora knew that the Chandlers had no other close family. Someone would need to make funeral arrangements.

"I wouldn't feel too bad," Cliff told Nora later that morning in his office. "Everyone knew Julia Chandler was crazy. We just didn't know she was crazy enough to kill herself." Cliff's meaty hand rested paternally on Nora's shoulder. "I'm only sorry you had to be the one to see it." Here the lawyer paused for a moment. "Still, it creates a few more loose ends to tidy up for us. You know Julia left all the property, intellectual and physical, of Jubal Chandler Music Ministries to you, right?"

Nora nodded. She twisted a piece of napkin that she'd brought with her from the tourist bar in her hands.

"Well, we can wait until you're a bit more composed for that," said Cliff. "Estates always have plenty of time. Our truly urgent mission at present is preparing Pierce for his arraignment. We have less than twenty-four hours left before he has to appear in court. And we have at least four hours worth of driving back to Asheville to decide what we're going to tell him to say. 'Cause from the way you've described him," Cliff settled down into the chair next to Nora. "Pierce isn't exactly the sharpest knife in the drawer."

Nora half-smiled at Cliff's shade toward Pierce. He half-smiled back, the kind of smile that said I-hope-you're-okay, but I-know-that-you're-not. Regardless, it gave Nora the strength that she needed to ask her next question. "Cliff, I know this is out of left field, but do you know a kid artist named Buddy Conway? He was the one I messaged you about yesterday, remember?"

Cliff bristled slightly at the change of subject. "Know him? Yes, I represent him. Why?"

"It's a long story," said Nora. "I'll tell you in the car on the way to Asheville."

***

By the time they'd passed Monteagle, Tennessee, Nora had told Cliff the whole story of what she'd seen in the mirror, hoping for advice.

"Nothing surprises me in this world," Cliff said, shaking his head. "But no jury in America will ever believe any of that, right? It's too far-fetched. To convict a man of murder based on some vision that the victim's wife *thinks* she saw in a haunted mirror? They'll think you're crazy. Plus, getting involved would create a conflict of interest for me, to represent both of you in the matter of Jasper's estate and the counterclaims that will inevitably be brought by Tommy Ponder and Buddy Conway. I represent them separately, on the new material that was released after Jasper's death, as well as his whole catalog from before. Tommy controls the copyrights on it. Jasper left you the cash on hand and Tommy the future royalties. If you try to bring charges against Tommy, it will look like you're just trying to get him put in jail so that you can have it all. The best thing to do is to just let it drop. Take the money from Jubal Chandler Music Ministries and just walk away. That should be more than enough for multiple lifetimes. The rest of it won't bring Jasper back, you know."

"I know," Nora insisted. "But it's not about the money; it's about the *principle* of the thing. I just hate knowing that Tommy *killed* him and is out there now benefiting from Jasper's work. There has to be *something* I can do."

"Let me stop you right there," Cliff said, his tone growing cold and precise. "It's that phrase. *The principle of the thing.* Way back years ago, when I was in law school, I remember the Dean telling us in our first-day assembly that the last thing you ever want is a client who comes in and says whatever legal action they want to start isn't about the money, but the *principle* of the thing. It's a red flag that your client is crazy and irrational. Now, do you want me to dismiss you as a client, Nora? Because you're crazy and irrational? After what you've told me today, I have perfect grounds to request that you be psychologically evaluated and to put all the funds that you stand to receive from Julia's estate into a conservatorship I control because grief has made you delusional. Why, you've even accused a trusted friend of Jasper's murder. I'd have no choice but to give you only a small allowance every month and restrict your access to the rest, just like Britney Spears. For the rest of your life. Is that what you want, Nora? For someone else to be in control? Because that's where we're headed if you pursue this matter against Tommy Ponder. Think very carefully before you answer."

Nora did think, for quite a while. She was glad that she was driving the car. It helped to steady her nerves and temper her anger.

She thought about all she'd gone through, helping Jasper get sober enough to work again. She considered what Julia told her about similar struggles with Jubal. Then, about how Cliff had always been so patronizing to her, both before and after Jasper's death. *How long had he known? Could he even have been involved?* Nora's mind reeled as she considered the possibilities of what the man sitting beside her in the car, a man whom she'd trusted for years, might be capable of. Even now, Cliff was trying to use twisted logic to explain his way out of the whole situation.

This was a trap, Nora thought. She could see it now, carefully crafted to leave her and Julia with no way out. A trap that, when sprung, allowed Tommy Ponder to get away with killing Jasper and using his work to help other, more stable artists with less baggage to build careers that would, in turn, add to his fortune. Even if Nora and Julia had been able to come up with additional, more traditional evidence regarding Jasper's murder, the plan was always to have them declared insane and the money taken if they came forward to the police. That must have been why Julia called her in the first place. To have another witness would have made her seem less crazy. Yet, whatever Julia endured over the years had wrecked her too completely even to allow herself to find an ally in Nora. In the end, Nora knew what she wanted. She did not want to end up like Julia. There was only one path forward to ensure that didn't happen.

"No, Cliff," Nora said softly at last. "I don't think I want that. If you'll just finish out whatever needs to be done for me to inherit from Chandler Music, as Julia wanted, I'm not going to pursue any rights to Jasper's catalog. Or what happened to him because of Tommy."

Cliff grinned, a tight-lipped smile of finality, as he breathed a sigh of relief. "Good girl. I'm glad that you're willing to listen to reason. Better to let sleeping dogs lie. Otherwise, they wake up pissed off and bite you in the ass." He slapped both hands down on the chubby thighs of his expensive suit. "Now, about this other thing with Pierce..."

Cliff's attempt at changing the subject was interrupted as Nora's phone rang. It was Hazel.

"Nora, you have to get back to Asheville as fast as possible. Something's happened."

"What else is new?" Nora replied, checking her bloodshot eyes in the rearview. "It seems like everything that can go wrong has, at this point."

"Well, I'm sorry, but there's a bit more," Hazel said. "Calista's gone through the mirror."

Chapter Twenty

After introducing Pierce to Cliff, the two headed off to rent a car and drive back to Durham. Watching them pull away, Nora tried to put her earlier conversation with Cliff out of her mind temporarily. Cliff was an excellent attorney, and no matter what else he was capable of, Pierce needed that type of intellect right now. *To keep an innocent man from looking like a criminal*, Nora thought, *sometimes it takes a real one.*

On the rest of the way over, Cliff decided that he would take Pierce back to Durham as soon as possible. He wanted to perform a little background investigation of his own. Also, Cliff wanted to hear Pierce's version of the events leading up to Vicki's disappearance in private to compare with the version Nora had already told him. Nora and Hazel remained behind with Sheridan, who was in the process of cleaning up the wreckage of the dance studio.

"It was just like this when I came down," said Sheridan, leaning on a broom and gesturing around the shambles of the main floor. Every window was smashed, as were the regular floor-to-ceiling mirrors behind the exercise barres. "I heard screams, and then this massive crash. So, I threw on some jeans and shoes, grabbed this old baseball bat, and ran downstairs. At first, I thought it was like a home invasion of some kind. Zelda, Calista's pig, was gone which kind of supported that explanation, because thieves usually steal or kill pets too. After I watched the security video, though... I believed it, but it was unbelievable, you know?"

"I can imagine," said Nora, straightening up to carry her full dustpan of glass shards to the trash. The three of them had already watched the security footage together. It had left more questions than answers. In the part that Sheridan mostly fast-forwarded through, Calista stood for over three hours, motionless and unblinking in front of the Blue Post mirror.

Then, there was a huge flash of light. Against the blinding background, they could see Calista being dragged by her hair, through the power of some unseen force, kicking and screaming into the surface of the mirror. As she disappeared and the mirror portal closed, every other piece of glass in the room shattered, including the security camera lens. Everything afterward was static.

"Where were you and Pierce during all of this again?" Nora asked Hazel.

"Pierce claimed he couldn't take a second night on the air mattresses. So we walked down the street and rented rooms. No offense, Sheridan, but I couldn't either."

"None taken," Sheridan said. "Nobody likes sleeping on a pool float on a floor full of resin. I told Calista that we should have booked rooms for you the first night too, but she was insistent. She wanted all of you to be together downstairs. I wish she'd felt comfortable enough to tell me why, though I see it now. She was afraid. But that's Cali. Always afraid of nothing, until it's too late."

Nora turned to Hazel. "Got any ideas on what we should do? We can't exactly call the cops on a ghost. Especially after all the suspicion surrounding Pierce. They'd just blame him."

"True," replied Hazel, pushing another large heap of glass fragments toward the center of the studio with her wide broom. "There isn't a whole lot of precedent for paranormal activity of this sort. I mean, we're not talking about a mere spiritual suppression or infestation while someone was astral projecting. This is an actual, physical abduction into another dimension. There simply aren't any guidelines to follow for it."

"Didn't you say earlier that if someone on the other side of the mirror had a deeply spiritual connection with the person trying to contact them, then they could still communicate?" Sheridan asked.

"Yes, that seems to be how it works," Hazel nodded.

"Well, I can't think of anyone who would have a deeper spiritual connection to Calista than me," Sheridan said. "When we first hooked up at the academy, it was my only time with a girl. I mean, I had kissed boys before in high school, but my gaydar wasn't really in tune then. So it always ended badly. I didn't trust my feelings. I kept trying to convince myself that I must be straight, because if I wasn't, why did I keep getting rejected by guys but not girls? Stupid teenage boy logic, I know. However, being with Calista just that once, waking up next to her the following morning, seeing her angelic face and beautiful body, and feeling no physical desire for her at all. Well, it made me know who I was. Afterward, I just fell into the charade of our relationship. Cali was so sweet and fun and understanding of everything else about me I couldn't stand the thought of losing her by telling her the truth for a long time. But she knew. Cali really always knew. She loved me anyway. Enough so that when I finally told her, it made what we had stronger. If I hadn't had Cali in my life, supporting me through all the big steps of when I came out to my family and everyone else, I don't know what I would have done." Here Sheridan trailed off in thought. "Anyway, I know she's your sister, Nora, but in a way, she's like mine too. That's why I think that I should be the one to go in after her."

Nora looked stunned. "You mean, you think that you can just go into the mirror yourself and bring her back?"

"That's what I'm hoping for," answered Sheridan, who resumed sweeping with vigor. "When I was younger and still trying to reconcile my identity with the Irish Catholic background I grew up in, I tried all sorts of things to come to some kind of internal settlement with myself and my spirituality. For a while, I was into metaphysics and astral projection. Along the way, I had a few, what I will call *experiences*." Sheridan paused to make air quotes with his fingers. "Enough to make me believe that spiritual flight was genuine. I haven't done it in a long time, but I could try."

Hazel agreed, "It's the best chance we've got. If you're up for it, Sheridan, I have another suggestion."

"What's that?" he asked.

"Since I think that this entity who took Calista is most certainly Gallows Meg and Gallows Meg was a purveyor of, shall we say, gentleman's entertainment, I was wondering..."

Sheridan interrupted her, his bright green eyes wide with realization of her plot. "You were wondering if I would be willing to present as female so that I could look like a Queen of the Night, and this horrendous Meg person would invite me into her world?"

"Precisely," said Hazel. "She's looking for recruits, since both of the people whom I know Meg to have attempted to pull into her world beyond the mirror were female."

"Honey, if you think it is any hardship at all for this pretty boy dancer to put on drag, *especially* to save his best friend in the entire world from some crazy dead bitch madam, then I'm afraid you don't know anything about me! I... am... in!"

"I knew I could count on you," said Hazel warmly, reaching for both of Sheridan's hands.

Hazel glanced over her shoulder at Nora. "You and I will stay out here. I think it's best to have at least one other person who is close to Calista on this side to help call her back."

To Sheridan, Hazel said, "And I will be here for you as well, helping to guide your astral flight. Since you've done this before, just follow your instincts. If you feel yourself getting lost, follow the sound of my voice. Sheridan nodded in assent, grasping Hazel's hands tighter. Nora put her hands around their double clasp, making it a triple.

***

The trio made quick progress that evening in cleaning up the dance studio and boarding its windows. Fortunately, Mondays and Tuesdays were their regular days to be closed to students. Except for the expected random passers-by gawking from the sidewalk, they were able to work complete-ly undisturbed. Also, it helped that each of them had a background in carpentry. Nora and Hazel from restoring antique furniture and Sheridan from summers spent as a teenager working with his father's construction company in New Hampshire. As they strolled down Patton Avenue to-ward Wall Street for dinner at the Laughing Seed Cafe, already a favorite of Sheridan's, who was a vegetarian, they were happy to see Zelda the pig come out squealing from her hiding place in an alleyway behind a dumpster. From the shallow cuts and scrapes on her back, they supposed she'd become scared and run away when the studio windows shattered. Zelda grunted happily when Sheridan bumped noses with her, as Nora had seen Calista do before. Nora could tell Sheridan was genuinely relieved to see the pig, even if he did immediately produce a sanitizing wipe to swab both his nose and the pig's afterward.

With dinner finished, the trio walked back to the studio. Sheridan went upstairs to clean and bandage Zelda's wounds and to settle his cat Isis in for the night. He also changed for the encounter. After an hour or so, he re-emerged in full drag.

"Why am I not surprised that you make such a beautiful lady!" said Nora, clapping as Sheridan descended the stairs.

Sheridan tossed his long, glossy auburn hair and posed dramatically for a moment at the top of the stairs. "Thank you, my darling, thank you. You're too kind!" He said, affecting an erudite laugh and blowing her a kiss as he rotated into a perfect three-quarter pose and pulled himself up to his fully statuesque height. "You can call me *Sher* tonight, honey."

"You look perfect. If Meg's able to see you, there's no way she could resist," said Hazel, scanning Sheridan from head to toe. Taking his cue from Hazel's description of ghastly Meg's own decidedly plumper, co-quettish colonial dame outfit, Sheridan wore a twinkling, emerald green, off-the-shoulder gown that trailed to the floor. The gown had a sculpted bodice and a thigh-high slit, exposing the dainty freckles on his otherwise distinctly muscular legs, which were covered in nude fishnet hose. To this, Sheridan added a brilliant rhinestone clip over one ear, sweeping his hair to frame his defined jawline. His makeup was flawlessly airbrushed to look glamorous but not overdone. Pleased with the effect, Sheridan strode over on sky-high heels to the chaise lounge that they'd moved to the center of the floor facing the mirror.

"With great beauty comes great responsibility," he said, enjoying one last preen before steeling his gaze as the muscles of his jaw became tight and hard. "Let's do this."

Chapter Twenty-One

An hour later, Sheridan lay breathing softly and steadily on the chaise lounge. His long, soft auburn curls drifted over its tufted back. Sheridan's hands lay crossed and relaxed over his midsection. The folds of his sparkling gown cascaded to the floor and contrasted with the lush purple velvet and gilded trim like something from a dream. To Nora, his peaceful expression reminded her of the Lady of the Lake from old paintings she'd seen in a museum as a child.

Nora and Hazel sat behind what once had been the one-way mirror of the dancers' dressing room behind him, off to the left of the main floor. They peered cautiously together over the sill. Hazel sat with her FLIR thermal camera in her lap, adjusting the settings. She reached up and put it inside a box that formerly held a new pair of toe shoes. The box now had a hole cut strategically in the side, with the lens of the camera directly behind. Hazel attached the camera through a second hole in the back of the box via an HDMI cable to the studio's regular security monitor. She'd set the monitor on the floor behind the half-wall, just in front of where she and Nora sat cross-legged. The digital temperature on the camera held steady at 72 degrees.

"How will we know when he's in?" Nora mouthed soundlessly to Hazel.

"Don't worry, you'll know. It's very noticeable," Hazel replied silently.

A few minutes later, a familiar fog began to gather around the edges of the mirror. Hazel motioned for Nora to get down and be quiet. But this time, Nora noticed, it was different. The fog began to spill out onto the floor, surrounding Sheridan's prone body on the chaise lounge. Nora saw him bite his lower lip ever so slightly, as goose flesh began to rise on his lithe, muscular arms, making the fine red hairs rise. She felt the room grow colder. Nora glanced at the display numbers on the monitor. 65 degrees and still falling.

The fog began to coalesce into the form of a woman. Judging from the shape of her ample bosom squeezed into a push-up bodice, Nora did not need Hazel to tell her that this must be Meg. The apparition's voluminous skirt billowed out, with its hem hovering over the floor as she rolled toward Sheridan like a ghostly tide. Meg's face was the last part of her body to take shape. Nora could tell Meg's bold features would have made her a striking woman in life.

Meg bent down over Sheridan. A tendril of hair fell from her updo as she put an ear close, first to his mouth and then directly on his chest to hear his heartbeat. Sheridan shivered but did not stir. Meg tucked the escaped curl behind her ear and caressed the side of Sheridan's face. Here, he squinted his eyes slightly but did not open them. Nora felt certain that Sheridan was merely feigning sleep, but it appeared to be working perfectly. Running her hand down his arm, Meg locked a firm grip on Sheridan's wrist. She smiled and then pulled. One solid, quick jerk, like a magician pulling a cloth from under a set table.

To Nora's surprise, Sheridan's silhouette slipped out in a long, fluid stream, reconfiguring in ghostly pallor by Meg's side. Sheridan's physical head fell to one side, in a slumber from which Nora was certain he would not awaken until body and soul were reunited. Still holding his hand, Meg gathered up her skirt with the other. As if getting up into a carriage, she stepped over the frame and right through the glass of the large mirror. Sheridan followed.

"And he's through," said Hazel, peering closer into the monitor screen. Lifting the lid of the box carefully, Hazel refocused the camera to zoom in closer to the mirror's surface.

"What is that?" whispered Nora, seeing the vapors behind the glass readjust to show an old saloon-style barroom. "Where are they?"

"The Blue Post," returned Hazel. "That makes sense because that's probably where Meg took Calista. A real ballerina would be quite a novelty among the other dancing girls."

"It does make sense," Nora nodded, as the bar, its patrons, and a small stage for the dancing girls began to take shape. Meg introduced Sheridan to a man with long, dark pirate curls and a strong Roman nose. The man was wearing a magnificent velvet coat and poet's shirt with a frilled doublet and scarf. As he reached to take Sheridan's hand to kiss, Nora could see that he had on a huge emerald ring made from what appeared to be two intertwined serpents.

Although the image was in grayscale, Nora could almost feel the heat of Sheridan's blush as the man pulled out a chair for him. They sat down. Sheridan gazed into the man's eyes and beamed. When Sheridan admired the man's ring, he took it off and placed it on Sheridan's finger.

"Sheridan's flirting with him!" Nora hissed. Hazel shushed her as the scene continued to unfold. Sheridan and the man with the serpent ring appeared to be quite smitten with one another, laughing and making the slightest excuse to touch, a knee here, a shoulder there. It was not long before Sheridan was beside him. The man's arm draped casually across the back of Sheridan's chair, just skimming his shoulders. Nora and Hazel watched their chatter ebb and flow until something seemed to catch the man's attention from across the room. The expression on his handsome face changed quickly from pleasure to suspicion. Sheridan noticed it too and looked at the man quizzically, then turned back toward the left of the room. Another group of men came through the door. Nora noticed the first man suggest with his eyes that Sheridan put his hand with the ring on it under the table. Sheridan, who picked up on the hint, complied.

"Oh no," breathed Hazel. "Those are the men who attacked Meg! The one in the front was the guy who slit her throat. That," Hazel tapped on the monitor screen. "That's the knife he used!"

The man with the knife strode across the room. He pulled out a chair at the table across from where Sheridan and the dark-haired man sat. Spinning it around on one leg, he plopped down straddling it and facing the two of them. He stared menacingly first at the dark-haired man, then at Sheridan, as the others pulled up chairs. Following suit, they surrounded the pair in a semi-circle, blocking their view of the stage. Calmly finishing his beer, the first man rose and extended his now ring-free hand to Sheridan, who accepted with his right but tucked his left in the small of his back. Nora saw Sheridan nervously twist the too-large ring around so that the massive gemstone was facing into his palm. The dark-haired man placed a protective hand over it, completely concealing the ring. He softly guided Sheridan to two seats at the short end of the bar closest to the right front corner of the stage. Although he attempted to be nonchalant and picked up his conversation with Sheridan once again, their interactions now seemed strained. Each cast nervous glances over at the group of men, who continued to watch them.

When the curtains finally parted on the tiny stage, a group of five women in can-can costumes, looking as if they'd come straight from the stage of the Moulin Rouge, stood in perfect dancer's attention. Although they were in heavy makeup and powdered to look just alike, Nora immediately recognized the one in the middle as Calista. Sheridan saw her too, and his eyes went wide as the predominantly male crowd rose to its feet to whoop and holler. Although they could still hear no sound from what was happening inside the mirror, Nora could tell from the exaggerated flourishes and heavy sweating of the piano player that the pace of the music was picking up. The girls began to dance. Higher and higher they kicked, as the rowdy crowd swelled closer and closer to the stage.

When one set a heavy boot upon its actual surface, Meg came from out of nowhere with what looked like a policeman's club. She whacked the man hard on the knee with it. He yelped in pain as the crowd parted slightly to let him fall hard on his back to the floor. Then, several other drunken men began pushing and shoving one another. Meg wove in and out among the crowd, smacking back anyone who came too close to the stage. Finally, one of the girls screamed, broke the line, and dashed off the stage and into the kitchen area behind the bar. A balding, fat ogre of a man chased her. Meg ran after them, clubbing people out of the way, left and right, as the remaining four dancing girls cut and ran.

Sheridan grabbed Calista by the arm as she streaked past. Recognizing Sheridan, Calista hugged him close. Sheridan whispered something into his companion's ear, and the man looked surprised but nodded in agreement. They parted ways. Sheridan and Calista darted out the same door through which Meg exited. The dark-haired man went out the opposite one, toward the street. Through the melee, the fellow whom Hazel recognized with the knife saw the dark-haired man leave. Pushing apart several fights, he gathered his crew. They huddled for a moment, then followed Sheridan's dark-haired man out the door and into the street.

"Oh God, I hope they're not after him!" breathed Nora.

"I hate to say so, but they probably are," replied Hazel. "Didn't you see the stare-down that they were giving him and Sheridan at the table? They're a vicious bunch. Sheridan's fellow looked wealthy. Like someone worth robbing."

Eventually, the fight died down. Meg returned grinning with something in her mouth. It looked like a piece of beef jerky. Opening the lid of an enormous jar on the counter, she spat it in and closed the lid. A few moments later, the ogre-like man whom Meg chased out as he pursued the dancing girl reappeared, clutching the side of his head. Blood gushed through his fingers. He gave Meg a wicked look, but she merely smirked at him and turned away.

"Holy cow! It's true!" said Hazel.

"What's true?" asked Nora, as Hazel zoomed the camera in again for a closer look at the pickle jar.

"There's this legend that Meg would bite the ears off men who caused a ruckus and then throw their ears in a pickle jar on the bar as a warning to others. Check it out!"

Sure enough, upon closer inspection, Nora could see what looked like dozens of ear remnants floating in the large jar.

The dancing girls, Calista, and Sheridan timidly followed Meg, one by one, out from the kitchen area. Sheridan spoke a quick exchange with Meg and Calista before hurrying out the door where the dark-haired man and those following him had gone. Meg handed out brooms and dustpans to the girls to clean up broken glass. Then, she trudged upstairs. Once Meg left, Calista called the other girls together. Nora could tell from her gestures that she was encouraging them to leave and go have a drink somewhere else while she finished the cleaning alone. Not needing too much prompting, they left by the same front door as the rest of the crowd.

A few seconds later, Calista cautiously laid down the broom with which she'd been so diligently sweeping and walked toward the mirror. Initially, it appeared that she was going to walk through easily. However, when Calista approached the glass and put her hand on the surface from the other side, nothing happened.

"I was afraid of this," said Hazel, standing up. "Come on. We have to get closer so you can call her."

Nora and Hazel stepped up to the mirror. Calista stared out and past them, searching the surface all over with bright, inquisitive eyes.

"What should I do?" asked Nora.

"Just call her name," said Hazel. "Call her name, put your hands on the glass, and push, like you're reaching for something through a sheet of plastic. Close your eyes and visualize your hands going through the mirror. Imagine yourself clasping Calista's hands tight. Then, just pull."

Nora did as instructed. She was surprised to feel the surface of the mirror begin to bend inward a little.

Hazel saw it too. "Don't stop! You're doing it!"

Then, with a rush like falling through ice, Nora's arms broke through. She plunged forward. Blinking at a stunned Calista, Nora put her head and the rest of her torso through. Straining to maintain her balance, Nora reached out for her sister.

"Grab her tight by both arms, and when I count to three, pull as hard as you can!" called Hazel. Nora felt Hazel's grip close around her waist so that she would be shoving Nora away from the mirror like a tackle pushing a football dummy. Nora linked arms with Calista, forming a fireman's grip. Looking up the staircase, Nora saw a figure at the top. *Meg!*

Just then, Hazel began to count down. "One, two, three, *PULL!*" She and Nora yanked backward with all their might. Calista jumped forward so that by the time Hazel said the last word, Calista was in the air. Meg jumped too. Shrieking as she reverted to spectral form and flew through the air toward Calista, Meg was too late. With a great tearing sound and a whoosh of air, Calista came tumbling out of the mirror, falling on top of her sister and Hazel in a heap.

Struggling to right themselves, Calista now stood in just her bodice, leotard, and underthings. The tearing sound, Nora realized, must have been Meg grabbing the back of Calista's fluffy can-can skirt. It had been ripped clean off.

"Sheridan!" Calista cried in a panic. Seeing her friend's lifeless body lying on the chaise lounge, she rushed over to him. Realizing that he wasn't moving, Calista cried out to Hazel and Nora. "What's wrong with Sheridan? Where is he?"

Hazel nodded toward the mirror. All three turned to face it. The abyss of its blank surface stared back at them.

Chapter Twenty-Two

"I've got to go back for him!" Calista sobbed after Nora and Hazel explained to her what had happened. Sheridan's cat shoaled endlessly around her father's inert form. Isis seemed worried, stopping to pat Sheridan's face from time to time, as if trying to awaken him, but to no avail. Zelda, also released from her quarantine upstairs after all the goings-on, was snuggled protectively in Calista's lap. She massaged the pig's face and back consolingly. "It's all my fault. If I hadn't gone in there; if I had been stronger..."

Hazel interrupted her. "No one's blaming you for anything. As I've told you, when Meg confronted me years before, it was all that I could do to prevent myself from being physically forced into the mirror. And I knew what I was up against, whereas you did not. One of the favorite tricks of a malevolent spirit is to mask itself as something the person loves. Most likely someone they lost and are longing for to entice them over to the other side."

Sniffing back tears, Calista agreed. "You're right. On the first evening that I saw her, I was alone in the studio, going over the combinations for some lessons the next day. Although I appreciate everything that you've done for me, Nora, in setting up the studio and all, it's been hard. I mean, I've always been pretty emotionally self-sufficient. So long as I had a pet," she dipped a nod to indicate Zelda, "and a few close friends, I felt fine. However, I never realized how much I would miss the company of other dancers. Even with Sheridan here, I'm so lonely. When I saw Meg's girls, I was intrigued by how different and also alike we were. It's as if we were going through the same steps to different dances across time."

"That's a very poetic way of putting it," said Nora, reaching out to rub Zelda's ears. The pig snuffled. "And I know you're appreciative. You've only said it umpteen thousand times. I just wish you'd felt more com-fortable reaching out to me. I would have come, you know."

"Yet, the infamous Hewitt Woman Stoicism strikes again," said Hazel. "I'm beginning to see a pattern here. All three of you grew up with a mother who constantly repressed her feelings. When unhappy, that seems more normal. God forbid that anyone in the twenty-first century allows themselves to admit that they are not happy, grateful, and mindful for a second. Tamping down happy feelings makes less sense until you unpack the idea a little. Happiness is a precarious state. It's always in danger of being lost. Therefore, to express happiness is also to express vulnerability. Since people who perceive themselves to be successful and powerful resist most displays of vulnerability, they also tend to resist happiness. If you'll forgive me for saying so, that fear of happiness appears to be the fatal flaw for the entire Hewitt family."

Both Calista and Nora replied affirmatively. Hazel continued, changing the subject.

"However, none of this is going to bring our valiant Sheridan back from the other side. For that, it appears I am finally needed."

Hazel went over to one of the storage cabinets and pulled out a yoga mat. Spreading it on the floor, Hazel sat down upon it, cross-legged. "Since I am the one most experienced in astral projection, I will go into the mirror to find him. Nora, I want you to speak to me periodically along the journey. Keep me on task, since everything there will likely be intended to keep me distracted so that I remain. Ghosts are the loneliest people in the world. There is nothing they crave more than human companionship. Calista, you take notes, both mental and physical, if we can find a notebook around here, of landmarks that I pass. You can call them out to me, should I become disoriented. It's easy to do, especially if I am waylaid by some type of confrontation. Soul travel can be very interesting but dangerous, as it leaves the host body open and vulnerable for possession. If either of you notice, at any time, that another spiritual entity has exited the glass and is hovering near either Sheridan or me, you must call us both back immediately. Hopefully, I will have already found him before that time, and we can make a safe retreat. Now, I'm going to lie down and try to put myself into a trance. Don't be startled if you see my spirit rise. Nora, you know what it looks like since you've seen Sheridan do it already. Calista can just watch you for cues as to whether everything is progressing as it should. Are we all agreed?"

The sisters nodded their heads, *yes*. Calista went to retrieve a pencil and paper. When she returned, she sat down beside Hazel, who was already lying flat on her back on the mat. Nora sat on her other side. After what seemed like an eternity, but was less than half an hour, Hazel's breath became very quiet and slow. Finally, a soft, white wisp of what looked like smoke began to rise over her face, gathering form. Then, Hazel's spirit sat up and looked at them. Her eyes burned with white fire as she put a finger to her lips for silence. Straightening up into a standing position, Nora saw the body of sleeping Hazel go completely slack as if she were dead. From this state, the shadow Hazel slipped soundlessly across the room and into the mirror without any resistance.

Once Hazel's spirit was inside the mirror, they could tell the scene was much different than the one they'd seen less than an hour earlier. The portal for entry and exit was still in the Blue Post. However, by the time the image was clear, Hazel was outside on the street. She walked with purpose, her steps definite and quick on the sidewalk. Nora and Calista exchanged glances, both wondering the same thing. *How could she know where to go?*

Fifteen minutes later, Hazel slowed her steps. To their astonishment, they could see a figure in a long dress kneeling over the man in the velvet coat. When the person in the dress looked up, Calista yelped. "It's Sheridan! He's alive!"

"But it looks as if his friend isn't, unfortunately," said Nora, studying the poor wreck lying mangled in the road. The man's once long, beautiful hair was in knots, much of it pulled back from his skull as if someone had been interrupted in the process of scalping him. Blood from an exit wound in his forehead cascaded down his noble face like water over the edge of a broken fountain. His luxurious velvet coat and frilled shirt were ripped to shreds, and his chest bled from dozens of stab wounds. As Nora and Calista watched, Hazel and Sheridan spoke to one another for a moment, then embraced. Hazel helped Sheridan to stand. Shaken, they turned and began to walk back the way that Hazel had come originally.

Instinctively, Nora called out to her friends. "Hazel! Sheridan! It's me! Nora! Can you hear me? Can you find your way back?"

At this, both looked up and around, as if they were searching for where the sound of her voice came from. Hazel gave a pained half-smile and whispered something into Sheridan's ear. He seemed as if he understood. As they progressed onward, Nora observed that Sheridan's beautiful dress was ripped and that he was missing his shoes. Also, as she looked more closely, Nora could tell that Sheridan had the beginnings of what appeared to be a black eye.

Ultimately, they made it back to the bar. After peering cautiously around to ensure that they were alone, they stood facing out of the mirror, just as Calista had before. Nora and Calista called to them. Then, each moving according to their intuition, they placed their hands on the glass. The pain was excruciating, like touching a hot stove eye, but it lasted only a moment. Almost at the instant of contact, Calista and Nora drew back. With their pull, the spiritual wisps of both Hazel and Sheridan slipped out of the mirror and back into their physical bodies, as easily as a magician drawing a handkerchief through his hand.

Awakening, Hazel and Sheridan took deep gasps of air, like swimmers surfacing from many feet below. They opened their eyes in unison. Nora and Calista ran forward to embrace them. Isis leaped into Sheridan's lap. Zelda, sensing all the excitement, raced around the room, squealing with delight.

As he came out of his trance, Sheridan grimaced like someone coming to after a horrible accident. He reached up and pulled his wig off. Throwing it to the floor with the manner of someone who was purely disgusted by the world. Nora and Calista looked puzzled. Hazel, perceiving the source of his frustration, spoke.

"Sheridan, what happened to Llewelyn was over three hundred years ago. I know the two of you felt a very strong connection. It was apparent even to us out here. There isn't anything that you could have done. The past is the past, and it is set in stone. No matter what we try to do here, fate will run over our best efforts as if they were stones in the street."

"Don't you understand?" Sheridan urged, "If I had been alive then, that could have been *me!* Llewelyn was beautiful, intelligent, refined, and gay, so they beat him into the ground for it. They would have stolen from him too if he hadn't already given this to me! He knew! He knew they were coming for him!" Sheridan held up his hand with the back facing them. On his third finger was the ring with two intertwined serpents, each holding one side of a gigantic emerald in its mouth.

"You tried, darling," Hazel said. "I admire you for trying. But as I said, it simply could not be changed."

"What happened?" asked Calista, sitting down next to Sheridan on the chaise lounge.

"Just before you and I ran into the kitchen during the fight, Llewelyn...Lew," Sheridan winced, "told me that he would run outside and pull his carriage around the back entrance to pick up both of us. It was just a small two-seat gig. He planned to ride the horse itself and put us inside. He was worried that the gang of men who sat down trying to intimidate us before the dancing began would attack us on the street as we left. He thought we'd have a better chance to get away safely in the gig. Anyway, as Lew waited for us outside, the gang came out. One of them tried to grab his horse's bridle and pull him down out of the saddle, so he cut the line on the gig and took off. The others followed on horseback. He'd gotten five or six blocks before they shot him in the back, and he fell. The horse spooked and ran away, leaving Lew lying on the ground. He was already bleeding out, but they jumped him anyway. They mutilated him."

Sheridan buried his head in his hands and told the rest of his story to the floor. "By the time I got to Lew, it was too late. I heard the shots. There must have been several that hit him. I kicked off those stupid shoes and ran. When I came upon him lying there, they were ransacking his body, ripping out his pockets. One even had his watch in his hand. I snatched the watch away from the guy and hit him as hard as I could in the stomach. He socked me in the eye, and I fell. I dropped the watch, and he grabbed it back. Then all of them ran away. My eye hurt so badly, I couldn't stand up, so I just lay there next to him. Lew tried to talk, but with every word, he was spitting blood. I could make out something about the ring, that I should hold onto it. Then, he was gone."

Calista hugged him. Sheridan held his breath, visibly trying not to cry.

"Sheridan, I'm very sorry. Do you have any idea who the man you met was?" Hazel asked.

"No, I don't. But I wish I did. It was as if... as if Lew *knew me*. Like we'd met somewhere before. He could tell immediately that I was in drag, and I could tell right away that he was gay and wanted me to know it. There was such an instant connection. It was uncanny."

"Most likely, you *have* known each other," Hazel explained. "In a previous life, you probably had a much longer relationship. However, because of

Lew's sudden death, we may never be sure. If you're interested, you could try to go back to an earlier time before his murder and see if you could find something that resonated."

"What good would that do?" Sheridan asked, standing up and pacing with frustration. "The longer I spoke with Lew, the more that I would care for him. The better I knew him, the more painful it would become to watch him die, night after night. If you say that there's no hope that anything I do could save Lew, why should I go through the pain? So that I would fall in love with him? And hurt even more than I do now?"

"No," said Hazel quietly. "So that you could learn to love Llewelyn from afar. Maybe recognize him again in the next life. If the two of you are truly soulmates, it *could* happen."

"I can't," said Sheridan, running his fingers repeatedly through his bright red hair, making it stand up again as usual. "I just can't take the anguish of doing it, knowing what will happen. If it's true that he's someone I'm meant to be with through time, then I'd rather wait and be surprised when the right time comes. So that we can live our lives without fear."

"That's a perfectly reasonable choice," Hazel replied. "Please forgive me. I certainly didn't mean to suggest otherwise. Every person handles love and its improbabilities differently." Here she stopped a moment and looked at Nora directly, as if she were just realizing something very important. Nora glanced back at her inquisitively, but the moment passed.

"Regardless, it's excellent to have you back. You're a very brave man, Sheridan. And again, I'm beyond devastated for what happened to Llewelyn. Although..." she pointed at the ring on his hand. "It does solve a local mystery that we've had in Wilmington for centuries."

"What's that?" Sheridan asked.

"The mystery of whatever happened to Llewelyn Markwick and his ring. Do any of you know the story? Nora, you should, if my former student performed her job as tour guide successfully. Mr. Markwick was a strikingly handsome Welsh merchant in the early days of Wilmington, who had a penchant for fancy clothes. Many assumed he was gay, although it has never been proven. Anyway, his most prized possession was a ring that was a family heirloom, a large emerald surrounded by two intertwined serpents. When he was attacked and murdered, many wondered what had happened to this fabulous gem. Now we know."

Hazel caught Sheridan's eye as he studied her. "On the night of his murder, Mr. Markwick felt threatened while entertaining an equally dashing Irishman at the bar, so he slipped the ring to his new fellow for safekeeping. Unfortunately, Markwick was killed just a couple of hours later. The ring was never found. Because..." Hazel gestured to Sheridan.

"Because he gave it to me. But how is that possible?" Sheridan asked, looking down at the ring on his finger in amazement. "You said time and fate couldn't be changed by going back through the mirrors?"

"That's true. It cannot be changed, only re-experienced. You and Mr. Markwick met because you were meant to meet. There was a past life connection between the two of you that plays variations on a continuous loop woven among centuries. As there also is between Gallows Meg and Calista, and perhaps even myself. Calista's connection is obvious. She once was one of Meg's dancing girls. My connection, I haven't yet figured out. Since Meg did not succeed in keeping me within her world, it could be because she had mistaken me for someone else. That happens sometimes in families, where there is a strong resemblance."

"So, I get it," interceded Nora. "If a person who is trapped in a mirror has a strong connection, whether in this life or a previous one, to someone outside, then they will reach out and try to communicate. However, if they don't..."

"Then their connection was never that strong. It was only a minor impression. They were not, as you might say, soulmates."

"I see," said Nora sadly, as she processed what that meant. Jasper had recognized and acknowledged his father's voice, but not the presence of either her or his mother when they'd watched his spirit in the mirror.

"Yes, I can see it too. Your wheels are turning." Hazel said, "I'm just as puzzled as you are as to what the connection might be between you and Alexander Hostler."

"Who?" asked Calista.

"No one," said Nora sharply, giving Hazel a look. "Now that you and Sheridan are both safe," she paused to check the time on her phone. "And it's almost dawn; I think that I should go lie down for a few hours. Then, I need to call Cliff. See how he and Pierce are doing."

"Aren't you forgetting something?" asked Sheridan. Nora looked at him questioningly.

"Um... what are we going to do about the whole portal to another world of murder and mayhem hanging on the wall over there?" he finished.

"Well, there's only one thing we can do about it," replied Hazel. "Sheridan, if you're certain that you don't want to go back and try to interact with Markwick again, and no one else has any desire to go back, then we should probably destroy it. Otherwise, Meg or who knows what all else will continue to have the opportunity to draw in anyone with a strong connection to what's on the other side of the mirror. There were four of them to begin with. Nora's mother-in-law has already broken one. So that only leaves this one and the two in Durham and Wilmington remaining, before Meg and her whole universe are most likely sealed away forever."

Sheridan didn't hesitate. "Calista, do you have any reason to ever want to go back inside the world of that mirror?"

"Absolutely not!" Calista exclaimed.

"Perfect. Thank you." Sheridan replied. Before anyone else could think or move, Sheridan picked up the large, antique brick that they sometimes used to prop open the studio door to let in the afternoon breeze. "Everyone stand back and turn around," he ordered.

Whirling like a discus thrower, Sheridan launched the brick as hard as he could into the mirror from about twenty feet away, continuing in his spin to a protective crouch on the floor as the glass scattered around him.

"So long, Lew," Sheridan whispered into the air, brushing his hands on his skirt. "See you in the next life."

Chapter Twenty-Three

Nora slept dreamlessly until Calista awakened her around noon. Sheridan and Hazel accompanied them down the street to the Sunny Point Cafe for breakfast. Finding herself hungrier than usual, Nora ordered the shrimp and grits, which were plentiful and delicious. She ate every bite.

They agreed that Sheridan would return to the studio to manage the day's dance campers by himself, while Calista would rent a car to follow Nora and Hazel back to Durham.

"Of all the cars in the entire world that you could have chosen," Nora said, shaking her head as her sister pulled up to the curb at the rental agency. "A Prius. I understand wanting to be eco-friendly, but why not a Tesla or something? They're electric. You can afford it, and it's just a rental for a few days anyway. Why not live a little?"

"Says the woman who has literally millions of dollars and yet drives a Tahoe," Calista chided. "I love the Prius! Plus, do you know how many rescue animals I could save at the no-kill shelter with the difference that I donated if I ended up buying a Prius instead of a Tesla?"

"I have no idea, but I'm sure you're going to tell me," said Nora wearily. Calista, although sincere about her love of animals and her desire to protect them, had worn Nora out over the years with her zeal for advocacy.

"I did the math. Five hundred! Isn't that amazing?"

"I'm astounded," said Nora. Although her tone was sarcastic, her surprise was genuine. She'd never thought about the fact that the choice to buy an automobile twice the price of what one would need cost the lives of five hundred innocent homeless animals. Only someone like Calista would think of something like that.

After they'd shared directions to the hotel where Cliff and Pierce were staying, they set out for Durham. Hazel insisted on driving Nora's Tahoe for the entire three hours. Calista followed in the Prius. Filled with warm grits and suddenly more exhausted than she realized, Nora fell asleep in the afternoon sun, like a cat on a windowsill.

When they arrived at the hotel, Nora awakened slowly and called Cliff's cell. "We're sitting outside of Dr. Yates's house," the lawyer said. "We were supposed to meet at four, but when we knocked on the door, he didn't answer. So, I called down to his old lab using the other number you gave me, but his assistant said that she hadn't seen him either. Is this normal? Is Yates some kind of absent-minded professor or what?"

"Not that I'm aware of," said Nora, slowly emerging from her catatonic state in the passenger's seat. Through the window, she could see Calista pull up in the Prius, get out, and begin walking toward the Tahoe. "I didn't know Yates at all when we met. He and my father were close. They worked together on the same experiments. As to his propensity for forgetfulness, your guess is as good as mine on that one."

"Well, since we're already over here, why don't you just meet us?" Cliff asked. "I'm choosing to believe that Yates *is* a typical professor and just forgot. Maybe he'll turn up soon."

Nora didn't like the hint of suspicion that she heard in Cliff's voice. Cliff once told her that the best trait a lawyer could have was an instinct for finding the truth when surrounded by lies. She didn't want to think about what his suspicions were regarding Dr. Yates, as every possibility was bad. Nora pressed the button to roll down the window. She gave Professor Yates's home address to both Calista and Hazel simultaneously. Following Calista's lead this time, their two-car wagon train pressed on eastward.

Pulling up in front of Yates's house, Nora realized something that she hadn't before. Dr. Yates had the most perfectly manicured lawn of any old bachelor's home she'd ever seen. The pansies, peonies, and petunias were perfectly placed, and each plant turned several happy faces to the sun. There was also a rose-covered arched reading nook, a koi pond, a beehive, and a gazebo surrounded by blue snowball bushes in full bloom. Nora noticed that the house itself was immaculate as she approached. Everything was painted, pressure washed, and in spic and span order. "What could cause a person," Nora wondered aloud to herself, "to cultivate such a garden that no one but he would see?"

"Loneliness," answered Hazel, not recognizing that the question was rhetorical. Nora had begun to realize that her new friend thought that every question pondered in her general vicinity required her response. It didn't bother her. Rather, Nora found it amusing and somewhat telling. She imagined for the first time that Hazel, who seemed to be such a self-sufficient authority on so many things, must also be lonely. They parked the Tahoe at the curb, got out, and approached the house. Cliff and Pierce stood waiting in the yard.

"I've been thinking about this," said Pierce, leading her toward the door. "Perhaps I can call the security company that operates these push-button door locks and get them to open it for me remotely. As if I were his realtor or something. I mean, you said he was really old, Nora. What if he's passed out somewhere and needs our help?"

Nora hadn't considered this possibility. She was surprised that Pierce had. It seemed such a thoughtful and unusual thing for him to worry about. A few moments later, Pierce had the security company on the line. Laying on the sweetness heavily, the operator bought Pierce's entire fabricated story. However, after the interview was over, Pierce seemed disappointed.

"What do you have to be sad about?" Nora asked as Pierce punched in the key code to the door lock. The door swung open with a click.

"It's always been too easy," Pierce replied. "The operator was a woman. My entire life, all the way back to elementary school, I've been able to leverage compliments to females to get what I wanted. I've always felt bad about it."

"I'd save your sorrow, young man, for a true occasion to share it," interjected Cliff. The attorney pushed past Pierce through the unlocked door and into the small kitchen. "Depending on what we find here, you may have one soon enough."

The interior of Yates's house was just as Nora and Hazel remembered from their initial visit. Old leather chairs, heavy dark wood furniture, and floor-to-ceiling bookcases that reached every peak of the tiny but impeccably clean little brick Tudor house gave the overall impression of the home of a very well-read hobbit. Although it wasn't anything even close to being in style with any trend in the past century, Nora couldn't help but admire the warm self-assuredness of it. However, the tranquility was short-lived.

"I've found Yates," called Cliff from the back room. "It's bad. Be careful not to touch anything as you walk in." Nora's heart sank as she walked toward the sound of Cliff's voice. Hazel and Pierce followed.

Cliff stood with his arms crossed, studying the bloody mess that had been the right side of Dr. Yates's head. Entering from the left side of the room, the silhouette of the left side of Yates's lean face looked perfectly normal. However, as Nora walked around to stand by Cliff, she almost became sick. The right side was nothing but a crushed mass of blood and bone. His blue eyeball had become loose in the socket, most likely from the bullet severing the tissues holding it in place. The eye hung halfway out like some vulgar impression of a Halloween mask. Bits of flesh and flecks of bone clung where they had dried on his polo shirt, a completely incongruous shade of robin's egg blue. Nora could see his teeth, in surprisingly good condition for a man over seventy, gleaming out of the patch of skin torn away from his jaw. Still caught in his death grip, the barrel of a Browning 1911 .38 caliber pistol rested with its tip on the floor. Dr. Yates's finger was still on the trigger.

"Dear God!" Nora gasped as something rushed past her, brushing her leg only slightly but making her jump all the same. It was Yates's large ginger tomcat. He hopped up onto his dead master's lap and sniffed with a forlorn look on his face. Then, the cat curled up on top of the desk, never diverting his intense yellow gaze from Yates's inert form.

"Judging from all the orange fur on the lap of his khakis," said Cliff, "I guess that's his cat. Poor devil." Cliff leaned in to read what Yates had written in the open notebook on his desktop. "Looks like he was working right up to the end."

Nora felt nauseous, but Cliff stepped aside for her to see. "Be sure not to touch anything," Cliff cautioned again. "We'll have to call the police in a few minutes. I just want to get an overall impression of the scene as it is before they arrive and inevitably bungle something."

Feeling more at ease when viewing the notes from Yates's intact left side, Nora stooped to read the lines at the top of the notebook page.

Upon re-examination of Subject 153, both in the presence of the two aforementioned witnesses and my later review of the glass that same evening, the findings captured at last by my employment of the infrared, heat-detecting video camera were nothing short of astonishing. They revealed...

Here, Yates's observations trailed off with a sharp downstroke of his fountain pen, leaving a tiny hole punched into the paper. Looking down, Nora could see the pen in question lying on the floor, just out of reach of Yates's left arm that draped limply over his antique desk chair.

"Don't you find it curious," said Cliff, pointing at Yates's left hand, "that the professor wrote left-handed, yet chose to shoot himself with his right? Especially in the middle of a sentence?"

Circling the chair again, Nora studied the gun in Yates's hand. "I find the pistol itself even more curious." Suppressing the sick feeling rising from her stomach, she knelt closer to study the portion of the pistol grip that was visible around Yates's palm.

Nora knew she had encountered a pistol of that type, with a striped zebra wood grip, only once before in her life. In a flash, she could see herself at ten years old, with her sisters standing on either side. All their eyes fixed on the gun as her father explained carefully to Vicki and her how it operated. Then, he cautioned Calista never to touch it, because "it wasn't a toy."

She remembered Calista being sent back inside to play while her father took her and Vicki out in the woods behind the house. Henry patiently instructed them both, in great detail, on the proper care that was to be taken with firearms. Although Henry had two long guns in the house, a shotgun and a rifle, which stayed tucked in a back corner of his half of her parents' walk-in closet, the episode with the pistol stuck in Nora's mind. It was the only time she'd ever seen her father holding a pistol. Vaguely, Nora remembered the unease that she'd felt when Henry initially placed the heavy pistol in her hands. As Nora fired once at the paper target that Henry had placed in the tree line, her wariness lessened. By the third shot, she felt almost normal. Last, Nora remembered her father smiling proudly as he came back from checking her shots, with the card in his hand. Henry pointed out the first shot, which was low and to the left, then Nora's over-correction, which had gone high and to the right. The third, she'd known even without looking at it, was a bullseye.

Nora swayed on her feet, thinking carefully for a moment. Her heart ached for the missed opportunity to know Dr. Yates better. Not just because of how he could possibly help in finding out more about Vicki or the mysteries of the mirrors, but because he had been her father's friend. Nora had so few memories of Henry, and it seemed with Bill's death, one more link was gone forever. She looked down at Yates's orange cat, which weaved himself ingratiatingly around her calves. As Nora reached down to pet him, she saw that his collar read, *Sydney Carton.*

As in, the drunken lawyer from Dickens's Tale of Two Cities, she thought. The mirror image of Charles Darnay, who was supposed to be the hero of the book. Straightening, Nora remembered that it was Carton who was the one willing to face the noose for the woman they both loved. After, he'd helped Darnay escape by using a disguise.

Cliff, growing impatient, broke into her reverie. "Are you going to tell me why the pistol is relevant, or are we going to stand here and pet cats all day?"

For the first time since Jasper's death, Nora forced herself to see Cliff for what he was. It had taken her the long car ride back to Durham to fully process it. After the initial shock of his callous reaction to the information she'd shared with him about what she'd seen in Jasper's mirror wore off, Nora was sure. She could not trust Cliff Tuttle at all. Something about his inability to demonstrate any sadness when faced with the death of a stranger was what did it. Although she'd leaned on Cliff like a friend for years, as her only protection from Jasper's mother and all the worms that came out of the woodwork squirming for pieces of her husband's estate, Cliff was still just an old Nashville huckster. He was not her friend. Like all lawyers, he was a mercenary. Useful, but someone who should be told only what was necessary.

"That's my father's pistol. I haven't seen it since I was ten." Nora said, then paused, before adding thoughtfully. "I was told that he'd shot himself with it."

Chapter Twenty-Four

The police came and went. They spent what Nora thought was an extraordinary amount of time questioning Pierce and an underwhelming amount of time dusting for fingerprints or doing any actual detective work. However, Pierce had an alibi for the entire window of possibility for Dr. Yates's death, so they let him be. As Cliff explained to her, "Police who attend a murder scene will do everything they can first to declare it a suicide and second, to railroad the most convenient suspect. Either path will lighten their workload." With neither of those two preferred options showing promise, the police merely gathered the evidence, took statements from each of them, called the coroner, and left.

As they were getting ready to leave, Nora excused herself to go to the bathroom. When she shut the door, Nora noticed Yates's faculty ID badge and keycard hanging from a lanyard on the towel hook. She could hardly miss it. On the bathroom mirror, there was a yellow sticky note, written in bold Sharpie with Yates's old-school copybook hand.

Don't forget your ID! An arrow pointed toward the door hook with a smiley face.

"Thanks, absent-minded professor," she whispered to herself. Having seen Yates use the keycard on her initial visit to the lab, Nora knew that it would come in handy, should she desire to revisit the lab again with Yates gone. Nora slipped it into her purse, washed her hands, and rejoined the group.

Since Pierce's initial arraignment was the next morning, Cliff made reservations to stay overnight again in Durham. "Should be pretty open and shut," the lawyer said. "I seriously doubt that any grand jury would indict with what little circumstantial evidence they have. Especially if

Harper is still willing to give a corroborating statement. She is, correct?" Cliff looked at Pierce for confirmation.

"Oh, yeah... she'll be there," Pierce replied, with an inkling of reservation in his voice. "I mean, I tried to call her to confirm it this morning. She isn't answering her phone for some reason, but I know she'll be there."

Cliff appeared skeptical at this, replying only, "Well, we'll see."

The remainder of the afternoon was a flurry of calls and making arrangements on when to meet next. Calista called Sheridan to check on him in the studio. He seemed to be managing just fine, so she told him she planned to go to Wilmington to stay with Nora for a few days. Hazel called her Gramma Dean to say that yes, she would be back in time for Wednesday bowling night. Ultimately, it was decided that Cliff would call everyone after he and Pierce made it through the arraignment so that they could plan to meet again regarding Vicki.

During this round of calls, Sydney Carton reappeared. "And where have you been?" Nora asked him as the orange tomcat should in an endless loop around Nora's ankles. The worried cat had disappeared completely during the police's visit. Although Calista made every possible overture of friendship, Sydney completely ignored her, preferring instead to attempt to win Nora over. When Nora picked up her purse at last to leave, the cat let out a loud trill of a purr and leaped in front of the door, flopping down in front of it like a draft-cozy to prevent her exit.

"It seems I have found a cat, poor thing," Nora said, picking up Sydney beneath his front shoulders to open the door. "What a bale of fur!" Sydney's ponderous rear end sagged limply toward the floor. Nora gathered the cat's bottom half up in her arms, cradling him like a baby. Sydney snuggled against her, purring loudly.

"Rather the other way around," said Hazel. "Since it's always the cat who finds you."

By the time the trio of women arrived back in Wilmington, it was dusk. Nora was only slightly surprised that Sydney slept curled up in her lap the entire way, not making so much as a peep. Hazel gathered her equipment and left for home a few blocks away. Nora instructed Calista on where to park her Prius around the back so that she wouldn't have to leave it on the street. Exhausted, Nora fumbled with her keys to unlock the front door. However, when she touched the knob, it was unlocked. *Shit*, she thought.

After everything else, did I leave the door open so that any random burglar could walk in?

Moments later, Nora realized that her fears were unfounded. Setting Sydney down to go in first, the cat ran inside, meowing loudly. As Nora entered, she noticed two things. First, there was a very old wooden captain's wheel lying in the middle of the parlor floor, directly underneath the spot where she'd often wondered about what kind of light fixture to place. Second, the little table in the entryway where she'd placed the last note, in what seemed like years ago, had a second note beside it. The shaky letters were scrawled in pencil, likely the one lying on the floor next to the table. Nora picked up the pencil and saw that the tip was broken.

At the top of the page, the note read, *I'm sorry for yelling at you. Please come back!*

Then at the bottom, *P.S. - Maybe try the wheel next?*

Calista entered behind her and pointed at the wheel. "What's that?"

Nora looked down, studying it, then back up at the ceiling. It *would* go nicely with the shape of the round-fronted room. "My next project. Alexander has chosen my chandelier."

***

After helping Calista load her things into the guest bedroom upstairs, she and Nora parted ways. Calista went to Whole Foods to pick up some salmon and couscous to prepare for dinner, and Nora left for her design studio to retrieve a lighting kit and tools. She'd ordered the kit and a handmade, wrought iron frame for a client who wanted her to make an artistic display of elk antlers into a chandelier. The client, a newly anointed second trophy wife, and her husband were attempting a compromise on the fact that he wanted his hunting prizes proudly displayed in the living room, but she would rather not be stared at by half a dozen dead animals. However, the client was in no hurry, and Nora could easily reorder another kit. According to her expert eye, the diameter of the metal frame and the captain's wheel should be a perfect fit.

Arriving back at the house with her supplies before Calista, Nora took time to explore for other possible signs that Hostler might have read her notes. Other than the fact that every one of the notes was lying on the floor, rather than attached to the walls where she pinned them, Nora found nothing. She considered uncovering the mirror but decided to wait until after dinner. She'd told Calista on the drive over about Hostler's ghost in her house. Calista hadn't seemed disturbed, despite her terrifying brush with Meg the night before. Still, Nora felt that it was best to wait at least until after they'd eaten dinner and rested to engage. The house seemed to almost pulse with energy as she walked through it. When she touched the edge of the looking glass frame through the quilt, she could feel its warmth.

He's waiting for me, Nora thought, smiling to herself. She was a little surprised to be looking forward to seeing him again.

By the time Calista returned, Nora was already elbow-deep in the wheel chandelier project. As she'd suspected, the wheel and frame were an ideal fit, each being exactly a yard in diameter. She'd drilled and screwed these pieces into place quickly. Within an hour, she had the lighting kit secured in place as well. Nora didn't even have to measure for equal distance, just boring the holes for the sockets behind each handle. As Calista bustled around the kitchen preparing dinner, Nora notched and strung the chains, counting the links so that it would hang straight. Last, she ran the wire, hiding the excess behind the metal cup attached to the ceiling.

"Are you already done?" asked Calista, seeing Nora putting the last bulbs into their sockets. She climbed down from the ladder. "Let's find out!" Nora said, walking over to the circuit box and turning the breaker back on before flipping the switch. The chandelier came on with a slight *click*.

"Marvelous!" said Calista, applauding tiny excited claps like a cartoon character. Nora knew this must be the same kind of applause that Calista used to celebrate when her students completed a new combination of steps for the first time. "You've always been so handy with everything. I wish I were!"

"I can teach you if you're willing to learn," replied Nora, knowing that Calista would never take her up on it. Although her little sister was supportive of her design work, she lacked the patience to create any for herself.

"I'll pass. Besides, why should I learn when I have you? Dinner's ready!"

The two sisters sat down to their meal. Despite her general lack of patience for anything else involving craftsmanship, Calista was an excellent cook. She'd had to become one after declaring in junior high that she would never eat meat again. This assertion also prompted Marjorie to declare that she refused to prepare separate meals for Calista, so if she wanted to eat *like one of those vegetarian hippie people,* she'd have to learn to do so by cooking for herself.

By that time, Vicki had gone off to college, so it was just Nora and Calista at home together by themselves most nights. Thus, Nora, who generally detested the mess of cooking, had eaten her way through several years of her sister's meatless experiments without complaint, cooking only the proteins separately for herself.

Eventually, during Nora's senior year of high school, their mother lost all hope for Calista after she declared her desire to become a professional dancer. Marjorie decided to punish her youngest daughter by refusing to buy any of the *special hippie foods* that Calista was used to preparing in her meatless lifestyle. Marjorie also refused to drive Calista to dance classes. So, Nora stepped in. From her weekend babysitting money, Nora started buying all the foods she knew Calista wanted. In exchange, Calista learned how to prepare animal proteins, even though she still didn't eat them. It was a practice so well established between the two sisters over the years that it now continued unstated whenever they were together, even though neither cooked for Vicki or their mother. Thus, when they sat down to dinner, Calista ate her salad and couscous with added lentils, and Nora enjoyed almost the same, exchanging the plant protein for salmon.

By the time they'd made it to the fresh strawberry pie, Nora decided that her sister might have recovered enough from her previous ordeal to be receptive to her proposal. "How would you feel about another mirror experiment tonight? You're completely free to say no, of course, but I thought you might want to see a harmless one. After everything, you know."

Calista chewed thoughtfully as she answered the question with two additional ones. "This wouldn't be the spirit Hazel was teasing you about? Was he the one who left you that wheel?"

"Yes, I'm almost certain he was," said Nora. "Of course, I'm intrigued about the wheel too. Where did it come from? How did he get it here? But also I was wondering, if he were indeed friendly, as he seems to want to be, could it not be possible that we learn some things from him?"

"What kinds of things?" asked Calista, getting up to prepare another cup of espresso.

"There are so many," Nora held up her hand to tick them off. "First, how do the mirror portals work? Second, why are some hot while others are cold? Third, why are some spirits hostile while others are hospitable? According to Hazel, Hostler and his friend Jocelyn were into all that Victorian-style spiritual stuff. Would it not stand to reason that his curiosity would extend after death? Couldn't it help us to find Vicki and possibly learn more about what happened to Dad and Jasper if we had someone with insights on the other side who was willing to guide us through what all of it means?"

"Oh, absolutely!" called Calista, listening from the kitchen as espresso brewed. She came to lean on the doorjamb with a dish towel in hand. "My only concern is what he might want in exchange for the information."

"What do you mean?" asked Nora. "Do you think there's some kind of ghostly *quid pro quo*?"

"Well, you never know. I mean, Meg seemed completely harmless too, at first. Until I became enthralled by her. Once she'd lured me into the mirror, it was too late. I was trapped." Calista went back into the kitchen and returned, setting a tiny cup down in front of each of them.

Nora blew on the espresso and took a careful sip. It was scalding hot. "I just don't get that feeling from him at all, though. I kind of feel like Sheridan was describing how he felt with Llewelyn. The more I've considered it, Alex's presence is a strange sort of comfort. Like seeing someone from high school that you'd completely forgotten about on social media. Where the initial contact is awkward and almost startling at first, but before you know it, you're going on like the old friends you used to be."

As Nora explained this, she saw her sister's attention drift away. Calista was peering into the parlor. "Look at the cat," she said.

Sydney was sitting directly under the wheel chandelier. Nora noticed that the cat was moving his head ever so slowly around in a circle. Nora's gaze followed his eyes upward, where she could see the wheel chandelier had begun to swirl, almost imperceptibly, counterclockwise.

"Sheridan told me once that a friendly spirit's energy will always move counterclockwise in the Northern Hemisphere, but if it's sinister, it will go the other way," said Calista, setting her espresso cup down noiselessly on the table.

As they watched, the circle of the wheel grew wider and wider. Sydney made a trilling sound and retreated backward, hiding under Nora's chair.

Within a few seconds, it was swaying as widely back and forth as a child's playground swing. Just as Nora was beginning to worry that the chain would break under the strain, a familiar fog began to gather directly under the chandelier, coalescing into a human shape. It gazed skyward with arms extended down and palms facing up in a reverent pose. Once the form was somewhat solid, the figure changed from grayscale to color. As he stood shimmering before them, the man's hard, skyward gaze softened and shifted to look at them. The otherworldly silver light faded from his eyes, which became a perfectly normal shade of slate gray.

"Lovely," he said, looking from one sister to the other. "Astonishing, and lovely."

Chapter Twenty-Five

"Thank you, Mr. Hostler," said Nora, as the spirit rippled like a calm ocean at low tide. Then by instinct, she curtsied deeply.

"The pleasure is mine, dear." Hostler stepped forward two paces and turned to gaze up at the chandelier. "Sam was always so insistent that it would work, but I had my doubts. Turns out the spirit can manifest through objects after all. Guess I owe him that twenty."

Hostler smiled the sort of smile that would have lit up a room if it weren't already illuminated by his ghostly form. Watching the shadow muscles of his face flex as a complex array of thoughts swirled, Nora had the distinct impression that Hostler was the kind of man who was always up to something. "I would kiss your hand; however, the nature of my being is unfortunately quite transitory of late. Thus, suffice it to say instead that I am charmed to finally make your acquaintance, albeit from a slight distance."

Hostler bowed graciously, allowing the soft, natural curls of his messy hair to tumble forward. He brushed them back with a slightly annoyed whisk of the hand, which Nora felt had been a habitual gesture in life. She studied him, oddly amused at his formal manners.

He continued, "I'm so glad you found my wheel idea suitable. I read your explanation of the significance of the..." He motioned toward the airplane propeller as he searched for the word, "...sky propeller? No, that's not right. Forgive me. I've not seen one. It's been a long time. Regardless, I thought it would continue the traveling theme that you've established for the room, whilst also allowing me to put a bit of myself into it. I trust that my suggestion was not too obtrusive?"

"Oh, no... not at all," said Nora, coming to sit down on the sofa closer to Hostler. Calista remained rooted to the floor where she was, gaping and wordless. Sydney the cat tucked himself as far back into the corner under the china cabinet as the walls would allow.

"I'm just happy that you've decided to share the house with me," Nora continued. "I mean, I completely understand what a shock it must have been to awaken to so many changes at once. However, I hope you know that they were all made with as much care and concern for preserving the character of the place as possible. I am an interior designer."

"A what?" Hostler asked, his handsome face crinkling into a frown.

"An interior designer. A person who remodels—changes—spaces to be more functional and aesthetically pleasing. My specialty is in historic preservation, so I've enjoyed bringing this place back to life." Nora stopped her explanation abruptly, sensing that she'd made an error in a speech that he might find off-putting.

"Yes..." replied Hostler, with a twinkle in his eye. "Back to life. Too bad the house can be reincarnated, just not me." Nora caught the joke as they exchanged glances. "Please do not fret over the fact that I am not corporeally present, Ms. Hewitt. I've had almost two hundred years to become accustomed to the fact that I am no longer among the living. There are some things I miss. Mostly food," he nodded in the general direction of the dinner table, where Calista nervously smiled at him, "and other tactile stimulations, such as petting an animal."

Sydney's intense feline gaze penetrated the air between them suspiciously from beneath the cabinet. "But there are welcome trade-offs as well. For example, I am no longer plagued by the pains of old injuries, nor am I fettered by the trappings of traditional transportation. I can go anywhere I please, at any time. I am a free spirit. My soul is like the wind. You must understand, Ms. Hewitt, that for a man such as myself, who spent a lifetime in logistics, this is quite a marvel, no?"

"Oh yes, of course," replied Nora, pushing herself up so that she was now seated on the very edge of the sofa.

"Splendid," said Hostler. "Once again, I hope that you will permit my intrusion. I surmise that you might since I am also a curious person. I couldn't help overhearing that you would like to ask me some questions regarding the nature of life after death. At least, as it exists beyond the surface of the mirror?"

Nora was puzzled. "You could hear us? Even without being here?"

"Oh, certainly!" replied Hostler, chuckling to himself, again with his eyes merry. "And see you. In all states. Although I remain a gentleman, rest assured, Ms. Hewitt. I restrain my gaze when I feel that it might be unwanted or inappropriate."

Calista snorted her disbelief. "Oh, I'm sure!"

Nora ignored her, although she crossed her legs in an unconsciously protective manner and tucked a stray strand of hair behind her ear. "That 's... very interesting, Mr. Hostler. But yes, I am extremely curious. After all that we've," she gestured to Calista, "experienced in the last few days. Not to mention what's happened with our sister Vicki."

"I've seen your Victoria," answered Hostler. "She is resting on my side, and she is completely safe. For now, anyway." Both Calista and Nora looked at him searchingly as he continued. "We could sit here and talk back and forth all night, or I could show you in person how everything works much more quickly. It all depends on how much you trust me."

Hostler's quicksilver eyes scanned from Nora's face to Calista's. The latter sister subtly shook her head. *No.*

Nora turned her gaze from her sister to Hostler. "I don't have the faintest idea why, Mr. Hostler, but I trust you completely. When shall we begin?"

Hostler offered his hand, with the tip of his index finger extended to Nora. "Now would be ideal, although you must forgive my touch. I understand that the heat of it is uncomfortable. Yet, the effects do not last, and the damage is small, so long as contact is minimal. All that is required to enter is a fingertip. The sensation will be no more than lightly brushing a stovetop."

"Then, let's begin," Nora said, reaching out to touch the tip of her index finger to his. They stepped under the wheel gingerly, as if making the first move in an elaborate dance. With a flash of white-hot light, they were gone.

Chapter Twenty-Six

Nora blinked open her eyes to a place that was and was not her parlor. Although the ship's wheel chandelier remained, it was lit with candles, not electric bulbs. The furniture was completely different as well. Expensive and immaculately maintained, Nora recognized that every piece was vintage Chippendale walnut. The upholstered surfaces were plush blue velvet, and the tops of the writing desk and tea table were white marble. Hostler caught her staring at the chandelier.

"That was always my favorite piece. Made it myself, out of the last ship I steered. Before that load fell and busted my knee. Never was quite the same after that. But I was over fifty. It was time, I suppose, to go around to the other side of the desk, even though keeping accounts was such a bore." He stopped, realizing that Nora was observing his chatter. "I shan't go on rambling. My apologies, but it does get lonely here, with no one to talk to. You're here for reasons of your own. Tell me what you'd like to know, and I will be more than happy to oblige." Hostler stood ramrod straight, almost as if at attention. His formal posture made Nora giggle, which in turn caused him to relax slightly.

"Well..." Nora began, as she circumnavigated the room, glancing here and there to take in random bits of decor, all decidedly masculine and nautical. "I suppose that we should begin with the journey itself. Why are some spirits able to enter and exit the mirrors? Also, why are some hot, while others are cold?"

"That's simple," replied Hostler. On the other side of the mirror, he no longer shimmered. Settling into the chaise lounge like a patient on an old-fashioned psychiatrist's couch, he began.

"If you've ever read *Beowulf*, you'll know that Hell, or at least the concept of a place of purgation during life after death as the pagan Anglo-Saxons understood it, is cold. Not hot, like the Christian Bible says. If a spirit has not yet relinquished its bonds with the earth and is still paying penance for its sins during life, it will burn with icy fire. Thus, its touch is cold. In contrast, a spirit that is fully purged will burn hot with a sense of recreation and rebirth because it has been released of its misdeeds and is once again prepared to re-enter the world of the physically living. Both kinds of spirits can enter and exit the mirrors whenever they have some unfinished business on the other side." Hostler folded his arms satisfactorily behind his head and snuggled into the back of the chaise. "What else do you like to know?"

Nora was taken aback by the simplicity of his answer, but she persevered. "Okay, so according to that description, *you* come through as *hot,* meaning that you are purged and ready to re-enter the world. Other spirits say, Gallows Meg, for example, remains cold, even many years later. So, this means that she still has something sinful left to purge, correct?"

"Not just something, my dear, but *many* things," Hostler corrected her. "The greatest sin of all, even more so than murder, is avarice. The willingness to do anything or destroy anyone for material gain and power over others. Lucifer coveted Jesus's position at the right hand of God and was willing to do anything to supplant him. The desire to deprive a rightful other of something and take it for oneself is the only sin for which there is no justification. One can murder in self-defense, steal because one is hungry, or lust because one has been rejected too many times to count. Yet, once their needs are met, such sinners are usually satisfied. The truly avaricious can never be satiated. They are always greedy, and it is this hunger that ultimately produces their demise. I knew Meg in her original life. She was a big, blustery Irish girl from a bad family. Her father was a sailor. He drank and beat her mother, who died young. Not even thirty. Meg grew up the oldest girl in a large family of brothers. She spent her youth raising and protecting them when other girls of her sort were catching husbands. By the time her brothers were old enough to fend for themselves, it was too late. Meg was an old maid. Working had made her muscular and tough, and she was tall with a distinctive face. Meg made her way as a dancer and courtesan, but she was smarter than the other girls. She saved her money. When the opportunity came, she bought the club she danced in from the old opium fiend who lost it for pennies. Turned it into the Blue Post. However, the journey made her hard and mean. Stole all the humanity right out of her, until she became as cruel as the men off whom she'd made a fortune. Still, Meg hungered for the things she'd never had. A caring family. Real friends. So now, she drags in kindhearted girls who've had that sort of life because she wants to turn them into similarly twisted versions of herself. Her anger will never be sated. Meg's cold heart burns with icy fire."

"That explains why she took Calista then," replied Nora. "She's the kindest, most genuine soul I know. And why Meg was attracted to Sheridan as well. He's also very gentle. It makes sense." Nora thought for a moment. "Okay, question number two. Your spirit burns hot, and you seem to know me right away. What is the significance of those things?"

"Again, easy," replied Hostler, rustling impatiently, moving his clasped hands from behind his head to rest on his stomach as he sank even deeper into the chaise lounge. "Although I was what some would call a rogue during life, I was not generally a bad person in spirit. I wanted nothing from anyone other than to have a good time. The sin of luxury is one of the easiest to wash away. So now, I come and go as I please. A free spirit, warmed by my wisdom of the world."

Nora pressed him, "That makes sense too. So then, if you're free to come and go as you say you are, your reasoning for choosing to communicate with me is... what exactly?"

At this, Hostler sat up properly on the chaise lounge. His face drained of amusement, and he ran his hands through his hair impatiently. "I was hoping you'd remember me on your own, and this would be more natural. But you don't, and it's not. So, I'll just have to say it. In my original life, you were someone else, Nora. Someone whom I loved very much, yet I didn't take it seriously enough. She married someone else, and then she died. That's it. That's my reason for choosing you. However, none of that matters now. This is another life, and you don't remember me."

Hostler's intense, silvery gaze burned so brightly that Nora had to close her eyes. Yet as she did, a flash of memory flooded her brain. A party. In this dining room that had been his and now was hers. A young bride and groom sat glowing at the head of the table. The groom looked strangely familiar, but Nora couldn't pinpoint why. Everyone was laughing and drunk, but Hostler more so than the rest. He got up to make a toast, weaving as he did so. The groom's face went pale, but the rest of the laughing crowd grew louder. Although she couldn't hear the words, Nora felt anger rise inside her. Not thinking, she rose, crossed the room, and slapped Hostler so hard his head snapped to the side. He fell off the side of the lounge. The burst of memory stopped abruptly.

Mortified, Nora helped Hostler to his feet. To her surprise, he was laughing. "Well, I certainly remember *that*, Ms. Hewitt." At this point, he doubled over, cackling. "Or should I say, the Right Reverend Mrs. Chandler? Formerly Miss Eleanor Jocelyn?"

Nora sat down hard on the floor. All at once, she knew who he was.

Chapter Twenty-Seven

"I t helps if I close my eyes. Is that okay?" Nora asked.

"By all means," Hostler replied. "I'm just happy to know that there is a way to prompt your recollection at all."

Nora sat in the blue velvet winged chair opposite the chaise lounge. Hostler perched on the edge of the lounge and studied her.

She began reciting to him the snippets of vision that scrolled before her mind's eye, like photos in one of those digital slide frames. "Sam was my little brother. The two of you were best friends. You had a crush on me for years. I knew it, but you were afraid to say anything because you thought I would find you impish and immature. That night when you embarrassed me, you proved as much. By then, I loved you. We had been together—slept together—in secret. But you weren't ready for marriage. I didn't want anyone to know what had happened between us. So, I married the Reverend Chandler just to spite you. He was boring and hypocritical, but I was in a hurry to escape the scandal that would inevitably result once the gossip started. He was in a rush to marry and get away too, although at the time, I didn't know why. We went West, into Tennessee, what was then still basically the wilderness. He said it was to minister to the Indians. In truth, he was about to lose his position in the church here because he was addicted to laudanum. Our marriage was unhappy and childless, barely consummated. He had so little interest in me or anything else because of the drug. Mercifully, he caught typhoid fever and died the following winter. I caught it too, nursing him. I lingered on with it until spring."

"Yes," said Hostler, leaning forward eagerly, hanging on every word. "Before you died, you had time to write me a letter." Hostler rose and stepped over to a small, ornate writing desk. He handed Nora a piece of paper. It had been mounted on a thin piece of board and covered with some transparent substance. Taking it in hand, Nora realized that it felt like an old-fashioned children's hornbook.

"You can read it if you like, but I'll tell you what it says. You realized your marriage to Chandler was a mistake. Now that you were a widow, you wanted to see if we could make amends. Not wanting to wait to send a reply, I took my horse and left that very day, but it was too late. Your fever took a turn for the worse. By the time I arrived, you were dead. Although I begged to bring your body back, Chandler's family refused. You were buried next to him in the family plot."

"The family plot?" Nora replied, realization dawning on her. "Of the Chandlers? In Tennessee?"

"Yes, from what I gathered during my discussion with them at your funeral, Chandler had several other brothers who were all successful to some degree in various business enterprises. He was the only minister and thus considered to be their poor relation."

"Oh..." Nora breathed, taking in this new information. "It could be. There was a family cemetery that Jasper showed me not long after we married. It was out in the woods near Franklin. The tombstones were so old and worn, we couldn't read the names. I remember asking him if he wanted to be buried there. He said no—he'd had enough of his family already in this lifetime. Jasper's wish was to be cremated, so that's what we did. His mother kept his ashes. They were still in her house, on the piano, when I was there a few days ago."

Hostler surprised her with a laugh, "Well, of course, he didn't want to be buried there. He already *had been*. You were too, by the way. I read that stone when it was new. The first one is in the second row if you ever care to go back to see it. They liked to put the wife at the husband's right hand in those days. He was the first to die in the generation after the family arrived. Yours should still be there on the outside row."

"That's metaphorical," Nora rationalized. "I always felt like an outsider there, even in this life. I suppose you know about Jasper too, then?"

"Oh yes, I know of Jasper Chandler," replied Hostler. "I saw him when he first crossed over and recognized him immediately. He's still burning cold, I believe. Lots of avarice in that man. He seethed with it for his more successful brothers during the first lifetime in which I knew him. He continues to seethe even now, albeit with jealousy for younger musicians this time. I would take you to see him, but I'm afraid it would not go well. Rather like the encounter that your sister had with Gallows Meg. He would only seek to trap you within his misery yet again."

"I understand," replied Nora, processing the thoughts that she had chosen to ignore. Not only had her relationship with Jasper been unfulfilling in her current life, but it was also an echo of their past.

Sensing her distress, Hostler changed the subject. "There is nothing to be done about Jasper. However, I *can* offer you some reassurance about your sister, Victoria. She is alive, you know."

"You mentioned that before. Where is she?" Nora asked.

Hostler turned his head to the side and stuffed his hands into his pockets. He seemed to be searching for the right approach. "I've never been good at putting things delicately, so I'll just tell you. You seem to have accepted the news about Chandler and his past fairly well. Victoria is in your mother's laboratory. She appears to be asleep or under the influence of some sort of sedative. Been there for days. Your mother and some other doctors brought her. As for taking you there, I'm not sure if I can. I've never transported a living human out of one mirror and into another that they previously haven't entered. It makes two levels of removal of the soul from the body. Quite frankly, I'd rather not risk it. I can show you, though, by peering through the mirror from this world into hers. That was how I first learned of where she was, anyway."

"Yes, I'm ready to do anything. If at least I know where she is, maybe then I can figure out how to rescue her in the real world," Nora said.

Hostler sighed. "Of course. You *are* on a mission. Yet, is this world so *unreal* to you?" He reached out, took the letter board from her, and turned it over. "One more thing before we go. Do you know why I mounted this letter to the back of a children's hornbook?"

Nora was so absorbed in everything else that had happened it surprised her to notice she hadn't considered a reason. "Sure, yes, now that you mention it. Why?"

Hostler smiled and showed her the reverse side. "This was mine as I was learning to spell. I struggled with reversing my letters, and it made me shy. You noticed me doing it when Sam and I would study together. You used to sit on the porch—the porch of this house—with me. You'd take my hand and make me trace the letter shapes with you. *Feel it, Alex*, you would say to me. *Each letter has a personality all its own. If you think about how its character feels every time you see one, it will help you remember*. And it did help, a great deal. That envisioning of the letters, and how they made me feel. I never recovered from your kindness."

As Hostler spoke, he turned the board back toward himself. Nora watched him trace the *A* in silence with his index finger. Sensing that she was watching him, Hostler's reverie was broken. He tossed the board hastily back onto the desk.

"Enough of that maudlin sentimentality for now. Let me take you to see Victoria."

Chapter Twenty-Eight

Hostler directed Nora upstairs to the room that she'd chosen for her bedroom. "When I lived here, this was the guest room. It faced the street and was slightly smaller. I slept in the room that is your study, I believe, judging by its contents."

They stood before the mirror.

"What do we have to do to make it work?" Nora asked.

"It's easier than you might think," replied Hostler. He put his right hand to the surface of the glass and motioned for her to come forward. "I simply place my palms like so and think about the place I would like to see. It has to be both hands to complete the circle of energy. You can either stand behind me and look over my shoulder, or..."

He sized Nora up visually. "You might get a better view if you were to stand in front of me since I'm a bit taller." Hostler noticed the skeptical look on Nora's face at the thought of being trapped between him and the mirror portal. "That is... if you trust me. If not, well, I can run downstairs and bring you the footstool to stand on, by my side."

"No, that's okay," said Nora, without hesitation. "I trust you." She stepped in front of him, her face about a foot away from the mirror. As he moved into position behind her, she could feel the unusual warmth of his presence. It was like standing very close to someone with a fever. When Hostler placed his left palm on the glass across from his right, the surface of the mirror began to glow. Nora could feel the dry heat of the air increase around her dramatically as if she had opened the door to a sauna.

"If it becomes too much for you, or you feel faint, you must let me know immediately. I don't want you to get burned," Hostler directed. "Holding the entry point open requires a great deal of energy, and that energy is discharged as heat. Although I can no longer feel the sensation, I have witnessed its effects. I've melted many a good candle by keeping it too near the portal as I was learning the methods of its operation."

Nora turned to him, "How long have you been trying?"

"About two hundred years," Hostler shrugged. "Since I died, I've had a lot of time on my hands." He grinned at her. When Nora smiled back, she closed her eyes. For a second, she saw herself standing with her back pressed against a brick wall, turning to face Hostler in the same way. Only she could see the wharf and the river running behind him.

"Your office," Nora whispered. "Outside your office. I came to bring you a book of poetry you'd seen me reading. As I was leaving, that was the first time we..."

"Kissed, yes. I still have the book. Coleridge." His eyes flashed with pleasurable recognition, and his grin softened. "I've memorized every line. Alas, now is not the time. To paraphrase Old Sam, we must not let the trance of the silver-eyed Mariner be abated. I can only hold the portal open for a few moments. Look!"

Nora spun to face the mirror. An image formed. The eerily bright translucence behind it reminded her of looking into the lens of an old-fashioned filmstrip projector, making all the figures moving before her dark. Squinting, Nora could just make out the shapes of what looked like an observation room. Cabinets lined the walls, and there was a hospital bed with various machines surrounding it in the center.

On the bed, a woman lay sleeping peacefully. Wired sensors were attached to her upper chest and forehead. Her head turned to the side, facing Nora, who recognized it was Vicki. Nora realized that she must be looking through the one-way mirrored glass behind which scientists sat to observe their patients. Although she'd never been there before, Nora felt as if she knew the place from hearing it described. It was her mother's lab. Moments later, Marjorie and several other doctors whom Nora didn't recognize entered the room, confirming her suspicion.

"Her vitals continue to be stable," Marjorie said to the youngest one, who was taking notes. "However, we won't know the permanent effects on her short-term memory until she awakens. Of course, she'll have to be willing to consent to the follow-up study afterward for us to be sure. Even if she doesn't, and she wakes up retaining her full faculties otherwise, we'll still have her current data as a test case. With that evidence, it will be much easier to convince other potential subjects that the treatment would cure their PTSD."

"I think that it's remarkable what you've accomplished with this woman," another doctor fawned. "Just think of it," the woman said, addressing the other doctors as she gestured to Victoria, lying on the table. "*Jane A* may be the first victim of a traumatic experience that psychiatrists will ever be able to help without years of drugs or psychotherapy. I mean, we've already been able to create a temporary state of drug-induced amnesia to help addicts break the cycle of memory reconsolidation. However, this is a whole different ball game altogether. What Dr. Hewitt has done, we believe," she glanced at Marjorie for confirmation. Marjorie returned a knowing smirk that Nora recognized immediately as her mother's *told-you-so* look. "Is to indefinitely suppress specific memories through selective destruction of particular neurons, while leaving the remainder of the patient's memories and brain function intact. Dr. Hewitt has removed the memories causing *Jane A*'s PTSD, allowing her to move forward with her life, uninhibited by the traumas of her past. In short, Dr. Hewitt has found the antidote to psychological poison so that it no longer inhibits her personality or professional performance."

"Yes, but what about the ethical implications?" said one of the younger female doctors, stepping forward. "Even though this new procedure might have the ability to help victims of severe PTSD, what is to prevent, say, the government from using it on soldiers? So they become more ruthless killers on the battlefield? Oftentimes, it's knowing that one will have to live with the consequences of one's actions that helps to uphold standards of morality."

"I concur," agreed another doctor, this one an older man. "Development of behaviors based on past experiences, whether positive or negative, is an essential building block of learning. What happens if one of those blocks is removed when a memory is erased? Does the whole tower of emotional development topple?"

"I hate to say so, but I concur as well," said the last doctor. "Although I applaud the brilliance of Dr. Hewitt's work, I can't help but think we're going to have a difficult time raising funds to further her findings through additional clinical trials at our institutions after her initial grant runs out. Having been on my home department's media team and the research council for years, I know there will be a lot of resistance from some of the senior faculty. Even here at Duke, some have been vocal in the past against university support of memory suppression and erasure experiments. They see it as a sort of mind control. Not to mention how it would play to the press if they were asked to put their spin on the issue. Dissension in the ranks looks very bad for any department, as I'm sure you know, Dr. Chance."

The doctor, who had begun the conversation praising Marjorie's work, appeared uneasy. She glanced at Marjorie.

"Dr. Smith," Marjorie began, with her face fixed into a condescending smile that matched her tone. "I know that there are outliers in every department who would rather rely on older methods, but we live in an era of technological innovation. It's no longer just publish or perish, but provoke controversy or perish, to keep one's position. With the government cutting back on funding for all the soft sciences and many of our professors aging, we've got to push the envelope. I hate to put it bluntly, but I knew the professor who would have been most likely to object for many years. He was suffering from early-stage dementia. That caused him to take an early retirement, and unfortunately, his life. I trust you heard about poor Dr. Yates in the news yesterday?"

"Yes, I did," Dr. Smith shook his head. "A tragedy. I didn't know he had dementia. Yates appeared perfectly sharp at the conference we attended together last year. Just the same old academic burnout that we'll all have at seventy."

"Or, just a classic case of male ego," Marjorie corrected. "Even though Yates was a psychiatrist, he was an old bachelor and valued his independence. He didn't want to be pitied, so he didn't let on that his mental faculties were failing."

"You must be right," said Dr. Smith, shaking his head sadly. "Still, I will miss Bill. Just as much as we all still miss Henry. They were the life of the department here at Duke. It's such a sad irony that partners who always seemed so jovial would end up like that, all these years apart. I'm sure you agree that the coincidence is bizarre, Marjorie, given that..." he stopped, excluding the obvious.

"Yes, of course," Marjorie brushed him off. She deftly turned the conversation back to making a case for additional research funding.

"I think that's about as long as I can hold it," whispered Hostler. "Step out and let me close the portal. You'll probably want to turn away from the light. It gets very bright when it narrows."

Nora did as instructed, slipping out from under Hostler's arm and turning her back to the glass. She could feel the heat of the mirror rise as the light blazing from its surface sharpened in focus like a laser and then was gone. Nora faced Hostler, who stood panting as if he'd just run a long distance. He slumped down cross-legged on the floor, exhausted.

"Please forgive my posture. Holding the portal open for that long really takes a lot out of me. I'm afraid that I won't be much good for conversation or anything else for a while."

"That's completely understandable," said Nora, instinctively kneeling to comfort him. She could tell that Hostler didn't want to be hovered as he waved her away. "No, no. Remember, you can't touch me. I'm still hot from it. You'll only burn yourself. Besides, you should get back to your sister. It's been hours in the terrestrial world. I'm sure she's worried sick. Besides, after what you've seen, don't you need to make some plans?"

"Yes, of course," said Nora, rising. "How do I get back?"

"Just go downstairs and stand under the chandelier. Be very still and quiet. Listen to see if you can hear Calista calling to you. She should be by now. When you hear her, put both of your hands on either side of the perimeter of the wheel and pull yourself up. You may need to stand on the ottoman to reach it. Close your eyes and visualize yourself slipping through a hole in the center and back into the other room. Be careful—brace yourself in case you fall. You'll be surprised at how quickly it happens. Do you feel ready?"

"Yes," Nora replied. "And thank you."

He smiled at her in a pained fashion. "Any time spent with you is always a pleasure, my darl..." Hostler stopped himself. "Eleanor."

Chapter Twenty-Nine

The next morning, Nora, Calista, and Hazel sat at a small table outside of Java Dog Coffeehouse drinking chai lattes.

"Let me make sure that I have all of the details correct," said Hazel. "After Hostler opened the portal from his mirror into Marjorie's lab observation window, you saw your mother trying to pass your sister off as an anonymous test subject for her PTSD memory erasure study. She acted very dismissively when Yates's death was mentioned, and also your father's. I don't like the inferences of any of this. From everything I know after having spent a lifetime in academics, some of us, unfortunately, are willing to stop at nothing to advance our work just for the sake of ego. As the saying goes, the battles in academia are so bloody because the rewards are so small."

"I don't like it either," echoed Calista, twisting the cup in her hand nervously. "I mean, Mother can certainly be ruthless when she wants to be, but this... I just can't comprehend how she'd be capable of any of it." She turned to Nora. "How do you know what Hostler showed you was real? He told you so many things that stretch the boundaries of credulity, even for someone like me, who wants to believe in everything." Calista spread her arms wide for emphasis.

"I'm not sure," Nora said. "I just get this feeling that I should trust him. What motive would he have to lie to me?"

"If he's who he claims to be, a spirit who knew you in a past life and is longing to reconnect, then none," said Hazel. "However, there is always the chance that a darker, more sinister force is in play. They sometimes appear disguised as more friendly spirits when people are in vulnerable and confused states of mind. As I'm sure you are now, considering everything that's happened."

"But he had a very direct answer for every question I asked him," Nora insisted. "Correct me if I'm wrong, or if it's a fallacy, but evil spirits don't usually respond to direct questioning. If they do, it's often with a riddle."

"That's true," agreed Hazel. "As far as I can tell, Hostler's given us zero reason to suspect he's anything other than what he purports to be."

"So, what do we do now?" Calista asked.

"The only thing that makes sense," said Nora. "We go back to Durham and check out Mother's lab for ourselves. I hadn't been there in years, but I recognized it immediately. Strangely, it's just a few floors above where Hazel and I were before with Yates."

"There will be security, though," said Hazel. "And we don't have Yates anymore to let us in."

"We may not have Yates," replied Nora, "but I have the next best thing." She rummaged around in her purse and pulled out the lanyard to show them. "His keycard."

Chapter Thirty

The main plan was Calista's, although Hazel added a few points as the trio drove back from Wilmington to Durham in Nora's Tahoe. When they called Pierce and Sheridan to explain, both men insisted on meeting them to help.

Thanks to summer break, the campus was virtually deserted when they arrived. Their entry into the Duke psychology lab building could not have been easier. One swipe of Dr. Yates's keycard, and they were inside the main door. Another swipe and a numerical code, written on the back of Yates's ID in Sharpie, allowed them in and out of Vicki's lab as well. There, they collected the third of Gallus Meg's Blue Post mirrors. Pierce and Sheridan wrestled the bulky frame through the elevator. They set it up against the line of cabinets beside the entry door of Marjorie's lab so that it could not be seen by anyone who entered the room.

As with most medical labs, there were a series of light switches in Marjorie's. Several spotlights were trained on the subject in the center of the exam room, while the others controlled the general overhead fluorescents. With a quick removal of the light plate and snip of the wires leading from the switches overhead, Sheridan disabled all the lights that did not shine directly on Vicki's sleeping form. Seeing her sister's pale, inert body, covered only in a white sheet and a hospital gown and bathed in a stark white spotlight, gave Nora the creeps. It reminded her of that old Rembrandt painting—*The Anatomy Lesson.*

"Nice to know all those years working for Dad finally came in handy for something," Sheridan said, trying to lighten the mood, as he screwed the light plate back into place.

Hidden by the shadows, they stationed themselves around the room. Calista and Sheridan to the right, on the side with Meg's mirror, and Hazel and Pierce to the left. Hazel set up her night-vision camera equipment in the furthest and darkest corner, directly opposite Meg's mirror. Whatever happened, the entire incident would be caught on film.

Nora crouched beneath the head of Vicki's hospital bed, invisible to anyone entering the room. Sitting with her back pressed against the front wheels of the gurney, Nora listened to her sister's quiet breathing.

After ten minutes, Calista whispered, "How long did you say we have to wait?"

"Not much longer," Nora whispered back. "According to what I saw from Alex's vision last night, Vicki's last dose of sedative was about twenty-four hours ago. Marjorie will have to come in soon to administer the next dose so that she doesn't wake up."

"So it's Alex now?" Hazel smirked. "That's progress."

"Shut up," returned Nora, louder than she intended. Surprisingly, her friend's teasing about her drop of Hostler's first name wasn't the thought that Nora dwelled on. Instead, Nora pondered the reasons why she called her mother *Marjorie* rather than some more familial name. Marjorie had always insisted on it, and Nora never questioned her mother's insistence.

A few moments later, a soft beeping sound chirped from the security door down the hallway. Someone had entered the building. Although Nora worried that her mother would return with the same entourage as the evening before, those fears were unfounded. Nora recognized her mother's hard steps alone as they clicked briskly down the hallway. She and Calista exchanged knowing glances as they shushed the room.

Every muscle in Nora's body tensed as she heard her mother swipe her keycard. Three soft beeps followed. When Marjorie flipped the light switches, only the spotlights over Vicki's bed came on. Peering out from the shadows cast by the gurney, Nora saw the puzzled look on Marjorie's face as she clicked the other two switches on and off again. Out of the corner of her right eye, Nora could see Calista creeping toward Meg's mirror. Kneeling in front of it, Calista placed both hands on its surface. Sheridan crouched beside her, with both hands firmly grasping the leather belt of her shorts. They turned in unison toward Nora and mouthed one word.

Now.

Nora rose to stand beside her sister's bed. "Hello, Mother."

Marjorie froze, her eyes wide with terror. "What are you doing here? How did you get in?"

Nora held up her left hand. "I have Dr. Yates's keycard. I know what you did to him. And to Vicki, that's obvious. My only remaining question is what you had to do with Dad's death."

Marjorie's face was stone. "Your *father*," she sneered at the word, "was on the verge of disgracing the entire family. All that nonsense about spirituality and things coming out of mirrors! If he had lived to publish it, he would have been the laughingstock of not just Duke, but the entire academic world. Henry was so selfish. He cared only for indulging his curiosity. It would have ruined us both. No one is going to hire a psychiatrist who's lost his marbles. And then where would that have left you and your sisters? I worked too long and too hard for..."

Nora cut her off. "But what if he were *right*, Mother?" She bore down on the word, noticing that Marjorie flinched as she said it. "What if he were, as you are now, on the brink of a discovery that would change the world for the better? I mean, wouldn't everyone be comforted by the thought of knowing there is life after death?"

"Ghost stories!" scoffed Marjorie. "Who's ever been comforted by those? Everyone knows that parapsychology is a pseudoscience. That's why Yates was marginalized and finally driven out of the department. But not before he'd drawn your father into his craziness. Yates was selfish too, far more selfish than I am. He wanted a companion in his downfall. All I wanted was to save your father's career, and mine, and by proxy, the lives of you and your two ungrateful sisters. What a mistake I made! Stupid Vicki," Marjorie gestured to her oldest daughter lying in front of her. "She idolized those idiots and was going down the same path. All of it had to be stopped. If I'd been as irresponsible as your *father*, I could have just left the three of you with him and gone out on my own. Would have been a hell of a lot easier!"

As she spoke, Marjorie stepped closer to Nora, who saw that her mother had a syringe in her right hand. *Vicki's sedative.* Nora thought, yet remained still.

"So, you're saying you killed Yates and Dad?"

At this, Marjorie cackled. "Oh, so you think you're going to get some confession out of me, is that it? Make our lives into some kind of sordid little true crime media circus? Well, think again, *Daughter*," Marjorie spat the last word. "I wouldn't give *you* the satisfaction of taking *my* career away from me now. Not you, or your father, or Yates, or anyone else. That's all I have left. I'm not saying a God-damned word!"

All of a sudden, a searing beam of light flashed from the right side of the room. Calista flattened herself face-down to the floor. Her palms remained planted firmly on the mirror. Pierce ran to the door as Hazel flew past Nora to the head of Vicki's hospital bed.

"What in hell!" exclaimed Marjorie, as a shadowy figure in a long dress materialized out of the light.

"Now!" screamed Nora. Pierce flung open the door, and Hazel shoved Vicki's bed as hard as she could through it. As the bed sailed by, Marjorie rushed toward Nora, with the hypodermic needle raised. They crashed into each other. Marjorie lost her grip on the syringe as she fell. The two of them wrestled to the floor. Stronger from years of lifting heavy furniture, Nora was soon on top of her. Marjorie fought back, clawing at Nora's face and throat. As the ghostly shape solidified into the body of the long dead madam, Nora rolled away from her mother. Marjorie snatched up the syringe and leaped to her feet.

Gallows Meg grabbed Marjorie from behind. There was a horrific ripping sound as Meg bit down on Marjorie's right ear and tore it away. Meg spat Marjorie's ear out onto the floor. Blood poured from the hole on the side of her head. Marjorie wailed in pain as Meg wrapped her thick arms around her waist, dragging her toward the mirror.

"Get down!" yelled Nora. Sheridan yanked Calista backward with all his strength, breaking her contact with the surface of the mirror.

"Hope you enjoy the dance hall from hell, Mother!" Calista screamed as Marjorie flew past.

The surface of the mirror flashed with intense brightness as the portal shrank to close. Marjorie and Meg hit the glass with an ear-splitting crash, shattering fragments across the room.

Moments later, the five of them lay panting on the floor. Hazel came to her senses first. "Remember, exactly as we planned. No one touches anything. Leave the mess as it is—it's our best defense. Be careful to step over the blood. We all have gloves on, but I don't want to take any chances. I'll get the cameras and edit this part out of the video. Pierce, you have the hammock in your backpack, right?"

Pierce put a trembling hand on the pack on his back and nodded.

"Okay, great. Take it out in the hall. You and Sheridan get on each end of it. Nora and Calista, you two lift your sister off the gurney. Let's go!"

They moved quickly. In a few minutes, they were outside the exterior door of the lab building. Hazel sent Calista and the men to the car with Vicki, who was just beginning to stir. She and Nora stood outside the door.

"Jesus, I can't believe it worked!" said Hazel, who was doubled over, hands on knees, and still breathing hard. "Drop the card, and we're out of here."

Nora stood looking dumbly at the card in her hand as if realizing at last what it symbolized. "But what about all the other mirrors? The work that Vicki left? Our Dad? Or Yates?" she asked.

"If Vicki was working with the mirrors, she'll have keys too," replied Hazel, between gasps. "We just have to wait for her to wake up and tell us where they are. Then, we should be able to get back in. Right now, what we need most is that dead man's access card in the dirt right in front of the door. That lets the police know Yates's death wasn't a suicide and that foul play was involved. It also forces the inference that your mother was kidnapped from her lab. Marjorie's severed ear on the floor will confirm it when they run the blood test. If we need to, I can send an edited video anonymously and..." Seeing Nora flinch at the thought of her mother's bloody ear, she stopped herself. "Too much explanation. I'm bad about that. Sorry. I'll be in the car." Hazel turned and sprinted toward the parking lot.

"No, it's all right," Nora said to the air. "There's nothing to be sorry about. Mother got what she deserved." Nora pulled Yates's access card out of her pocket.

Or did she? Nora thought. All those years in graduate school. Then the initial fight to get an entry-level position, only to have to struggle again years later to regain it after the birth of her daughters, albeit at a lower salary than her similarly experienced male colleagues. No wonder Marjorie was so bitter. Nora thought about all the times that she, her sisters, and her father, Henry, had gone on vacations together. In contrast, her mother worked extra hours to prove *what* exactly? That she was equal to her male colleagues only because she was willing to push harder, to compromise her morals, to generally do *more*, just to compensate for being a woman?

Nora knew that her father and Yates experienced none of those problems. Being men, whether married or bachelors, rich or poor, they simply glided from one phase of life to another with little, if any, resistance at all. For a few seconds, Nora stood looking at Yates's smiling face staring back up at her from the ID photo. She remembered her mother's face on an identical keycard, now lost along with her into the hellish abyss of Meg's world beyond the mirror. Having seen it dangling around her mother's neck innumerable times, Nora remembered Marjorie's expression on it was tight and stern. Marjorie's ID photo looked like a person in a Depression-era photograph, although she'd always lived a comfortable, upper-middle-class lifestyle.

That kind of resentment, Nora concluded. *That kind of pain. That was how monsters were made.*

She dropped Dr. Yates's access card in the dust and ran to join her friends for the drive back to Victoria's house.

Chapter Thirty-One

"How long will she sleep like that?" asked Calista. She held open the door for the other four to carry Vicki into her home office. They sat her down on an overstuffed armchair. Although Vicki shifted a bit, as if she were soon to wake up, her eyes were not open. Nora looked around, taking in the perfect order of her surroundings. Her father Henry's mirror leaned up against the bookcase, standing in stark contrast as the only object out of place in the room.

"Probably less than an hour now," said Hazel, checking her watch. "We left around 10 pm. Since she missed her last dose, it should be any time."

"Considering what I overheard about Marjorie's experiments, though, I wonder what state she'll wake up in? Will Vicki know us?" asked Nora.

"I kind of hope not," said Pierce. "If anything good comes out of this, I'd like the opportunity to interact with her again, sans hatred. It would make things easier for the boys too."

"Not to mention much easier on your wallet for the divorce proceedings, if she can't remember all of the nonsense you were up to," smirked Sheridan.

Nora shot Sheridan a look, but he turned away. In the car on the way back from the lab, she'd heard Pierce texting up a storm but couldn't tell whether it was to Harper or his attorney, Cliff. Regardless, neither of them responded. Now that Vicki appeared to be safe, albeit still sedated, Nora could see Pierce glancing anxiously at his phone every few minutes.

"Waiting for the President to call, Pierce?" Nora asked.

"No," Pierce said, sheepishly putting the phone away in his pocket. "It's just..." he paused, as Nora watched the struggle over whether to tell the truth or a lie flash plainly across his blandly handsome face. He decided on half. "I can't seem to get Cliff on the phone. I want to tell him that we've found Vicki, and I... need to make another call too."

Nora interrupted him. "Let's hold that thought until she's awake and cognizant. Why don't you go make that other call now, though? Better yet... go check in person to see how she's doing. You wouldn't want to regain an ex-wife only to lose a girlfriend."

Looking like an unruly child who'd just been dismissed, Pierce turned slightly red in the face. As he turned to go, Nora called after him, "Remember, not a word to the police or anyone else until we know what the state of Vicki's memory is. We've all agreed."

Just as Pierce was about to say something in return, Vicki blinked and slowly opened her eyes. As she gradually gained focus, Vicki's gaze settled on her middle sister. "Nora, come here," she whispered. Nora crept closer toward Vicki as she reclined in the chair.

"What is it, Sis? How do you feel?"

"Like I have the worst hangover in the world," whispered Vicki hoarsely. She stared fixedly at Nora. "Why do you look so old? Is this a dream?"

Nora chuckled softly, "Well, because *I am* old, Sis. And no, this isn't a dream. How old do you think you are?"

Vicki's brows knitted as she struggled to raise the answer from behind a fog of memory. "Sixteen?" she guessed.

"A few years more than that, I'm afraid. Try forty and then some."

"Geez, that's old," said Vicki, coughing slightly. "Who's he?" Vicki pointed at Pierce. "Do I know you? You're pretty cute, but I get the feeling that I don't like you for some reason."

"Probably because you don't," said Pierce, stiffening.

"Well, I'm sure you won't know me, because we've never met, but I'm Sheridan. And I think I'm going to make things a bit less confusing by taking the cute unlikeable one home. Then, I'll be back for Calista. How's that sound?"

"Sounds good," said Vicki groggily. "I'm already tired of looking at him anyway."

As they exited the room, Hazel tried to stifle a laugh but only half-succeeded. "I think I'll go and get you a glass of water. Be right back." Dismissing herself, Hazel whispered to Nora, "I think your sister's going to be more okay than usual, all things considered."

With just the three of them left in the room, Calista and Nora knelt on either side of their oldest sister, who seemed to be gaining awareness by the minute. They prodded her with questions as gently as they could, trying to hold back curiosity.

"When were you born?"

Vicki answered this question easily. "July 4, 1976. I was a bicentennial baby."

"What year is it now?"

This one caused Vicki more difficulty. "1992?"

"Who is the president?"

"Bill Clinton. Although I'm not sure if I like him either. He reminds me of that other man who was in here. The cute one."

"Do you know where you are?"

Vicki shook her head, *no.*

"Can you tell me what your job is?"

Here, Vicki looked confused again. "I don't know if I have one right now. Last summer, I led a beginning violin class at a camp for inner-city youth."

"Oh wow, that was the summer between when I was in 2nd and 3rd grade. When I broke my wrist in gymnastics class," said Calista. She looked worriedly at Nora, who shushed her.

Vicki looked directly at her younger sister. "I told you that you weren't ready to flip off the balance beam on the dismount, but did you listen? Nope. You're lucky you didn't break your neck." Vicki coughed again slightly. Nora wondered if Hazel was purposefully lingering in bringing the glass of water to give them time alone. Nevertheless, she persisted.

"So, you play the violin? Do you think that you might be able to play something for us?"

"Maybe," said Vicki. "But not right now. My arms are too tired."

"I understand," said Nora, taking her hand reassuringly. "Could you tell us the name of the tune that you are working on?"

"Vivaldi's *Four Seasons. Spring.* It dances," Vicki smiled dreamily.

No wonder she remembered that one, Nora thought to herself, remembering the days that she and Vicki, before Calista was even born, would hear the tune wafting under the door to her father's office. It was his "little celebration song," as Henry used to say. He only put it on as he was finishing work for the day and tidying up his home office. When they heard it, the two of them would stand by their father's door, waiting for it to open. As soon as it did, they'd spring upon him, and Henry danced them around the room.

"I wonder if you could hum a bit of it for us now?" Nora asked.

"Oh Nora, I know you know *that* song!" Vicki complained. "I'm not a singer. Why are you asking me all these silly questions?" Vicki tried to sit up fully and drag her feet off the ottoman to the floor. Then, she attempted to push herself up to stand. She sank back down with a thump, looking dizzy.

"Just humor me, will you?" Nora was relieved at seeing some of her sister's familiar independence back. "You don't have to sing, I said. Just hum!"

Vicki made a sassy face and began to hum the tune in an exaggerated, mocking fashion.

"Nora, look!" said Calista, pointing at the mirror across the room. Henry's desk mirror. Its surface began to glow. Nora could feel the temperature in the room rising ever so slightly.

"Sis, can you walk over here with me? Closer to that mirror. Do you see it?"

Vicki nodded, still slightly groggy. She seemed to sense the energy coming from the surface of the mirror and was drawn to it. "If you two would help me, yes."

"We will help you; don't worry. Cali, can you take her arm on the other side over there?" Calista nodded. The three of them moved in unison to sit in a row, cross-legged, before their father's mirror. Without saying a word to one another, the three sisters grasped hands. Nora took Vicki's left hand in her right, and Vicki took Calista's in her left. Then, Calista placed her right palm on the mirror's surface, while Nora did the same with her left. The glow behind the glass swirled and coalesced into a form that all three recognized immediately.

"Daddy!"

From the other side of the mirror, Dr. Hewitt dropped his pen as he looked out at them.

"My girls!" Henry exclaimed, "To what do I owe the pleasure of this surprise?"

"We miss you!" Calista blurted.

"And we're here to warn you," continued Vicki.

"About Mother," finished Nora. "But I think you already know."

Dr. Hewitt's expression darkened. "Of course, I know, my darlings. I was there. But all of that is so far gone into the past now. No one can change it. What I'd rather talk about is where *you* are. The lives of the living are my only concern now, aren't they, Vicki?"

To the surprise of Nora and Calista, Vicki nodded. Dr. Hewitt continued. "Vicki's told me a good deal about herself and her life. Quite frankly, I'm flattered that she continued to follow in my footsteps. But what about you two? What has happened?"

Nora responded automatically, "I'm an interior designer in Wilmington. Calista was a dancer in New York, but she had a hip injury a few years ago that shortened her career, so now she runs a children's dance studio in Asheville."

"Both honorable professions," replied Henry, nodding encouragingly. "So, what brings the three of you here to me today?"

"I called you," replied Vicki, startling her sisters with her clarity of expression. "They made me hum our song, and I did. Today, I have a different question for you, though, than usual."

"What is that, my dearest one?" Henry asked.

"You know what has happened to each of us without you. What I've always wanted to know was what would have happened to us if you had remained alive. Would we be the same?"

Henry shook his head. "I think that you already know the answer to that, Vicki. Of course, you wouldn't. It's the struggle without me that's made you into the strong women you are today."

Nora could see her sister regaining her sense of self as she pressed on. "Yes, Daddy, I know. But don't you agree that my work on your experiments would have gone much better if I had had your guidance? Or if Nora had been able to count on your support for her design career, instead of mother's condescension? How much more could she have achieved? Or Calista..."

Here Henry dismissed her speculation. "Quite the contrary, Vicki. I am sad to say that *none* of your lives would have been possible if I had remained alive. It was your mutual stubbornness and the strength that you found together in rebelling against your mother's domestic dictatorship that made each of you who you are. I was always too soft with each of you. If I had lived, you would have been led to believe that every man in your life would treat you with love, kindness, and respect. As such, they would have run over you because you would have been more easily deceived. However, having to rely on each other without me to advise you made you wary. That alertness made you stronger and more self-preservative."

Vicki scowled, looking even more skeptical. "How can you be so sure? And how are we to know that we can't just step through this mirror right now and start all over once again?"

Henry looked down sadly. "I hoped that it would not come to this, but I will show you. However, be warned. Once I do, it must be the last time any of you will see me. It is not a thing that is to be done."

Nora and Calista leaned forward in unison, the word *stop* just beginning to issue from their lips. Vicki was too fast for them. "Show me," she said.

Instantly, the scene in the mirror changed. No longer were they watching their father in his office. Instead, they saw a cramped, cluttered apartment. Calista gasped as she saw herself waddling and pregnant, with one baby on her hip. Another screamed and wriggled to free himself of his highchair. An overweight, prematurely balding man in a white sleeveless T-shirt at least a size too small for him with coffee stains down the front yelled and smacked her bottom.

"That's Brent Bailey!" she exclaimed. "How did he get so fat? And why..."

Before Calista could finish, the image whirled and changed. It became a scene of Nora and her still-alive mother-in-law, Julia. They were sitting on the puffy white leather sofas, drinking iced tea in Julia's massive living room, at her Brentwood mansion, along with a dozen almost identical women. Each was dressed to the nines, though their looks were ruined from dieting to razor thinness. Nora could see that her face was emaciated and drawn, devoid of all expression. The Junior League logo was printed on several papers that they passed around, nodding and murmuring passively. As Julia crossed and uncrossed her spindly stems, the other women, including Nora, unconsciously followed her, as if they were all synchronized swimming to unheard music.

Once again, the image swirled and reformed into Henry sitting before them. "Now, don't you see what I was trying to explain?"

"But where was I?" cried Vicki. "Both of their lives were terrible, I know. Calista married her no-account has-been high school football player boyfriend and started shooting out babies. And Nora became an automaton slave to her rich mother-in-law, but what about me? I did everything right! I was everything that you and Mother thought I should be!"

"That is exactly why I had nothing to show you, Vicki," Henry replied patiently. "With both of us present in your life, there would have been no room left for you to develop your character. Although Calista and Nora would each have made mistakes regardless, you are correct in one thing. You made none. You pleased everyone. As a result, you were a complete erasure. If you must see it, behold! Here is where you would have been today, Victoria, with both your mother and me to please, to the detriment of yourself."

The image darkened and recentered on an empty stretch of dark blue water, beyond sight distance of any land. "I don't understand," stammered Vicki. "Is that the ocean? Why?"

"Because even in death, you were unable to have an independent thought. Your actual life would not have been drastically different had I lived. Yes, you would have followed me into psychology. Yes, we would have enjoyed more success together. But you still would have married Pierce. Only after a lifetime up to that point of completely deleting yourself to please both parents would you never have had the gumption to stand up to your husband when he began cheating. Instead, you would have entered into a series of plastic surgeries. Although intended to make you look younger and more appealing, those would have killed you before the age you currently are now, of a blood infection. That's why I have nothing to show you, Vicki. Because there can only be an adult *you* without *me*. Dead, as I am, you only have one parent to please and the other to rebel against. The dead are the easiest audiences. We are not anything you remember us as being. As your life stood until a few weeks ago, at least you were able to retain half of it. But if *I* had lived... there would have been *nothing* left of *you*."

Henry paused for a moment as Vicki began to cry softly. "If the three of you learn nothing else from having me as your father, then learn this: The looking-glass theory is real. We become not just a part of our environment but inextricably woven into the very fabric of it. Our reactions to expectations placed upon us, whether positive or negative, make us who we are. From Vicki, nothing but greatness was expected. However, it was greatness on her parents' terms, not her own. As a result, she achieved many things but lived a life that was hollow and unfulfilled. Hopefully, now that those negative memories have been erased, Victoria will be able to discover her true nature at last."

"But how did you know..." asked Nora. Henry interrupted her.

"I have only a few moments left, so I must hurry. Calista had nothing expected of her but folly, except by one person. That was her sister, Nora. Thus, because she received nothing but negativity from her mother, who was the only parent she truly remembered, Calista gravitated toward the artificial construct of another mother, who believed in her talents and supported her beliefs. However, since the two of you were a child guiding another child, Calista never truly grew up. Regardless, she manages to bring joy and light to everyone she meets because she never had to bear the burdens of adult responsibility on her own."

Calista glanced over to Nora, who for once, was paying her absolutely zero attention.

"Then we come to Nora," Henry said. "You know that you were named for my mother, Eleanor, yes?"

"Yes, I do," said Nora, watching her father. Henry began to shimmer. From her interactions with Hostler, Nora knew that he was running out of energy.

"Your name was apt because you have played the role of parent that neither your mother nor I was suited for. You raised your little sister and later rescued a husband... but how long will it be, Eleanor, before you begin to redirect all your boundless energy toward yourself? For your entire life, you've been calm between the storms. It's time to make some waves."

The fog began to gather behind the glass, signaling to all that their time was almost up. Henry spoke directly to his oldest daughter. "Vicki, break bonds with your sisters' hands, and set your palms against the glass. I have one last gift for you before I go. However, I warn you. It will hurt." Obediently, Vicki placed her palms on the surface of the mirror. She cried out as the heat seared her flesh, and a flash of light flared. Vicki drew back in shock as the glass crumbled into shards beneath her hands. When the light dimmed, Vicki curled into a fetal position on the floor, cupping her burned hands protectively into her lap. Nora and Calista relaxed and lay flat on the floor beside their sister. None of them moved for several minutes.

Slowly, the door of the office creaked open. Hazel peered in. Seeing the trio lying motionless, she dropped Vicki's glass of water. It shattered on the slate floor.

Chapter Thirty-Two

The next morning's ride back to Wilmington was quiet, save for a few short calls. Hazel drove while Nora rode shotgun. According to Pierce, Harper, it seemed, had gone back to her family in Mobile. She'd dumped him and quit her job, refusing to give any reasons. Nora thought she knew why. A young girl chasing the mystery of a much older boyfriend simply was not capable of managing such stress.

Although Pierce seemed down, Nora felt that his sorrow was superficial. Harper was not a match for him. Even Pierce could see that when he was forced. Nevertheless, he'd driven Vicki home. It seemed that Vicki's memory loss had been restored by her contact with her father. Yet, she'd managed to retain her instant dislike for Pierce. Nora noticed that Vicki chose to sit in the back seat behind him as they pulled out of the drive.

Sheridan and Calista returned to Asheville. Before she left, Calista confided in her that she didn't think she was cut out to live in the South again. However, Sheridan wanted to stay and run the studio alone while she returned to New York. Nora agreed that this was best. She reassured them both that her support of Sheridan's sole ownership would carry on, regardless.

The last series of calls was made by Nora to Cliff, who never answered. At last, she was able to get ahold of Daphne, Cliff's assistant, who claimed that there was no record of any client by the name of Jasper Chandler ever having been entered into the firm's database. Nora had figured as much. She felt sure that if she followed up through any other kinds of records, she would reach a series of dead ends. Cliff Tuttle was an attorney who had the kind of power and influence to make almost anything disappear if he wanted to. Nora was just glad that Cliff seemed to have decided to leave Julia's bequest to her alone. Whatever his motivations might be, she thought it best not to inquire, given his implied threats during their previous conversation.

Although a small part of her was angry that her inheritance from Jasper's catalog had evaporated, a greater part was happy to be free at last. Nora *could* go back to see her name on the tombstone in the Chandler family cemetery; she was certain of that. Or she *could* fight Cliff and Tommy Ponder in court for her rightful share of Jasper's copyrights. But what good would come of it? Nora had her home, her business, and her family back. More money would add nothing to her life. Rather, it might subtract by causing her to become lazy and too easily satisfied. Ultimately, Nora opted for a clean break and never called Cliff's office again. She sold the Chandler estate that Julia left her through an online auction service, signing all the paperwork digitally, and donated the two tired old horses to a dude ranch that assisted addicts in recovery.

Back in Wilmington, Nora exchanged tired goodbyes with Hazel. They promised to meet for brunch again at the riverfront on Sunday. Too exhausted to notice anything as she staggered back into the house, if Nora had looked up, she would have seen the glaring absence of one particular item in her parlor. The captain's wheel chandelier had vanished.

***

Nora slept late the next morning. She had no idea what day or time it was when she awoke.

After showering and drinking a first cup of coffee, Nora dressed in her favorite swim outfit: a vintage-style navy two-piece with white shorts and a sweetheart front tank over the top. Sydney, her new ginger cat, meowed for attention. Nora fed him and engaged in a round of *Oh no, where did the string go?* with a spool of her measuring twine. The chubby ginger feline finally flopped over on his side on the floor, panting and out of breath. Nora toddled off to Java Dog for a macchiato and a muffin. On her way home, she flip-flopped slowly past the lazy world of Wilmington as it drifted by on a Sunday morning. Elderly couples trundled along in their Cadillacs on the way to church. Skater kids glided deftly by among the green spaces between the north and southbound lanes of Market Street. No one was in a hurry.

After breakfast, Nora drove down to Wrightsville Beach. Parking her car in one of the many lots near the beach houses south of Johnny Mercer Pier, she set off northward on the sand without any particular destination in mind. Popping up her umbrella, Nora staked out a place far enough away from the throng of families trying to get in one last weekend before school began, but still close to the water. Lying belly down on the warm sand in the shade, Nora slept until lunch. Then, she walked up to a little pub on Lumina Avenue, had a grouper sandwich and two beers, and returned to her spot on the beach. There, she napped again until almost dusk. As the evening tide began to roll in, Nora took her wakeboard out to bound over the waves. She noticed that every person around her was a child, or at most, a teenager. All the other adults remained on the shore. When it became so dark that she could no longer tell the difference between the waves and the horizon, Nora gathered up her things and walked back to her car.

At home, she showered off the salt and sand, then put on light-washed denim jeans and a white asymmetrical off-the-shoulder organic cotton summer sweater. She considered getting a bottle of wine, decided against it, and settled in with a mug of orange sherbet instead. Exhausted, she collapsed into bed earlier than usual still wearing all of her clothes. The cat... her cat... Nora corrected herself, snuggled up under her arm, placing his fuzzy cheek against hers. They slept in the same way for hours.

When Nora awakened, Sydney the cat was gone. As she peered under the bed and around the room, Nora saw that not only the cat was missing, but the rest of her furniture as well. Instead of her regular bedside lamp, there was a small nightstand with one candle burning. The usual comforting glow of streetlights had faded to almost dark. Nora slowly realized she was no longer in her own time.

"Alexander?" she called. "Alex, do you know where I am?"

There was no answer. Picking up her keys from the nightstand where she left them, Nora noticed that they were different. Instead of her multicolored vinyl keycaps, there were a series of skeleton keys. Each had a crude letter scratched on the surface. *H*, she guessed, was for *Home*. There was an *S*, probably for *Shop*, along with several others. Beside the keys, in the place where her phone had been, was a note scrawled in hurried pencil. Nora recognized the spidery hand.

Have gone to the cemetery. Meet me there when you awaken. Hurry! - AH.

Thumping down the stairs, Nora was not surprised to see an antique grandfather clock standing next to the wall, underneath where Nora's retro-futuristic steampunk clock had been. The face of it read ten minutes to midnight. Her mind reeled for a moment. Then, she knew where she needed to go. *Of course! The cemetery at St. James Church.*

Looking around for her purse, but unsurprised when she did not find it, Nora locked the front door of the house with the key marked *H*, slipped the key into the pocket of her jeans, and headed down to the cemetery.

The street from her house—*their house*—as Nora reminded herself, to the cemetery was covered with pebbled gravel, not asphalt. It crunched beneath her sneakers as Nora walked swiftly across it. The candles lit in the lamps gave only a halo of light through the sweltering fog. Nora realized that if she hadn't known the street already, she would have been lost.

From the corner adjacent to the cemetery, Nora could see two men. One, whose head of thick dark hair was full of dirt and twigs, was just barely visible as he stood shoulder-deep in a grave. Wrestling this way and that, he appeared to be trying to work something free with a crowbar. The other, whom Nora recognized from the looking glass, had curly red hair. He held a shovel and scanned the landscape, chattering nervously. When the red-headed man turned her way, Nora crouched down behind a privet hedge, like a rabbit.

"I think I've got it, Louis. Throw down that chain. I'll put the links between the lid and the box so that I can pry the rest of the nails out all at once."

"I thought I saw something more beyond that hedge yonder," Louis said. His voice trembled as he tossed a length of chain down into the hole. A series of pops and creaks emanated from the grave as Louis, swinging his lantern left and right, called out. "Show yourself! Be ye spirit or man, I command thee to tell me who you are!"

"Jesus Christ, Louis!" growled the dark man's voice from within the grave. "Do you want to bring the whole town down on us?"

"No, well, of course not, but I..." Louis stammered, searching for the right explanation. "I read in *King James's Daemonologie* that you're supposed to force an evil spirit to speak its name so that it will go away."

"Whose evil spirit are you speaking of, exactly?" asked the voice. With a grunt, the dark-haired man boosted himself up to sit on the grave's edge. Nora recognized it was Hostler. "It can't be poor Sam. There wasn't an evil bone in his whole body. Here!" Hostler handed Louis one end of the chain as he took the other, walked around to the other side of the grave, and motioned for Louis to step back.

"When I count three, I want you to pull as hard as you can. We can pop the lid right off."

"Alex, are you sure this is a good idea?" Louis implored. "Those dreams, they could have been anything. Grief, panic... and you drink too much! What if it's just that?"

Alex dusted his hands off on the thighs of his pants and straightened up to look at Louis. "Not for three nights in a row. It just can't be. Sam believed in all that life-after-death stuff. Me, I thought it was pure hooey, like all the rest of religion. But these dreams, Louis! These dreams will not leave me be. If Sam is in there and he's resting peacefully, we'll put the lid back on and fill in the grave, just like I promised. He was my best friend, Louis. I know you were close too. I have to be *sure* he's dead in there. Don't you want to be sure, Louis?"

"Of course I do," replied Louis. "It's just..."

Hostler interrupted him. "A grim business, I know. I know. But five minutes, Louis. In five minutes all of this will be over. We'll probably be standing here, filling Sam's grave back up with dirt, and making light of my stupid dreams. Can you give me five more minutes, Louis?"

"Alright," said Louis, giving the streetscape one more worried glance before dropping his shovel in the dirt and picking up the other end of the chain.

"Good," replied Alex, taking firm hold of his end and wrapping the chain links tight around his fist. "Here we go then. Together on three. One...two...*THREE!*"

The men heaved backward in unison as if in a tug of war with death. Nora heard a series of pops, which she supposed were the nails coming loose, followed by a loud cracking sound as the lid of the coffin came off. Alex and Louis staggered to regain their footing. Glancing at each other, they stood bent over and breathless. Louis motioned for his friend to move forward first. Alex stepped up to the side of the grave.

"Jesus Christ! It was true!" Hostler exclaimed, sitting down hard on the slab of a tombstone behind him. Louis rushed forward to see. At the edge of the grave, he stopped and turned back, pulling a handkerchief from his pocket to cover his mouth and nose as he coughed and gagged. Louis collapsed onto another gravestone next to his friend.

"Oh Alex, you were right! How I wish you weren't, but you were right. He's... Sam was..." Louis struggled to name the abomination delicately.

"Buried alive, yes. I can see it now. Just as he said in my dream." Alex pulled out his handkerchief to mop the dirt and sweat from his face.

"So, now what do we do?" asked Louis, visibly trying to hold down the desire to vomit.

"The only thing we can do," answered Alex. "Cover him back up properly. Tell his family what we've seen. We're too late to save him. Or rather, I was too late. Sam's dead because of me."

"You mustn't blame yourself, Alex!" said Louis, sliding closer and cautiously putting one arm around his friend while keeping his handkerchief over his nose with his other hand. "You've been telling me about your dreams for days. And Sam's father. But no one listened. They all thought you'd gone crazy with grief. Hell, I did too. Besides, even if you went down the very first morning after you had the dreams, you couldn't have opened the coffin by yourself. Think of how much effort it took, even with the two of us together. One man can't open a grave on his own. The dead are put down so deep for a reason, Alex. They're meant to stay buried."

Alex shifted and put the dirty handkerchief back into his pocket. He stood and walked again to the graveside. "Logically, I know you're right, Louis," he said, looking down. "Even if I had come that very morning, what then? Sam's back was broken. Even if he'd lived, he would never have walked again. He'd have been a burden on his family. Sam would have hated that. Death was better; I agree. But not under these circumstances. Sam deserved better. At least to die without suffering. Perhaps under a heavy dose of laudanum or something in his sleep, but not this." Hostler shook his head. "Sam didn't deserve this."

Walking around to kneel near the head of the grave, Alex peered closer to see Sam's face. "No, Louis. Sam and I made a pact, and I broke it. Whichever one of us was the first to go would come back and tell the other what was on the other side. I was drunk when I said it, so I thought nothing of it. Sam was serious. He believed in all that stuff. Mesmerism and life after death and the whole lot of it. If only I had believed too, but I didn't, Louis. I failed him. Just like I failed his sister, Eleanor. I sent them both to their deaths."

"In both cases, how could you have known?" Louis asked, still sitting on the headstone. "Eleanor was perfectly healthy when she left for Tennessee. She seemed quite content that she'd saved her reputation by marrying that minister. No one could have foreseen that he would play the Devil to her, or that she'd catch the fever and die so quickly. As for Sam, you were there for him until the very end, or at least as much as you knew. He died in your home, Alex. You were standing right by his side when the doctor pronounced him dead. What more could you have done? Contradicted his doctor's pronouncement? People would have thought you were mad!"

"I could only have done one thing differently," said Alex, settling back onto his haunches. "I could've been a different man than who I was, Louis. A better man. If I hadn't kept Sam out drinking until long past when he should have been home, then he and his wife wouldn't have quarreled. He wouldn't have ridden off half-crazed and drunk in the middle of the night. He wouldn't have fallen from his horse. If I hadn't been such a lecherous braggart, then I would have been able to contain myself and what I desired. Or at least, been more discreet about it. Then Eleanor wouldn't have had any reason to run away with that God-forsaken minister. If she hadn't been out in the wilderness, Eleanor might not have gotten that fever. Even if she had, she would likely have lived because she would've had access to better doctor's care."

"I'm not so certain about that," said Louis skeptically. "If the best doctor here can't even tell a dead man from a live one, Eleanor's chances may have been poor, regardless."

Alex looked at Louis sternly, but his friend continued. "I'm sorry, but it's true. Typhoid kills most people, with or without a good doctor. As for what you could or couldn't have done, I think anyone would say that had we been given the benefit of gazing into a crystal ball at the future consequences of our present actions, we might all choose to live our lives quite differently. The only thing you can do, for Sam or Eleanor, is to let their goodness live inside you. If you think that you could be a better man, well then be one. Let that be your testament to their memories."

Alex nodded. He motioned for his friend to come and kneel beside him at the grave to pray. Realizing what he meant to do, Louis followed. Alex bowed his head.

"Dear Father, I come to you for the first time in many years, and in the company of my best living friend, Louis Toomer, to swear that I will honor the memory of my dearest friend, Samuel Jocelyn, and his sister Eleanor, whom I loved more than life itself. In their honor, I will become a better man and try to be as they were. I will give up drinking to excess, gambling, needless luxury, and all the other ways of the flesh that are known frailties of spirit. I will come to this graveside and pray, as often as I am able, for forgiveness from these things, for not being a faithful believer in salvation and the life after this one, and for the strength to exist as a good and wholesome spiritual being. I swear this oath, as I prepare my friend for his reburial, so that his soul may at last find eternal peace. I appreciate this opportunity to have my eyes opened and to work toward forgiveness while it is still not too late. Amen."

"Amen," echoed Louis. Then a few seconds later, "That was the right thing to do, Alex. Shall we begin seeing to the rest of it then?"

"Yes, and let's be quick about it," replied Alex.

Easing himself back down into the grave, Alex joined the broken wood of the coffin lid as best he could to the bottom. As he attempted to align the top, Hostler couldn't help but stare at his friend's hands and face. Sam's eyes were frozen open in terror. The ends of his fingertips were ground down completely, exposing the bone. Dried rivulets of blood encrusted his hands down to the wrists, where it formed a sort of scab over the fine white linen of his cuffs. Although Alex attempted to gently press them down to his sides, rigor had set in. As a result, Sam's hands remained stiffly in front of his face, as if shielding him from the terrible reality of his fate. Sam's face was covered in flecks of gore, which Alex tried to clean off with his sweaty handkerchief. Here, his efforts fared better, as the damp cloth re-liquified the blood enough to allow him to wipe it away. However, his attempt to close Sam's eyes failed—the rigor again. Alex folded the handkerchief bloody side in, tucked it into the back pocket of his trousers, and shut the lid of the coffin. He pounded the nails back into place with the side of the pry bar he had used to loosen them and hauled himself out of the grave.

Filling in the space with dirt did not take nearly as long as it did to dig their way down. Within an hour, Alex and Louis were tamping down the last clods of earth. Exhausted and sweating, they embraced and said goodbye. Louis took his leave alone on foot, heading south toward the riverfront. Nora watched silently as Louis's labored stride carried him away.

Chapter Thirty-Three

"You can come out now. I know you're there," said Alex loudly as he crossed the street, wiping his dirty hands on the sides of his pant legs.

Nora stood and stepped from behind the hedge. "How long did you know?"

"From when I first got out of the grave. I wanted you to see all of it so I could explain afterward why I brought you here," replied Alex. The sweat still glistened off him in the moonlight.

Nora realized that Alex didn't shimmer as before. Instead, he appeared solid. She had so many questions but began with the easiest one. "You look different. There's no shimmer. Why?"

"Here, I am in my own time," Alex said. "Time is a fluid construct. Everything that *has* happened is *still* happening, as is everything yet to come. However, I *shimmer*, as you call it, in times that are not my natural ones because the events that shape those unnatural times are perpetually in a state of flux. My very existence there could be obliterated forever if any one particular action in the past changes, setting off a chain of events. But here? In the regular, paced time of my natural life, I remain solid. That is, so long as I do not do anything that significantly changes the consequential progression of later actions. If I did that," here Alex made a small exploding motion with his hands as he breathed out. "*Boom*. I might obliterate myself."

"So, if you're not supposed to change anything, at the risk of erasing yourself," asked Nora, "then why go to the trouble of bringing me here, to show me these things?"

"Because I wanted to explain and apologize, not change, some things about the nature of our relationship. In the hope that such knowledge might offer you some comfort in the future. Let's walk down to the river-front as I tell you, shall we? Some of it might be easier to comprehend fully when you see it in person."

As they fell into step with one another, Alex reached out to take Nora's hand. Cautiously interlacing her fingers with his, Nora was surprised to notice that his touch was neither hot nor cold. A soft breeze stirred the canopy of tree branches above them, causing a small shiver of tension to release through her body. It began at Nora's temples and coursed down her spinal column to the soles of her feet, giving a slight tingling sensation all over. Nora almost pulled her hand away. Alex grasped it more firmly, sending a second wave through her nervous system. It wasn't an unpleasant sensation, rather like the reawakening of nerves one felt with the first sip of a cold beer after a long day out in the hot sun.

"Do you feel that?" Nora whispered to Alex, leaning closer so that her lips almost touched his ear. "What is it?"

"Our mutual energies cycling together," Alex replied. "It's more notice-able here. Even though I am in the correct time, my body is still not fully corporeal. In actuality, the physical me, or what will be left of it during your lifetime, is back in that churchyard, not far from where we were with Sam."

They reached the riverfront walkway. Alex stopped in front of a large, salmon-colored building.

"Keys?" Alex asked, holding out his hand. "In this world, I still have to use them, which is why I left them on the nightstand."

Nora handed over the keys. Looking up at the building while Alex unlocked the door, Nora knew that she had been there before. Scanning the long wooden dock with many boats bobbing along beside it on her right offered no clues. However, when she looked down at the brick street, Nora realized where she was.

"This is the market street where I first met Dean Goodnight!" she ex-claimed. "Where I bought Meg's mirrors!"

"You are correct," Alex said, smiling at her revelation. "Do you recognize anything else?" Nora glanced around again, looking a bit perplexed. Alex took both her hands gently. "Close your eyes and then tell me what you see."

Nora did as instructed. With her eyes closed, she envisioned the salmon-colored building again. Only this time, instead of the small, cubbyhole panes, a long series of bay windows wrapped around the build-ing. They were flung open. Soft, gauzy curtains billowed inside as a gentle breeze blew in. Through the open windows, Nora could see an abundance of handmade, wooden furniture, elaborately carved with mermaids and other nautical designs. A woman with her hair piled high on top of her head brushed briskly over the room with a feath-er duster. In this vision, Alex walked over to an elaborately dressed couple, beaming with pride as he introduced them. When the woman turned to curtsy and began speaking with the couple, Nora gasped. The woman was herself.

Nora's eyes flashed open, where they met Alex's intense gaze. "What did you see?"

"My studio! Only I wasn't myself. And you were..." Nora trailed off.

"*Our* studio," interjected Alex. "Or perhaps *you* are more correct. *Your* studio, which produced custom furniture made with *my* lumber. So, yes. *Yours, mine,* and *ours.* In that version of our lives, anyway."

"I don't understand," said Nora, shaking her head. "What are you talking about? What version?"

"In alternate versions of time that constantly interweave themselves with our own, we are presented with a world of options. Each of them shifts like sand, dependent on choices that we make and remake. Visions of our circumstances perpetually revise themselves according to whether or not our choices remain consistent."

Seeing her eyes clouded with confusion, Alex pressed Nora's palms, and she felt the energy pulse through her body. "Close your eyes once more," Alex instructed. "Let go completely of any thoughts you have about what I just told you. Then, tell me what you see."

Once more, Nora closed her eyes. Instantly, she was transported again. In this version she watched as a woman, herself, but with a paler, very drawn face, stood in a worn black dress with a bundle of papers in her hand. The bright, salmon-colored exterior of the building had faded to an anemic puce hue, and the large windows were boarded over. Speaking to a rather shabby, rotund gentleman, she handed him the sheaf of papers and walked away silently down the dock.

"What happened to us?" Nora asked, blinking her eyes open again as the vision ended.

"That was our enterprise, about ten years after the vision that you witnessed before," said Alex. Nora noticed that he could not look at her this time.

"Your half of the business, the furniture, was doing so well that I got cocky. I fell back into my old ways. Drinking, gambling... I lost it all. Because I didn't have the heart to tell you, I shot myself instead. Right here." Alex tilted his head back so that Nora could see under his chin. There was a perfectly round, white scar centered beneath his jaw.

"That's what I've been trying to tell you, Nora," Alex said, lowering his chin and training his gaze back on her. "I've been through our story dozens upon dozens of times. It always turns out to be some version of the same. No matter what I do, I am still who I am. I can only disappoint you."

"If that is true," said Nora, withdrawing her hands as she walked through the door. "Then why tell me at all? What purpose does it serve?"

"I have to be free of it, Nora. The guilt and shame of disappointing you. I need your forgiveness." Alex motioned for her to follow him inside the building. As she stepped over the threshold, he struck a match. Using a taper candle, Alex lit the series of lanterns around the room. Nothing was inside the massive expanse of the warehouse floor but space. Alex turned to face her.

"So that I can go forward. Or rather, so that *we* can go forward. Oh, Nora, you have no idea how many times I've tried to think of some way to draw you here, to this place, and at this moment, to say how sorry I've been! For years, I thought that the key lay in keeping my promise by your brother's graveside. That I could return after death to that evening where I first embarrassed you at Sam's engagement party to make amends, and then everything would be all right. Only it wasn't! Even if I *had* held onto my promise then and *tried* to be a better man, it was impossible. Even with the benefit of hindsight, and even if I behaved myself one particular night. Sooner or later, I always ruined things. In the lifetime that I just showed you, we had a very successful business together. I ran the lumber company, and you turned it into beautiful pieces that were in demand all over the South. I was proud of you, of course, but I became jealous that my wife outshone me. I went back to drinking and generally doing anything that I could to pull attention away from you and back onto me. I neglected my part of the business and overspent all that you had earned. And when

I couldn't face you afterward, because I still loved you and admired you despite my foolish pride, I shot myself."

"Then I became a widow, penniless and in debt. I died of the fever the next year anyway because I couldn't afford a doctor," said Nora, as a wash of emotions flooded over her with the realization. She reached for Alex and buried her face into his shoulder.

"But this is the last one," Alex whispered, holding her. "And that is a promise this old liar will have to keep. Because once a spirit reveals the other worlds to the living, he can never relive them again. He must finally move on, into a new life."

Nora straightened to look at Alex, realizing what he implied. "That's why you brought me here," she said. "To make me remember all that we were and know all that we could have been. So that I will know you in the next life when we meet again."

"Yes," Alex said, breaking the embrace. He clasped Nora's hands in his once more. "I've tried for almost two hundred years to rewrite the past, and it can't be done. No matter how well-intentioned people are, or how willing they are to change. They might buy themselves a short span of happiness, but fate is inevitable. Fortunately, we are given the gift of time to come to an understanding of this in the afterlife. Where we work and rework as ghosts all of the far-reaching possibilities we wished our lives might have had, and enjoy the gift of peace at the end. The peace of knowing that we will meet those whom we truly love in the next life when the slate is at last wiped clean."

They walked down to the dock. Alex helped Nora across the threshold of a riverboat. Palm to palm, Nora saw without closing her eyes what it had been in a previous scene of their other life that he had shown her. Alex led her by the hand to the ship's wheel. Nora could see that it was the same one that she'd fashioned, many years later, into the chandelier in her parlor.

Nora turned to Alex, who began to shimmer. His clothes changed. As the outline of his body began to blur, Nora could see the clean cut of a dark suit. She looked down at her clothes, where the briefest outline of a white, flowing gown caressed her body to the floor. They were standing there just as they might have on their wedding day.

"I forgive you," she whispered.

"Thank you," Alex said, bending down to take Nora in his arms. Nora watched his eyes turn from warm gray to ghostly silver as Alex's shape began to flicker and fade. "I won't be able to speak with you again in this lifetime, but look for me in the next. Wherever you seek to find yourself, there you will always find me. For my dearest Eleanor, *I* am your looking glass."

As their lips touched, a beam of sunlight broke through the early morning mist. Then, like a vapor, Alex was gone. Nora stood, once again in her modern clothes, with one hand on the ship's wheel, as the whole world spun into ether.

Waking again into her world, in her bed, Nora saw that it was dawn. She rushed downstairs and flipped on the lights. The ship's wheel was still in its place above her parlor, gleaming with electricity.

Instantly, Nora knew what she must do. Taking the largest hammer from the toolbox that she kept in her office, Nora smashed the looking glass and collapsed crying onto the floor.

Chapter Thirty-Four

Although the next few months felt like a whirlwind, by Christmas Nora's life settled down once more. Vicki moved to Baltimore to take a new research position at Johns Hopkins before the ink was even dry on her divorce. The 'Munks arrived home for the holidays from college, determined to take a gap year off in Colorado to *ski and reassess*, as Vicki put it. The boys seemed unfazed by their parents' separation. Pierce agreed to split everything down the middle, so there was little to fight over. He closed his real estate office and semi-retired, buying into a condo development firm in Florida.

Calista returned to New York to start an MFA in dance so that she could become qualified to teach at the college level. Although she enjoyed being an educator, Calista missed her dance friends and the city. Nora supported the move, paying for her sister's tuition and another apartment.

Sheridan, in contrast, chose to remain in Asheville. At first, Sheridan tried to insist on paying rent or taking out a loan to buy out Calista's half of the studio. Nora flatly refused. Sheridan became like a brother. Nora enjoyed knowing that she had at least one family member still in the state. Sheridan's patient, paternal demeanor made him a huge hit with students. After a lifetime of living in the city, he enjoyed having a whole new world of the outdoors opened to him. Nora thought that Sheridan's decision to remain in Asheville also probably had a lot to do with the handsome architect that he'd met at an independent business brunch hosted at the Biltmore. She'd invited Sheridan and his plus one to her holiday brunch, and hoped for the best.

As for Nora, her dreams of living the leisurely life of a small boutique owner were ruined by her studio's popularity. By October, demand was so high for her work that she'd had to hire two full-time assistants to help. In November, Nora began looking for a larger showroom space.

Nora wasn't surprised that the warehouse she had seen in her dream about Alex went up for sale the weekend before Thanksgiving. She was walking back from lunch one day and saw the Realtor putting out the sign. Nora stopped her before she got back into the car and asked the price.

"Would you like to see inside?" the Realtor asked. She was very young and very pretty. Nora wondered how long she had been a Realtor. "Sure," said Nora, already knowing full well what the structure contained.

The space was exactly as Nora remembered it. Empty, save for the marks on the floor indicating where walls were during previous incarnations. The pony-tailed Realtor read from her notes that in its most recent life, it had been a crafting co-op, where local artisans could rent booths. "It also says that its original use was as a lumber warehouse, and then later..."

"A custom-made furniture store," finished Nora.

"Wow!" The young lady's blue eyes went wide. "You must be psychic or something!"

"I just had a hunch," said Nora. "Looks like a furniture store. Plus, I think I heard about that lumber warehouse situation. The original owner was a man named Hostler, was he not?"

"Get... out... of... town!" said the young Realtor, exaggerating the gaps between her words. "Look right there," she pointed to the name beside the space designated for the *Original Owner* on her clipboard list. It read, *A. Hostler.*

"I think I'll stay," Nora said to the Realtor. "I'll take it if the sellers will agree to a full-price offer."

"Oh, I'm sure they will," the Realtor gushed, pulling out her phone to call them. "They're in a pretty big hurry to unload it. I think somebody must have died or something."

The following week, Nora signed the papers. The warehouse was hers. Having the extra space was excellent news not only for Nora but also for Vicki. Duke was pressuring her sister all through the fall semester to *do something* about clearing out the storage space for Yates's lab. The older professor had passed without a will or heirs. Vicki was the younger faculty member who knew his work best, so she stepped in. The issue was resolved in early December by a day's trip to pick up all the mirrors and to put them into storage at Nora's new warehouse. The sisters made a pact to tell no one else about the experiments conducted by their father, Henry, or Dr. Bill Yates. On that point, they all agreed that their mother, Marjorie, was correct. It wasn't worth risking Vicki's career to allow her to be associated any further with the entire situation.

"What are you going to do with all of them?" Vicki asked Nora, as they stood sweating and surveying the once-vast space. It seemed much smaller, crowded by the aisles of mirrors. Shrouded in their white boxes, they almost covered the warehouse's entire top floor.

"Same thing that I do with all of the other pieces—sell them," replied Nora, nonchalantly.

"Don't you think that's irresponsible? Won't people just bring them back?" Vicki asked. "They're not exactly *normal mirrors*, you know."

"Who's going to return a mirror to the place that they bought it with that as an excuse? *Sorry, I can't keep this; it's haunted.*" Nora shrugged. "Probably no one. They'd be scared people would think that they were crazy. Plus, who's to say that the person who buys each one might not have their reasons for doing so? To learn something about themselves, like we did."

"I was just concerned that it might create a liability for you. But you're right. I hadn't thought about it that way," Vicki said. She and Nora had spent many hours on the phone dissecting their encounters with the mirrors. Ultimately, they concluded that, if what Alex said was true, the spirits in any particular mirror chose to reveal themselves purposefully and only to certain individuals.

"Perhaps that's all part of it, though," Vicki continued. "The necessary turning of the wheel of fate. If so, this space that you've created provides a sort of platform for that to occur."

"I like to think so," agreed Nora. "None of this would have happened if I hadn't recognized that very first mirror as being so similar to Jasper's and then bought it from Dean Goodnight in the street market."

"That's very true," replied Vicki, shuddering slightly. "I might not even be here if you hadn't. Nora, I wish there were something you'd let me do to thank you for..."

Nora cut Vicki off, "For saving my sister's life from our crazy mother? Please. I'm just happy that it's brought us closer again. Besides, I have everything else that I could need."

"That's true too. Whoever would have thought that other crazy old bat would have left you the rest of the *Chandler empire*?" Vicki made air quotes around the last two words. "You always told me that Julia hated you."

"She did!" insisted Nora. "But not for the reasons I thought. Julia hated me because she hated herself. She saw that I was becoming like her, married to Jasper. Which is too bad. I don't think she'd have been such a monster if she hadn't been reacting to everything she'd put up with out of Jubal first, and then Jasper, for all those years."

Vicki nodded. "It's a shame. Julia was right to be angry that you'd fall into the same pit as she did if she saw a lot of herself in you. Classic case of looking-glass theory in action. We become not only what we see but also what is expected of us. Julia probably grew up taking care of a drunk absentee father, then became the wife of a drunk absentee husband, and finally a mother to a drunk absentee son."

"Or to paraphrase Nietzsche, *whoever fights monsters should see to it that in the process she does not become one herself. For if she gazes long enough into an abyss, the abyss will gaze back into her.*" Nora said as she turned toward footsteps coming up the staircase behind her.

"Since when did you start spouting philosophy?" asked Vicki, as the door opened.

"Since she heard it from me," answered Hazel. "Is there anything more gratifying to a teacher than to hear her lessons being quoted as she enters a room?"

Nora rolled her eyes at her friend. "Yes, you're a regular fountain of wisdom. Is Dean downstairs?"

"Yep. You know Gramma Dean... she'd never admit that four flights of stairs are three too many. She's pretending to look at new pieces downstairs while I come up to fetch you."

"Well, let's not keep her waiting," said Nora. "Will you stay for dinner, Vicki?"

"No, I really should get to the airport. The flight back to Baltimore leaves at seven."

"I can drive you after I speak to Dean if you like," said Nora.

"You'd better let me," said Hazel. "Gramma Dean wanted to take you out to her warehouse to see something she's found. You know what an odyssey that is. Half an hour out there, then she has to root around and find whatever it is she's looking for. She claims it's important, though, so who am I to question?"

"Uh oh," said Vicki, exchanging glances with the other two as she gathered up her things to follow Hazel out the door. "God only knows what that could be."

"Ain't that the truth!" replied Nora, switching off the lights as they all went downstairs.

Chapter Thirty-Five

D ean Goodnight switched on the light in the office of her warehouse.
The shelves, which lined it from floor to ceiling, were filled with
every possible antique trinket, and a great number of rare books. Seeing
Nora staring at them in amazement, Dean cackled. "Didn't peg me as the
literary type, eh? I thought Hazel told ya I used to own a bookstore."

"She did, but..."

Dean didn't let Nora finish. "You thought I only sold 'em but didn't read
'em, eh?"

"To be honest, I didn't give it that much thought."

"Very few people these days give anythin' enough thought. But here,"
Dean said, opening the top drawer of her desk and pulling out a small,
flat cardboard box. "I found this in an old trunk at an estate sale a few
weeks back. Kept meanin' to give it to ya, but you was busy. Hazel told me
all about your little encounter with who was in that lookin' glass at your
house, so I thought ya might want it."

Nora looked at Dean curiously for a moment as the old woman lit a
cigarette and fitted it into her long holder. Dean gestured for Nora to open
the box.

Inside was a much yellowed and moth-eaten handkerchief. Parts of it
were stained a brownish color, like dried blood. It had been folded carefully
around the other object in the box. Even though the handkerchief was in
poor condition, Nora recognized the monogram.

"*A.H.!*" Nora breathed. "Where did you find it?"

Dean took a lengthy puff before answering. "Told ya. In an old trunk
full of other junk. The trunk itself I already sold. Pretty basic ol' steamer
trunk. Nothing special. Just random jumble sale-type stuff inside. That
was wedged up in a little compartment under the lid." Dean motioned at

the handkerchief-wrapped object in Nora's hand. "Not in the original box, of course."

"Of course," said Nora, as she carefully unwrapped the almost crumbling handkerchief from around the object. Tucked inside was a small silver shaving mirror. It had tiny feet that folded down in front and a little stand on the back so that it could be propped up on a table.

"Was just like that, not tarnished or nothin', when I first found it," Dean said. "Thought it was pretty strange 'til I put two an' two together with that story Hazel told me 'bout your gentleman friend."

"How much do you want for it?" Nora asked. Her eyes stated clearly that she was willing to pay any price.

"Ehhhhhh..." replied Dean, tipping a bit of ash onto the tray nearby. "I think *free* is the only fair price for it. It should belong to ya."

Nora reached out to hug the older lady. "You have no idea how much this means to me."

"Aw, I think I do," said Dean. Pulling back from the hug, she reached into her desk drawer and removed a second object.

"This," Dean said, clamping the cigarette holder firmly between her teeth and holding it up for Nora to see, "is the driver's side mirror from a 1949 REO semi-trailer truck. Biggest piece left of it that weren't burnt to a crisp after the wreck. Other than me, of course. Didn't have no seatbelts in those days. When it jackknifed, it slung me straight out through the windshield. That's why I part my hair over t'other side." Dean ran her gnarled hand over the right side of her wrinkled face. Nora could see the white line of a flat, thick scar that ran up from just over the outside tip of her eyebrow and into her hairline.

"Damn near peeled my face off. My poor Jimmy wasn't even that lucky. Hit that tree so hard it pushed the engine block into the cab. Steerin' wheel crushed his chest. Still to this day, I dunno what he saw in that road when he turned 'round to cause him to jerk the wheel so. Jimmy was a great driver. Drove tanks all through the war, only to come straight home and die in that damned truck. I was a fool to want to go ride with him. Should have stayed home with Lil' Jim where everybody said I belonged. But I was crazy for him an' crazy to be out of the house. Hadn't been much after Lil' Jim was born. If I hadn't been there distractin' him, well," Dean sighed heavily. "It might have been a different story. But it wasn't, an' so that's how it was. Jimmy was stuck under the wheel when the engine blew. Don't think he felt it, though. At least, I didn't hear him scream. That's been one of only two things that consoled me through the years 'bout the whole thing. This is the other." Dean waved the truck mirror at Nora.

"I know anyone else would think I was crazy. Maybe I am. Considerin' your circumstances, though, I'm gonna to tell ya like it is. I can see him in it sometimes. Jimmy."

"Really?" asked Nora, hopeful and disbelieving at the same time. "Under what circumstances?"

"Whenever I'm alone, holdin' it, an' thinkin' 'bout... ya know, our life," replied Dean. She laid the mirror down on her desk and picked up her cigarette holder again.

"Does it show you good times or...?"

"Oh, I learnt real quick to cover it up before it got to the bad part. Just saw that once, an' it was more than enough," said Dean, taking a puff. "Up to that part, though, we was just laughin' an' flirtin' 'round in the cab. Ya know, rollin' down the highway an' talkin' 'bout life. After he died, the truckin' company acted real sorry about it. Gave me plenty of money. Turns out it was a malfunction in the fuel line that made it blow up like it did in the wreck. Otherwise, Jimmy might have lived, just with a bunch of broken ribs or somethin'. I didn't have to work, but I needed a place to go an' feel useful every day, at a place I felt like goin' to. So, I opened a bookshop. Ran it for almost sixty years before I could tell that damn Amazon was gonna put me clear out of business. Was a great choice at the time, though. I've always loved to read, ever since I was a girl. Even though 'cause of the war, I quit school after the tenth grade. Went to work in a war factory. Lotta girls did in those days. The only other things we was expected to do was get married an' have babies. Did the marryin' part. Married the best fella I could find. Never felt up to doin' it again. We had Lil' Jim, who was a peach of a boy when he was young. Havin' the shop was the best way to work an' still take care of him. He wasn't even two when his Daddy died. I couldn't have left him with some stranger all day, an' gone off to some other job. It would have been too lonely for me an' him. Sometimes, though, in those mid-afternoon hours, when it was slow in the bookshop, an' Lil' Jim was off at school, it was too quiet. One day, I don't know why, I pulled that mirror out the drawer. Just like I did a few minutes ago here with ya, an' I started talkin' to it. Then all of a sudden, there was Jimmy, plain as the nose on your face! Talkin' back, just like we was in the truck that day. At first, I thought it was a dream, or that I was delirious from the heat. I got scared. I flipped it over an' put it away. Eventually, I came back to it, over an' over. Whenever I felt like I needed to talk to Jimmy about anythin', like when Lil' Jim passed or when I came down with this ol' COPD. My Jimmy was still always there to make me feel better. Not that it was ever the same, but it helped, if ya catch my drift."

"Oh, I do," replied Nora.

"Well good, I thought ya would." Dean sniffed loudly and took off her cat-eye glasses, swabbing them on the hem of her navy polo. Nora could see that her eyes were red, but she ignored the tears that came.

"So, just one more thing, an' I won't take up all the rest of your afternoon listenin' to an ol' woman, but I think it's important ya hear it. All that shit you three was yappin' 'bout when I was downstairs." Dean paused to breathe on her glasses and swabbed more decisively again. "All that shrink theory nonsense. It's all bunk. My Daddy was a drunk an' he beat my Momma within an inch of her life on a nightly basis. She went through life like a kicked dog nine days outta ten. *But I did not.*"

Dean popped her glasses back on and pointed at her chest with both thumbs. "Big Jim never drank a drop that I saw if it wasn't in fun, an' he certainly never laid a hand on me. One other ol' boy I dated before tried that once, an' I slapped the fire outta him. Put a stop to that right quick. I was never afraid to speak my mind on anythin'. Used to worry about it a little when I was young an' tryin' to be cute. A bunch of girlfriends an' I went to this little gypsy fortune teller down in Mobile once. Oh, an' she told all of 'em everything they wanted to hear about this feller an' that feller. Who was whose soulmate, an' all that rot. But then she came to me. I guess she could tell that I thought she was full of it. She looked me dead in the eye an' told me. *For some people, there is no one.* Ya know what I did then?"

"What?" Nora asked, spellbound.

"I laughed as loud as I could right in her face, just like this." Dean let out a wild cackle. "Then I told her, 'Shows how much ya know, ol' gypsy! I'm already engaged. What do ya think of that?' An' ya know what she said next?"

All Nora could do was echo, "What?" again.

Dean calmed down to a hoarse whisper. "She said, *what fate has written cannot be rewritten. For some people, there will always be no one.* I didn't think a thing of it at the time. Four years later, when I woke up in that hospital bed, an' they told me Big Jim was gone, though, I thought of nothin' else for days. *For some people, there is no one.* Her words hung on me like a curse for years. Until after I opened the shop, an' on those quiet days when Lil' Jim was in school. Those girlfriends who'd asked all those silly questions of that gypsy kept comin' by every day, wantin' my advice on what to do about whatever those same fellers, by then their no-account husbands, had done wrong to 'em. Day after day, they kept comin' until finally I had a revelation. Havin' no one but myself was just fine most of the time. Just damn fine!"

Dean's cigarette had burnt out to its end. She plucked it from her holder to stab it out in the ashtray. "So, I don't ever want to hear ya worryin' 'bout it, Nora. Bein' alone. Ya know what I mean?"

"Absolutely," said Nora. "And thank you. For everything. Especially this." Nora put the small silver mirror back in its box, hugged Dean one last time, and headed home.

***

That evening, Nora had a glass of wine and wandered around her house. She considered all the little projects she'd left to do until her week off after the holidays because she'd been so busy at the studio. Although her house was decorated impeccably for Christmas, it was all for show. Nora's thought that making her house part of the Tour of Homes might bring in more business worked better than she planned. Everyone wanted to visit the home of the new designer in town for inspiration. Looking at the stacks of elaborately wrapped gifts under the tree, Nora noticed all the tags indicated they were for other members of her family. Vicki hadn't bought her a Christmas present since she'd declared her atheism upon entering medical school. Nor had Calista. Every year, she voiced her disdain loudly for the overly commercial nature of the holiday season, despite accepting whatever gift Nora chose for her anyway.

Flipping on the television, Nora settled in to watch the ending of the Albert Finney version of Dickens's *Christmas Carol*. It had always been her favorite. Studying her living room as the credits rolled, Nora realized that she'd decorated possibly a hundred such rooms throughout her career in traditional English Christmas style, even though she'd never been to

England. In fact, Nora pondered, she hadn't been on a vacation of more than three or four days since she'd graduated college and first became a designer. Setting her wine glass into the sink, Nora flipped through her phone and deleted every project on her list of to-dos for the week after New Year's. In their place, Nora added one item, *Look up flights to London*, and went to bed.

Snuggled in next to her cat, Sydney, who'd taken to curling up under her arm like a child's teddy bear, Nora reached over to her nightstand to turn off the lamp. She smiled as she saw the reflection in the little shaving mirror that Dean had given her. A handsome gentleman with soft, dark, wavy hair slept there without a sound, as he would for the next fifty-nine years.

Acknowledgements

My life has had many separate eras, all of which have contributed in some manner to the writing of this story. In my twenties, I worked as a tape room intern at EMI music publishing house on Music Row, and as a broadcasting intern for Cumulus Radio. From those experiences, I learned many lessons not only about the music (lower case) BUSINESS (upper case), but also human nature in general. During my childhood, I spent most of my time with my grandmother Roberta and her friends, who had known one another since they were teenagers. Unfortunately, like most of those ladies, she was widowed young and never remarried. However, being women of America's greatest generation, they worked in factories, riveted ships, drove trucks, and stoically did whatever it took to carry on with their lives, build careers, buy homes, and raise children. Thus, it is to their tenacity, determination, and resourcefulness that I dedicate this book.

Additionally, I would like to thank my editor, Raigan Nickle, for catching all the details that I tend to overlook, especially when it comes to portraying the Southern dialect consistently, and my designer, Marta Obucina, for creating another amazing cover. Also, shout out to the super cute Black Cat Shoppe and its Ghost Tour of Old Wilmington. Their excellent guide introduced me to the tales of Gallows Meg, Samuel Jocelyn, Alexander Hostler, and all of the other restless spirits who haunt this volume. Finally, much thanks and love to my partner Andrew, without whom many of the intricate details of modern technology needed to prepare literature for presentation to readers would totally escape me, and to my cat, Jim Nightshade, for always being there to listen and offer emotional support.

About the Author

Vivian Catfield is the pen name of Dr. Candace Ursula Grissom. She holds a PhD in English from Middle Tennessee State University, an MFA in Creative Writing from Sewanee: The University of the South, and a BS in Music Business, also from MTSU, among other degrees. Born in North Alabama, she lived in Murfreesboro, Tennessee for many years. Currently, she resides in Cincinnati, Ohio with her partner Andrew and her cat Jim Nightshade. Outside of literature, her interests include acting, exploring haunted history, and spending time outdoors. Looking Glass Theory is her second novel. If you enjoyed it, please consider checking out her first novel, Keys in the Dust.

Also by Vivian Catfield

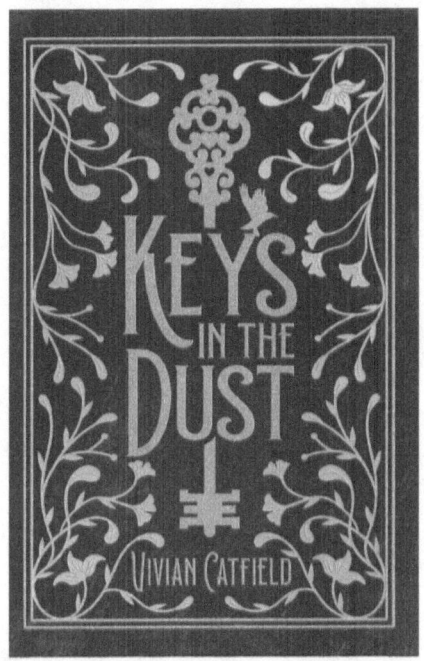

What if one silver key could unlock your power—and your destiny?

Willow Todd never expected a mysterious key to lead her to Rookes College, a hidden school of elemental witchcraft on an island shrouded in a magickal glamor. As a Spirit witch, Willow enters a world of natural magick, sisterhood, and ancient traditions—where students bond with animal familiars and harness the power of Earth, Air, Fire, Water, and Spirit. But Rookes isn't just a sanctuary. A deadly hurricane is coming, threatening to destroy both the island and the balance of the Otherworld. Guided by mentors inspired by historical heroines, Willow and her coven must raise a Cone of Power to defend their home. As Willow's magical gifts awaken, so does her connection to Elliott—a mysterious Spirit witch with a broken past. Together, they'll discover that love, nature, and unity may be the most powerful magick of all.

Also by Vivian Catfield

Who can you trust after finding out that your beloved was a liar?

Grieving her husband Ethan's murder, private detective Shiloh Foley finds
two dead women in Eden Park. The investigation reveals a shocking secret:
Ethan, a Cincinnati police officer, knew about the cover-up of a horrific
sexual abuse scandal at his elite local prep school. Now, the victim seeks
revenge as the Prophet of Eden Park, building a cult in the city's abandoned
subway tunnels to systematically terrorize and eliminate his attackers. With
a team of unlikely allies, including a nun, a teacher, a social worker, and her
assistant, Shiloh struggles against family betrayal and fights political
corruption to uncover the truth and she races to stop the Prophet's deadly
plan before it's too late.

Also by Vivian Catfield

Which wolf will win the battle raging inside of you?

On the eve of the Colorado Gold Rush, Mae Ulrich, a strong-willed, progressive heiress from Maine, leaves her home with dreams of starting a frontier school.Plagued by prophetic nightmares of vicious beasts, Mae's idealism is destroyed when she uncovers a ruthless plot to steal Native American lands and gold.Traveling west with a saloon keeper and a fur trader, Mae bonds with a mysterious cowboy and a gifted student. When a violent attack forces Mae to confront her fears, her shocking connection to the beasts is revealed. Embracing her inner darkness, Mae fights for justice in a gold-hungry nation, questioning the costs of change in a brutal pre-Civil War America.